3 June '78

Dear Nikki —

I'm so delighted by
& grateful for
your enthusiasm for
my book!

My thanks!

All best —
Sheila

HANSEL *and* GRETEL *in* BEVERLY HILLS

WILLIAM MORROW AND COMPANY, INC.

NEW YORK   1978

HANSEL
AND
GRETEL
IN
BEVERLY
HILLS

A NOVEL BY
SHEILA WELLER

Portions of this book originally appeared in *New Dawn* magazine.

Grateful acknowledgment is made for permission to reprint previously published lyrics of the following songs:

"Fly, Robin, Fly," by Sylvester Levay and Stephen Prager. Copyright © 1975 by Edition Meridian Butterfly. All rights reserved for the U.S.A. Administered by Midsong Music, Inc. Used by permission.
"The Party's Over," by Comden, Green and Styne. Copyright © 1956 by Betty Comden, Adolph Green and Jules Styne. Stratford Music Corp., owner of publication and allied rights throughout the world. Chappell & Co., Inc., and G. Schirmer, Inc., Publishers. International copyright secured ALL RIGHTS RESERVED. Used by permission.
"Guess I'll Hang My Tears Out to Dry," by Jules Styne and Sammy Cahn. Copyright © 1944 by Chappell & Co., Inc. Stratford Music Corporation, owner of publication and allied rights throughout the world. Sole selling agent: Chappell & Co., Inc. International copyright secured ALL RIGHTS RESERVED. Used by permission.
"Younger Than Springtime," by Rodgers and Hammerstein II. Copyright © 1949 by Richard Rodgers and Oscar Hammerstein II. Williamson Music, Inc., owner of publication and allied rights for the Western Hemisphere and Japan. International copyright secured ALL RIGHTS RESERVED. Used by permission.
"Be Thankful for What You Got," by William De Vaughn. Copyright © 1973 by Downtown Music Company. Used by permission.
"I'll Always Love My Mama," by Kenneth Gamble, Leon Huff, J. Whitehead and G. McFadden. Copyright © 1973 Mighty Three Music, administered by Blackwood Music, Inc., BMI. Used by permission.
"Just Friends," by Sam M. Lewis and John Klenner. Copyright © 1931 Metro-Goldwyn-Mayer, Inc. Renewed 1959 Robbins Music Corporation. All rights administered by Robbins Music Corporation. Used by permission.
"Fly Me to the Moon (In Other Words)." Words and music by Bart Howard. Publisher: TRO. Copyright © 1954 Almanac Music, Inc., New York, N.Y. Used by permission.
"What a Difference a Day Makes." English lyrics by Stanley Adams. Copyright © 1934 Edward B. Marks Music Corporation. Used by permission.
"Chain of Fools," by Donald Covay. Copyright © 1967 Pronto Music, Inc., and 14th Hour Music. Used by permission.
"In the Midnight Hour," by Wilson Pickett and Stephen Cropper. Copyright © 1966 Cotillion Music, Inc., and East Publications. Used by permission.

Library of Congress Cataloging in Publication Data

Weller, Sheila.
    Hansel and Gretel in Beverly Hills.

    I. Title.
PZ4.W4475Han [PS3573.E45714] 813'.5'4 77-27123
ISBN 0-688-03302-4

BOOK DESIGN   CARL WEISS

Printed in the United States of America.

First Edition

1   2   3   4   5   6   7   8   9   10

1

"DON'T MOVE! DON'T OPEN YOUR EYES!" RONALD COMMANDS, releasing his hands from the soufflé of suds on my head.

"Is this a stickup, darling?"

"It's your lash, Lil," he sighs, dabbing his fingers on my left eyelid. "It's all unglued and falling off. How many times do I have to tell you? The hair comes *before* the face."

"The hair comes before the face," I recite. "Now can I open my eyes?"

"Not . . . just . . . yet." He pats my lid decorously.

"Ronald," I groan, "Benny Chiu wants blind items, not a blind publicist."

"Li-il, I am trying to rescue your face."

So I sit obediently now on my fake-fur bathroom stool with Clairol Blue dripping down my neck while Ronald presses his motherly fingers over my eyelid.

"If you don't hurry up with that fakokta eyelash, I'm going to look like a melted ice-cream cone."

"Oh, bitch, bitch, bitch." He sighs, merrily put upon. "Did I teach you how to bitch, darling?"

"Did *I* teach *you*?"

His fingers smell of peroxide. Squinting my right eye open, I see them fuss spiderlike with my face, their blond hairs tickling my nose. Through the endless wall of mirrors I see his body sway to the soul music station he always sets my radio to—his forty-year-old belly making gaps in his body shirt; the tiny gold stud he had pierced in his left earlobe glinting along with the fake crystal beads that hang from my bathtub ceiling. Wistfully, he sings over and over with the silly radio voices: "Fly, robin, fly—up up to the sky . . ."

"What are you, leading a kindergarten choir?"

"Just another fairy's mantra, darling," he answers. "Except the way things have been going at Studio One these days, I need the Concorde to get me off the ground. *Now*," he says, "I am going to have to pull this silly lash off and start all over again."

He yanks at the lid.

"Owww!"

"Sorry, darling." The lash is pronged in his fingers like a specimen butterfly. "What did you use on this, anyway? Rubber cement?"

"Sima put it on for me." There must be some extra use I can get from the obsequious UCLA exchange student who rents my daughter's bedroom, aside from discussing the Six-Day War.

"It's not enough that that whimpering little Arab stuffs your refrigerator with her smelly olives? She has to play Erno Laszlo, too?"

"She's a very sweet girl, Sima is."

"Oh, Lil," he laughs, "you'd say that about anybody who's giving you eighty-five dollars a month."

I shrug. "This is true."

Ronald reaches across the porcelain counter for the magnifying mirror he stole for me from his shop. "Now, darling," he says, turbaning my head with a towel, "before I start the rinse-out, I am going to teach you how to put on an eyelash —the right way."

The blown-up face in the mirror winces back at me. It does not look attractive wincing. It looks nervous and graceless and frightened and two months away from fifty-four.

"Ronald," I ask, "remember those old Ethel Merman specials where this whole chorus line of young guys in top hats and tails prance around the old dame and then hoist her up on their shoulders? Ronald, is that us?"

"Lil," he reminds me softly, tucking the errant strands under the towel, "I've used your shoulders, too."

But now, looking at this face full of ill-disguised lines and pores and freckles—one eyelash on, one eyelash off; my eyes anxiously searching my face for humor, or, failing that, for dignity—the old dame comes tumbling down.

I push the mirror aside. "Later for the eyelash," I simply say.

"Lil, please don't be negative," he says, softly easing my head into the sink. "I mean, you are *going* to get this job, darling. You are going to snow that phony Chinaman with your wit and your charm and your elegance. Honey, you've *lived.* You were the belle of the ball when he was just a little pisher cutting maraschino cherries."

"But this town is full of sharp young women who've been doing publicity for all the new restaurants."

"They're just silly, hungry young flits, sweetheart. You're a *woman.* He is going to love you. Benny Chiu is going to *love you madly.* Now think like a winner, darling."

"Oh, Ronald," I sigh under the whoosh of tap water, "you'd make a great high school basketball coach."

"Would that I could be, darling. Would that I could."

As Ronald's fingers gently coax the soap out of my hair, the phone rings.

"Oh, God. It's Sylvia again."

"Every ten minutes." Ronald shakes his head. "What does that woman think she is: a labor pain?"

"Get rid of her for me, will you? Say I'm under the dryer?" But as he lifts up the receiver with his soapy hand, I raise my head from the sink. *I changed my mind,* I mouth, with urgent, flappy gestures, *I'll take it.*

"Sylvia, I can only talk a minute."

"Lil, don't wear the pantsuit," she launches in, as if we had never hung up. "Wear the black tunic from Saks."

Ronald pouts impatiently. *I'll just be a second,* I mime to him—my head crunched sideways, squeezing the wet phone to my wetter cheek, while Sylvia explains: "It goes *over* the hips instead of stopping *at* the hips, if you know what I mean."

"Okay, Syl, okay."

"And tell him you'll do a noodle-eating contest. Phil's sister-in-law can get it into the Beverly *Citizen* at least."

"Sylvia, have you ever heard of first things first? I want to convince Benny that I'm alive before making with all the corny ideas."

"What's corny?" Sylvia barks. "Listen, when I was doing publicity for Romano's, I had a linguine-eating festival. I even got a man from the Guinness Book of Records to come. Now *that* was a coup."

Ronald's lips contort noiselessly: *Hang up!*

"It ended up he couldn't publish the results," Sylvia goes on, "but did it hurt to have him there, with his British accent and everything? Lil, I'm telling you, gimmicks are the *bulwark* of publicity."

"Sylvia, I don't mean to insult you, but working three months for nothing for that little Italian dive in the Valley doesn't make you a Professor Emeritus of Public Relations."

"All right, don't listen to me," she huffs.

"It's not that I'm not listening, Syl. It's just that I'd like to have a nickel for every old broad in this town who'll stick stamps on seven-cents-off mailings for Chicken Delight and call herself a publicist for it." I pause. "And I wish one of them wasn't me. I'm nervous about seeing Benny again."

"*Why nervous?*" she croaks. "Look, anyone who worked the bar in a red monkey jacket at your own private parties is forever in your debt. It's like an adultery claim." Oh, God, the inevitable simile. "With photographs. You've got him by the balls."

"Sylvia," I correct her, "I'm going in hat-in-hand. The old days are over." It wasn't enough that Morty had to divorce me, he had to die on me, too? "I can't borrow against my past. They've changed the lousy currency."

"Amen to that, darling," Ronald whispers. "Amen to that." Then, for Sylvia's benefit, he whines loudly: "Lil, if you don't get off the phone *this second*, your hair is going to be so matted I'll need to borrow a rake to comb it."

"What's he bitching about?" Sylvia grumbles.

"Look, Sylvia, I've got to hang up."

"All right, Lil," he tries again, louder this time. *"Be* a Rastafarian. See if I care."

"What *is* he talking about?"

"I don't know, Syl, but I'm late. And Ronald's got to get back to the shop. I've got to hang up."

"Okay, but just remember this." I hold the phone away from my ear. "Ask Benny for a straight salary, not commissions. What Morty didn't give you from the real estate you can earn back in two years."

"Good-bye, Sylvia." I hang up.

"I swear," Ronald breathes, raising his big-toothed comb to my hair, "without the Civil Code that woman would be mute. Does she discuss her custody settlement with the delivery boy from Gelsen's?"

"For all I know, she discusses mine."

The difference between Sylvia and me is that when Irv left her six years ago, she became one of those professional divorcees—plumbing her own legal wreckage for cocktail party chat, leafing through other women's wrecks for footnotes. She's turned into a sort of Rona Barrett of alimony gossip, a Rod McKuen of interlocutory metaphors.

She found her calling.

And I found Ronald.

"Darling," I say now, patting his hand as it combs through my hair, "thanks for helping me get rid of her."

"One good turn deserves another. I mean, who else would have made my phone ring and ring and ring all last Saturday night when I was trying to impress that hot little chicken?"

"Who else would you have asked?"

"Oh, Lil," he laughs, spanking a clean towel in the air. "We *are* birds of a feather."

"Yeah, the crow and the woodpecker. I caw, and you peck heads."

"*Crow?* Gimme a break." He tucks the towel in the neckband of my dressing gown. "You're a fabulous, fabulous raven." He bends to get eye-level with me, squints in the mirror as he slowly centers my head just-so with his palms. Then he picks up his scissors. "Now, darling, we are going to *make you shine.*"

"What about the eyelash?" I ask as he snips.

"Don't worry. I'll put it back on for you."

"You sure you know how?"

"Honest to God, Lil. You think I roomed with that silly queen for three months to learn how to change hubcaps?"

"Darling," I laugh, "I'll never doubt you again."

"You shouldn't, you know," he says softly, preoccupied with the snipping and squinting.

"Ronald," I ask in a small voice, after a silence, "was I being . . . nudgey today?"

"Don't be silly." He flaps his hand in generous dismissal.

"I'm sorry if I was."

"Lil, I've been nudgey with you plenty of times."

"Just a couple."

"A *couple?* Either you've got a bad memory or you're being awfully charitable."

"I'm putting that last remark on record for the next time you call me a stingy kike."

"I take it back," he says, plugging in his blow dryer. "You just have a bad memory."

"What I love about you, darling, is you're always good for a compliment."

"When you're still trucking around at my age, pet, you better be good for something."

He sighs.

I smile.

And I lean back and feel the warmth of his blower caress my neck like a Puerto Vallarta breeze.

卐

I'm scared.

I'm scared, and I should have worn the tunic, like Sylvia said.

"Yes, I have an appointment with Mr. Chiu?" I say to the smart-looking woman in the silk jumpsuit who comes out to greet me.

"Lillian Resnick?"

I nod.

"Of course." She smiles warmly. "I'll run and tell Benny you're here."

Instantly I feel better.

Though, on second thought, she may be just patronizing me. Maybe Benny said, "Lil Resnick? Funny old dame. We go back twenty years. Called the other day, something about publicity work. Yes, she was a publicist once. Look, I'll give her lunch, shmooz with her a little. Be nice to her, will you? She was a jewel, as they went. She was a—"

Li-il, now honestly.

You're right, Ronald. I'm getting all worked up over nothing.

Darling, just sit down, relax, and for God's sake, keep your fingers out of your hair.

I sit down on a teak and velvet settee and stare at a little stone lion of some dynasty or other who is gurgling a waterfall out of his mouth; at a wall of framed pictures: Benny smiling in on various dining celebrities; Benny graciously presenting a check to the March of Dimes girl; Benny sticking chrysanthemums into a Rose Bowl float of a dragon.

In front of me, a whistling bartender is slicing limes, and Mexican busboys set up tables—just like they did at Ciro's when I'd saunter in on those afternoons—God, was it really twenty years ago?—straight from the hairdresser, the caterer, from driving the cleaning girl to the bus. Doris the hatcheck would smile up from that little pile of cardboard tickets she was sorting on the Dutch door ledge of her closet. Sandy the cigarette girl would hail, "Lil, how are you?" Al the maître d' would pleasantly inquire, "Another party tonight, Mrs. Resnick?" his hands clasped behind his back.

I'd smile to them all—the brightly generous smile of the favored patron. Then I'd call out, "Benny, you ready?" And out he'd trot in those quick, anxious little steps of his, his red uniform swinging from the coat hanger he held high. "Sorry to keep you waiting, Mrs. Resnick." So grateful to moonlight, so grateful for the lift, so grateful for anything I could do.

"Lillian. My God, it's been a long time." Shaking his head, smiling like a pleased uncle, Benny walks toward me now in slow, confident steps. "How *are* you?"

"Good, Benny." I smile. We hug. "And you? How've you been?"

"Can't complain." He sits down next to me. "Except that I haven't heard from you since I opened this place." His tone is like a tweak on an impish child's nose. "You know, I've had a whole pot of Lobster Chiu with your name on it simmering on the stove for about three years now."

"I've meant to come by, Benny. Really I have."

"The Chinese have a saying: Without those who held the ladder when you started your climb, you're left on the top rung alone."

"Well, I've certainly been following your ascent. I mean, the post-Emmys dinner anyone can do. But a banquet for that touchie-feelie group in Topanga? Now *that's* what I call success."

He's tickled. "You caught that? On Channel Eleven?"

"You bet I caught it. In fact, I was afraid if I got any closer to the screen I'd catch something else. That guru character with the beard to his navel. What did they do? Clone Sterling Hayden?" Benny laughs. "When he started talking about Oriental food's effect on sex, I expected to walk into Rexall's the next day and find your bottled Egg Drop soup right up there on the shelf next to the lecithin."

"Lil, you haven't changed."

We both smile fondly.

"Neither have you, Benny. Never missing an angle."

"Your ex-husband hit the nail on the head, remember? 'You don't fool me for a minute, Benny. You're not Chinese, you're just a Jew with a . . . a Jew with a . . .' "

"A Jew who's been wearing a tight bathing cap."

"Right." He shakes his head. "God, what we laughed at back then."

"Yes," I muse along. "Back then." When bad jokes were just part of the luxury, not part of the survival.

"Now." He takes both my hands in his and stands me up. "Let me give you a nice seven-course Cantonese lunch and we'll catch up."

"That sounds delicious, Benny. But can I take a rain check on six of them? I'm on this diet."

"Diet? You? Lil, you're looking marvelous."

I smile modestly. "Thank you, Benny." Then drop my
eyes to the floor to escape his painful graciousness.

"So you're back in publicity?" he asks, as we slide into a
corner booth.

"Well, more or less. It's been, well, actually, a good few
years since I've been with an agency. But I've been doing
freelance in the meantime. Just little things, small accounts.
A young actress, Gwynneth Coburn-Coxe? You probably
never heard of her." Stop with the self-effacement already.
You want to run yourself into the ground?

"I think that's wonderful, Lil."

"So when I heard you were going to open a new place at
the Marina, I thought"—is this shrug convincingly casual?—
"well, why not give a call. I mean, I was pretty sure you'd
have a big agency doing it, but, you know, why not? At least
to say hello."

"I'm delighted you called, Lil. Really. And there may be
some way we can work you into it."

"Benny, look. I don't want to put you on the spot."

"You're not putting me on any spot."

"*Really?*"

"Of course not." He smiles reassuringly. "Lil, let's have
a drink, and you tell me about you. Business can wait."

"Business can wait?" I squint. "Is this the anxious little
busboy I used to know, who read his USC restaurant manual between making vodka gimlets? Success has made you
a very smooth man, Benny."

"Nah, I'm still the nervous little coolie. I just hide it well.
Under that bathing cap. Seung!" He hails a passing waiter.
"Bring us a bottle of private-stock Beaujolais. So Lillian,
what have you been up to all these years?"

"What have I been up to?" I take a long breath. "Well, let's see . . ."

I feel like a stumped quiz show contestant. Pressured to arrange the right answer for the prize when all I really want to say is: Benny, I've been living off my investments and going shopping and getting my hair done, and sometimes I feel like the dolled-up old broad who arrived just as they were singing, "The party's o-verrr, it's time to call it a day . . ." and who stands and pouts at the schmutz left on the hors d'oeuvres tray and finally says to herself, Okay, either eat it or pass—but don't bitch.

I remember last winter, when Ronald took me out to dinner after my hysterectomy—as we sat at La Scala and clinked champagne glasses and I told him funny hospital stories and he laughed and I laughed, I suddenly thought, Jesus, sometimes it takes all my energy just not to feel neutered, just not to feel orphaned.

Now, summoning that energy again, I answer Benny: "Well, I've moved—to a lovely two-bedroom on Lasky Drive. I did it mostly in wicker and antiques—not heavy, like the old house on Oakhurst. Wicker and antiques and about forty plants."

"Where'd you get the green thumb, Lil? You were the lady who used to call your bougainvillea pansies."

"Oh, you Orientals with your flower fetishes. Listen, those bougainvillea, the way they looked? They should've been flattered." Good, I've got him laughing. "No, but seriously, I love the new place. That house on Oakhurst was just too big. Who needs a two-story remodeled Spanish on a 600 block? I mean, first we squared off the arches, then we rounded the arches, then we tacked on the lanai, then we put up the Regency front. One more face lift and that house would have qualified for Blue Cross." How am I doing, Ronald? Am I doing okay?

"Anyway, the new place is perfect for me. And it's big enough for Andrea, when she comes to visit. She's twenty-five now, can you believe it? After college, she decided this town was one big freeway and eighty taco stands. Or was it one big taco stand and eighty freeways? You know how they talk. I miss her a lot, but what can you do?"

"What *can* you do?" Benny empathizes. He nods approval to the waiter for the wine. "The Chinese have a saying: Everyone's land of milk and honey is past the last horizon."

"The Chinese have a saying for everything, don't they?"

He laughs. "Lil, was it you who used to say, 'Benny, if you can't make it in the restaurant business, you can always write copy for Hallmark'?"

"Either me or Morty, I can't remember."

He smiles. I smile. "I know, Benny. God, the dreadful jokes. But, except for the end, those were sweet, sweet days."

"They were," he says. "To you, Lil." Raising his wine-glass. "One of the great hostesses, one of the great ladies."

"To you." I raise mine. "And to the new restaurant."

The wine goes down warm into my empty stomach. I feel young, relaxed, hopeful.

"Will you consider postponing that diet, Lil?" he cajoles.

"Well," I smile. "For an old friend . . ."

As we eat, my mind races back to that party we had New Year's Eve, 1965. Ciro's was gone by then—most of the other clubs on the Strip as well—so we borrowed Benny from the La Cienega steakhouse where he was then the afternoon manager.

I was wearing a rust-colored chiffon and the new ruby earrings Morty had just bought me for Christmas, and we had a Sinatra record on, and I was singing along, "When I want rain, I get sunny weather. I'm just as blue as the sky . . ." as I mingled with our guests, hugging, laughing, toasting, drinking, greeting.

Someone squeezed my arm. I turned and embraced Ray Bleiberg, our bachelor friend and collector of Dunes Hotel showgirls. "Lillian," he said of the tall, bosomy brunette at his side, "I'd like you to meet Alana Martin."

"So nice to meet you. I've heard so much about you," the girl said sweetly.

"I was just telling Alana," Ray explained, "how sometimes if we're all around a piano and someone pulls out the sheet music to *Call Me Madam*, you get to work on it and if we all close our eyes, we swear we're hearing Merman in the flesh."

"Flesh? Who goes to work in the flesh?" Morty moved in with a wry smile. "Ray, are you pimping my wife again?"

The two men bear hugged.

"Alana, this is Morty Resnick. We only tolerate him because of his decent scotch and his marvelous wife."

"Tell me, Alana," Morty kibitzed back, shaking her hand, "why do gonif contractors always wind up with the most beautiful women?"

"To protect them from shyster lawyers," Ray returned. Then, after the laughter, "We were just discussing Lil's impersonations, Mort."

"Listen," Morty said, squeezing me proudly, "it doesn't hurt to have a little extra talent in the house. The way my man at Shearson Hammill is falling asleep at the wheel, *she* may end up going out and supporting me."

"*If* you can get me out of the house on time for work," I piped in, carving an opening for Morty.

"Ray, have I ever described what it's like getting Lil out of the house on time? This you wouldn't believe." He loosened his grip on my shoulder to illustrate. "First she goes through her purse three times. Then she changes her clothes twice. She's got one foot out the door—all this is happening while I'm waiting for her in the car, you understand—she's got one foot out the door and then Sylvia calls. She's talking to Sylvia, she decides she has to change her dress again, which means she also has to rearrange her purse. By the time she comes out, I've got beard stubble."

"I keep telling Morty," I sighed in exasperation, "just keep an extra shaver in the car."

Ray laughed. Alana laughed. And Morty hugged me like Burns hugging Allen as the curtain goes down.

Bits, bits, we were always doing bits. "It's what you get for hanging around with frustrated comics at the city desk," I said to Morty when I first met him. It was back in '47, and I had just left my job at the *New York World Telegram* to go to the Coast. Morty had just been made a junior partner in a firm that specialized in show business. Each night, he'd crawl out from under the law stacks and go down to Ciro's to reclaim his better self, the fellow on the third barstool in any Damon Runyon story. (There was enough teenage Brooklyn romantic left in Morty to be ashamed of his stolid profession.) I was there at ringside one night, laughing with friends, pretending the man I loved wasn't 3,000 miles away and engaged to another woman. The waiter delivered a note: "Do my glasses need cleaning, or are you really Ann Sheridan?" "No," I scribbled back, "but anything can be arranged for a price."

We fell in love in a way that was so sweet, so perfect, it made everything before seem excusable, everything after seem just. Five months later, we decided to get married. We asked Morty's best friend, Irv, and Irv's very pregnant wife, Sylvia, to come along and be our witnesses.

"How about Tijuana?" Morty suggested.

"With Sylvia?" I said. "Are you crazy? The customs guard on the way back will arrest her for smuggling Crenshaw melons."

"This one," Irv drawled, rabbinically, "this one is a handful, Mort."

"I'm prepared," Morty said. And he smiled at me with such pride, such tough tough tenderness.

And it was that pride that I would feel when we gave those parties ten, twelve, eighteen years later. Who cared that the chasm had already opened? That during the week Morty was distant and condescending, shouting *neurotic! neurotic! neurotic!* (so loud, so often that Andrea started singing the word to the tune of "A-Tisket, A-Tasket")? When we were standing there with our drinks and our friends— talking as halves of a whole, as George-and-Gracie, Hennie-and-Milty, Man-and-Wife; when every line, wink and nudge had a history; when he'd squeeze my shoulder and smile— I felt it as I'd heard it that night: *I'm prepared*, sickness or health, I take this woman, I have taken this woman, yes.

I left Morty with Ray and Alana and continued circulating, singing, "Friends ask me out. I tell them I'm busy. Must get a new alibi . . ." I felt a tug at my sleeve.

"That one, with the French twist," Sylvia whispered, nodding in the trio's direction. "I'd keep an eye on her."

"Come on, Sylvia. She's just a nice, boring Midwestern girl with legs that go up to her armpits. Like every one of the rest of them Ray brings around."

"Yes, but she's hungry."

"Oh, Syl, really." I shrugged off her cloying suspicion and went to the bar.

"How's it going, Benny? Ice holding up?"

"Fine, Mrs. Resnick, plenty." Automatically refilling my glass. "A wonderful party, Mrs. Resnick."

"Thanks, Benny. But Benny?" I smiled. "Come on, I'm not that old. You can call me Lil."

"Now here's the situation with the new restaurant, Lil." Benny's voice jolts me back. "We're refurbishing the place now—nice old seafood place on the pier. Publicity-wise, it'll be another five months before I'm ready to make any announcement. I know from experience that premature write-ups only help the competition. You know, you're taking two steps, the Luau and Jade West will take four. It's a hot area, the Marina."

I nod.

"Now, I'm turning the P.R. over to Shroeder and Klein. I don't like going the big-agency route, but with independents—and I certainly don't mean you, Lil—but with independents there are always complications. Work overload. Personality clashes. Column plants against my patrons' wishes. You know, just general tsuris."

"As they'd say in Peking."

"Exactly." He smiles. "Now, what I can do, what I'd like to do, is recommend you to Bill Shroeder. As a sort of per diem adjunct to the account."

Sure, sure. I can just hear it. Hiya, Bill? This is Benny. Listen, I'm sending over a swell old dame. Do me a favor and give her something to do, okay? Some plants for the Sherman Oaks papers? Let her leak our color scheme to *Southland Flatware Suppliers Monthly*, write some puns for Skolsky? She's funny, you'll love her. Just bill me.

"But Shroeder and Klein are the top agency in the business, Benny. I can't just breeze in there: recommendation, no recommendation. It's a favor, and I appreciate it, really I do, but I'm just not on their level."

"Of course you are." Oh, the munificence power affords. "Will you at least think about it, Lil?"

"Yes, of course. And thank you."

But then what did I expect? That Benny would give me work any other way? *Assertiveness*, Edith and Andi both said, like it was the name of a new religion. A religion for the prideless and the young.

"You can call me any time, Lil. Give me the word and I'll notify Bill. You're from a very important part of my past, you know. And Lil," he adds gently, "in case you were wondering, and I didn't want to bring it up, but I'd like you to know: They never came in here, the two of them. In fact, I didn't even stay in touch with Morty. I liked him, you know I liked him, but, well, the Chinese have a—"

"Benny." I smile and touch his wrist. "Thanks, but, please, you don't have to bother. I mean, Morty wouldn't even have appreciated it. He used to throw out the fortune when he opened the cookie anyway."

"All right, Lil." But his understanding chuckle doesn't quite dissolve the subject we've just broached. "She was nothing like you," he presses on, loyally. "You couldn't laugh at anything she said."

"Well, men need different things at different times in their lives, I guess. Oh, God, listen to me! Now *I* sound like the Chinaman."

He enjoys that for a minute; then he squints, as if trying hard to remember something. "I've even forgotten her name. Agatha, was it?"

"Alana," I correct, grateful for his intentional slip. "I hear she's remarried now, to some plastic surgeon." He opens his mouth as if to form a response to that little irony—but that's enough of the past for right now, enough of his thick consolation. "My God, this lobster is good, Benny."

"See what you've been missing all these years you stayed away?"

I smile and nod. I take one more bite; then, so as not to be tempted to finish it, I push my plate away.

As I walk through the glass Deco doors, Gwynneth's huge straw hat looms up from the *Interview* magazine splayed on the reception desk. The half of her face that isn't covered by those giant sunglasses greets me in a Quaalude smile. "Hey, Lil, how ya doin'?"

"I don't know. Yes, I do know. Not well."

"Ow, wow, bummed out? How come?"

"That's what I have to talk to Ronald to figure out. Is he free now?"

"For you? Always. Just sit down. Mellow out. Let me get him."

She turns around and peeks past the shoji screen to where Ronald and five other people like him are snipping and combing to quadraphonic disco music. "It's cool," she reports.

But he seems addled to me: hunched over to comb out the Rapunzel hair of a beatific-looking brunette.

"I *would* get the one who's testing for the remake of *National Velvet*," he mutters under his breath.

I scan her waist-length hair. "Is she riding it or playing it?"

"Who knows, darling," he sighs as I follow him to his supplies tray. "It's been madness since I left your apartment. Sheer, sheer madness." He pouts over the implements laid on the white towel, serious as a surgeon. "Oh, where is my number-three comb? Why don't they *organize* things around here?" He picks up a comb. "My two o'clock was forty minutes late. My three o'clock brought her Lasa. My three-thirty had a positive seizure over the fermodyl. 'Goat placenta?' she says. 'You're putting *goat placenta* in my hair?!' I felt like saying, 'Darling, relax. Before they did your hysto, you had one yourself.' But never mind that, darling. What happened with Benny?"

"Well, first of all, no job." He purses his lips, empathetically annoyed. "And second, I don't know. I felt like a performing bear. I just—"

"Darling," he says nervously, "I want to hear *all* about it, but if I don't blow her immediately, she snarls and mats. Here." He hands me a movie magazine and jerkily wheels his tray of rollers. "Read about Chad Everett's heartbreak. Just fifteen minutes, I promise."

"There really isn't much to say," I persist, trailing him back to Miss National Velvet, "except he was young and calm and I was old and nervous. Churning out shtiks for dear life. And I *know* he could see through it. *Anybody* could." I raise my voice to be heard over his blow dryer. "But what else could I do? At my age, nobody wants to hear your fears. They'd rather suffer through a bad Phyllis Diller routine and be done with it. You know what I realized when I left Benny? I realized why I hide when I see someone from the old days. Why I bury my head in the menu if someone who knew Morty and me sits down across the counter from me at Nibblers. Why I put on my sunglasses and pay without eating. You know how I tell you how silly I always feel when I resort to that?" Somberly, his eyes fastened on the brunette mane, he nods. "Well, it's not so silly. It's just too much effort to lie. And too much humiliation to be watched while you're lying."

"But that's all in your head, Lil," he says as he's said so many times before. "You've *blossomed* on your own, darling. You know that. Those dolts from the old days are still moldering over the ninth hole at Hillcrest. They're too boring to be camp, darling. You're a gem."

"Oh, Ronald, you're just saying that."

"I mean it, Lil. I mean it."

I hunt his preoccupied eyes over the curtain of dark wet hair he's unsnarling. I know I shouldn't clutch like this, shouldn't pump him for flattery when he's so busy, but I just can't help it. "I don't know," I wonder. "Did I keep my dignity with Benny? It gets harder and harder to tell. Do I have any dignity left to keep?"

"Do you have any dignity? Are you kidding?" He pulls me aside and cocks his head to the thin young girls mirrored all around us: their wet hair splayed on brown towels, their mouths full of canteloupe, their chins high with pride. "You have more dignity—more soul—in your left earlobe than any of these little chippies have in their whole anorexic little bods, darling. You know that, Lil. Don't I always tell you?"

"Do you ever," I smirk, shamed by the comfort. "And do I ever ask."

"Well, darling," he croons, making a grand gesture with his big-toothed comb, "we've all got to get our little strokes where we can. And speaking of strokes—"

"I think I hear a blue joke coming on." I peck him on the cheek. "I'm sitting down."

"Oh, Lil, you're *awful*," he laughs, swatting me on the rump. "Isn't she awful?" he asks Miss National Velvet.

Miss National Velvet giggles politely over her strawberry

kefir. I sit down in one of the white bentwoods they use
instead of clumsy barber chairs, listlessly pick up the magazine.

"Darling, it's a scream," he calls out over the dryer.

"What's a scream?"

"Chad Everett's heartbreak. Page 14, I think."

"Who wants to read about Chad Everett's heartbreak?"

"Then get yourself a *Vogue* and read about Diane Von
Furstenberg's maid's room."

"God, in that case I'd rather read about Chad Everett's
heartbreak."

I open the magazine, close it, put it down. Taped to the
mirror in front of me is Ronald's certificate. "Undernoted
having paid the statutory fee is hereby licensed under the
business and professional code to operate as Ronald Halvorsen, cosmetologist," it says, alongside his picture. He hates
that picture ("but one day," he sighs, "one day I'll get my
Scavullo replacement") but I'm rather fond of it. In those
pious, supplicating eyes that mugshots always give you, I see
the chubby Minneapolis kid he is always telling me about.
The one who joined the Russ Tamblyn Fan Club under
his sister's name just to get the 8 by 10 glossy. The one who
was rejected from theater arts school when he froze during
a reading of the Odets scene he'd practiced a month. The
one who "couldn't even come out of the closet, darling,
without banging my head on the coat hangers first." Ronald
has taught me that nothing is too sacredly shameful, too
sacredly painful not to be restored by the wisdom of self-
mockery. Yet it is in his lapses in that language—lapses like
the eyes in this photograph—that I love him most.

He is secretly so earnest—most of all when he talks about
Raulito, the Nicaraguan orphan he sends checks to every
month. Two years ago, Ronald spent almost a thousand

dollars having the boy's curvature of the spine corrected. I only know that because one day while I was going through his drawers looking for a nail scissors I found a thank you letter from the Agency, along with a picture of the bewildered child on crutches, wearing a denim outfit Ronald had sent. "A thousand dollars! My God, Ronald, how sweet of you," I said when he came back in the room. "Why is it sweet of me?" he'd snapped, as if I had challenged his integrity. "Parents spend forty times as much on their own kids. I'm not such a limpwrist that I can't meet responsibilities, you know."

I pick up the out-of-focus Polaroid of the child he has propped in its silver frame against a glass jar of cotton balls. "Is this a new picture?" I call out.

"Yes. Isn't he something?" He comes and peers proudly over my shoulder at the blurred snapshot. "I'm going shopping for clothes for his ninth birthday after work. I'm trying to figure out what size he is now."

"Don't they say in the letter?"

"Who had time to shlep down to Taco Bell to get it translated? After the Dear Sponsor, it's all in Spanish."

"Sylvia's maid's from El Salvador. I could bring it to her tonight."

"No. No time." He shakes his head briefly, righteously. "I want him to get the clothes by his birthday and I don't trust the mail delivery in that crazy country." He doesn't trust Sylvia, either. Or her maid. "I'll get him size twelve pants. He can always grow into them. Yes. Twelves." He nods his head, as wonderfully self-serious as his idea of a real father saying, "Dartmouth, son. Take Dartmouth, not Yale," and goes back to his customer.

Over the whir of the hair dryers, Gwynneth's spiked '40s heels make clicking noises on the linoleum. Her French jeans are skin-tight; her man-tailored shirt is unbuttoned half the way down and knotted at the midriff. Between that unvarying outfit and the unvarying wide-brim hat, she looks like Rosalind Russell at both ends and Harry Belafonte in between.

That's Ronald's description. He said for me to use it on the press release I'm writing for her. Gwynneth Coburn-Coxe. Age: 28, with the sunglasses; 35, without. Onetime British boarding school girl. Onetime child bride of Sutton Place investor. More recently, neo-actress, aficionado of surf bums, stenciler of T-shirts. Latest incarnation: voracious though late-blooming Lesbian and (temporary) beauty parlor receptionist. Take on life basically reducible to three expletives: "mel-low," "looove it!" and "Noo way." Looking for contemporized Diane Varsi part. Or *any* part. Can be found in her run-down Porsche and occasionally in various borrowed living rooms in a litter of empty amyl nitrate poppers and spent, boy-bodied girl friends.

Gwynneth taps Ronald on the shoulder. Wearily, his hands working National Velvet's mane into six hairclipped clumps, he bends his ear.

"Lil, come here," she calls gaily.

"Oh, don't bother Lil with that," Ronald complains.

I put down the movie magazine and walk over.

"Lil, I've got this new friend, Edwin. You'll just looove him." Gwynneth always shimmies on her vowels. "He's a black actor. Sooo bright. Sooo together. He did *Othello* in summer stock for years."

"He did *Othello* like I did Tadzio in *Death in Venice*," Ronald cuts in. "Lil, he sells plumbing equipment in Santa Monica."

"Ronald, don't be a piss, darling. You know that's only temporary. Anyway," turning back to me, "I was just talking to him on the phone and he was saying how he wants to get a publicist for film jobs. And I said I know this fantastic woman he'd just adooore."

I happen to have met Gwynneth on one of those rare nights I let Ronald drag me to a discotheque. Since then, she's been under the impression that I'm a collector of eccentrics. Or, God knows, maybe she thinks I'm one myself.

"Oh, I don't know, Gwynneth," I say. "I've never done publicity for a black Othello. Or a white one, for that matter. Does he wear those shmattes with the slit at the neck? Or can I sit down for lunch with him without feeling like the ambassador to Kenya?"

"A dashiki? Nooo way. Listen, the night I met him he was wearing this tweed jacket and like this bowler hat and reciting all this weird poetry. I mean, at Studio One? Don't you love it? I looked at him and thought"—shaking her smiling head almost religiously—"this one is *off—the—wall.* Oh, you'll just looove him, Lil. I'll call him back right now."

"Who is this guy?" I ask Ronald, after Gwynneth goes clicking back to her desk.

"God knows. Some stud with a gimmick." He dismisses it all with a flap of his hand. "She procures for him or he procures for her. Or *some*thing. It's all a bit too much for my poor little head to take right now. Let me just comb this one out and let's get out of here."

Two hours later, we walk in the twilight down Rodeo Drive, laden with Ronald's gift-wrapped packages for Raulito.

I turn to him. "Have dinner with me? I can unfreeze a steak."

"I wish I could, Lil, but I've got this thing I can't get out of."

"A date?" I ask hopefully.

"Maybe I *can* get out of it. I'll call him and say—"

"Look, Ronald, if it's a date, don't you dare break it for me. Who is he?"

"Oh, just some person I met the other night." The sigh is not felicitous. He is tired, disappointed, and tired of his own disappointment. "A window dresser or something at Penney's. He's making a dinner. I shouldn't have even accepted."

"Why not? What's so wrong with him?"

He can sense a scolding coming on. "He's just not my type," he says tersely.

"He's pursuing you, so of course you're not interested, right? You finally meet someone who's acting decent and interested so there *has* to be something wrong with him. You're going to throw away some perfectly nice person to go pining for some cruel little hood who'll make you drop forty dollars before he even gives you the privilege of being stood up at some dive in Hermosa Beach. Am I right, Ronald? *Am I right?*"

"Oh, Lil," he sighs, as we enter the deserted parking lot. "Why did I ever make you so hip?"

"I beg your pardon, darling. Who told whom that she was the hippest yenta he'd ever met?"

"You were. I mean, you are. I mean—oh, you know what I mean, Lil. Sometimes I love it when you nag, but other times—"

"*Constructively* nag," I correct.

"Sometimes I love it when you *constructively* nag, but right now, it's just . . . I'm exhausted. I mean: *What can I say?*" He shrugs his whole body in perturbed surrender. "You're *right*. I've spent the whole day thinking about a little punk who'll probably dump all over me, if it even gets that far. You're right, you're right, you're *right*."

Under the dim streetlights his face suddenly looks as vulnerable as in that silly beautician's license. And suddenly I want it *not* to be. Clutching this ridiculous wet doggie bag of lobster that Benny gave me, watching Ronald's tired eyes, I want all his levity back, his silliness, his sarcasm. There is an unwritten rule in this friendship of ours that we can't both feel defeated at the same time. We need one another for the rock at the other end of the seesaw, that weight where the body used to be. So many times we have grasped at bad jokes, sloppy puns, *anything* just to restore that buoyance so sweetly false it's merciful.

"I'm sorry, darling," I say softly. "I was being hard on you. Do you want to tell me about him? The kid?"

"Oh, he's just a mechanic," he says, sheepish with self-contempt. "A kid from Riverside with Pennzoil on his jeans and three hundred tools."

"Well," I shrug, "at least you can bring him by to fix my broken toaster."

"Oh, what a hunk, Lil. The face of an angel, I swear." He sighs. "This doll is a sucker again."

"So don't be a sucker," I whisper. "Put him out of your mind."

"But he said he'd call."

"But they *all* say that. I hate what it does to you to believe it."

"What can I say, Lil? This one said it like he meant it."

"Come on, Ronald. Some dumb punk with grease on his T-shirt? You're waiting for *this*?"

"But, Lil, you *know* I was destined to be Stella Kowalski."

I close my eyes for a couple of seconds, then look at him pleadingly. "Does it always have to be a joke on yourself? *Always?* Just this once, be good to yourself. Please? Forget him?"

"Come on, darling." He takes my arm. "I'll walk you to your car."

"Will you just *try* to be interested in the guy tonight?"

"I will, darling." He pats my arm as we walk. "I promise. What are you going to do tonight?"

"Watch television, I guess. Go to sleep."

"I'll call you at eleven to see how you're doing," he says, opening my Mustang door.

"I'll be okay."

"I'll call anyway."

"Now don't you get worried about me. I was the one who was worried about you, remember?"

He pecks me on the cheek. I close the door, turn on the ignition, the lights, adjust the rearview mirror. Ronald's car lights flash behind me. He follows me out of the parking lot. I turn right. He turns left. And we drive off to our separate nights down the clean and silent street.

2

IN THE DAYS WHEN I COULD STILL AFFORD TO BE SMUG, MORTY
and I would sit watching *This Is Your Life* on Wednesday
nights. There was Ralph Edwards, like a shaygets Moses,
clasping that scrapbook like the Talmud while his poor
guest, who until that moment had probably been doing her
damndest to forget most of her past, sat captive in the folds
of a fat tufted couch. Some echoey voice would blast out a
cloying remembrance. The guest would swoon with anguish
helplessly disguised as delight. The curtain would rise and

out they'd rush: the daughter and son-in-law and children; the son and daughter-in-law and children; the limping grade school piano teacher they exhumed and flew in, the cheery-faced geriatric boss from the first job; the whole rosy-cheeked, twinkly-eyed bunch; smothering the poor victim on the sofa, crowding on the arms of the sofa, leaning on the back of the sofa, spitting in her face with nostalgia and reverence.

"Edwards is like a goddam cop," I once nudged Morty. "Billyclubbing them all into formation with that scrapbook. I bet the poor shmuck in the middle will be the first to beat out for a scotch."

Morty laughed. We turned off the set.

I was young then. I could jeer at it, I suppose, because I took it for granted. I always assumed that the way you were eased into late middle-age was on a sedan chair hoisted up by the people in your life. You could look back and see the whole long thread. What hadn't been so good then would be filmed over now by affection. They always promised you that: that warm, hazy reconstruction, that summing-up, that *forgiveness*. A big goyish overstuffed couch crammed with everyone you ever touched, hurt, loved, laughed with. Those who formed you, those who mattered. Those, at the very least, who survived. A scrapbook of your life. A life.

"Remember *This Is Your Life?*" I ask Ronald, opening my eyes from my reverie.

"Oh, God, yes," he laughs, forking strands of my hair through the plastic bleaching bonnet. "The one where they were always giving out Norge refrigerators and Sara Coventry jewelry. And that fat frog with the mustache who put on the crowns."

"No. *This Is Your Life* was at night. You're thinking of *Queen for a Day*."

"Oh, darling, why didn't they let me be Queen for a Day? I don't want the Norge refrigerator, but I'll take the little hunk who lifted it in on his back."

"I used to laugh at *This Is Your Life*. But now it's not so funny. It was sappy, it was shmaltzy, it was all of those things. But it made you think you'd earn something by the time you were my age. That you at least had a family."

"Sometimes it's better not to have one," he says softly. "It spares you the guilt."

"But your mother understood, you said."

He takes a long sigh. "What else could she say? As long as my father died before he could know, she was grateful. She could soak up the grief for the two of them, just the way she was always soaking up those circles of water under his beer mug, and carry it all to her grave. Darling, you've probably never had the thrill of meeting a genuine Lutheran haus-frau. They wear their suffering just like their aprons. It hangs from their tits to their knees. No, she never understood. Why should she be expected to? I only wish she never had to know."

"What about your sister?"

"Never asks. When I come to St. Paul every two years, I'm the perfect Bachelor Uncle for two weeks. Chaste as a nun, darling. Chaste as a nun. She asks me questions like does Ann-Margret wear a fall and should she buy Polly Bergen's Oil of the Turtle. Deep down, darling, she *knows* she has a sister. I think she gets off on it. But that husband of hers. Straight? Dense? Darling, he makes Jerry Ford look like Oscar Wilde. Everything but the moosehead over the fireplace. One day he took me putting—don't you love it?: *putting*—and he said he had this embarrassing question to ask me. And then he bent over. Bent over! Well, darling, can't you just see me dying? I swear, I thought he was going to drop his pants, right there on the golf course. But he moved his hair away from his bald spot and asked: 'Uh, Ron, between you and me, what can I do to stop this, uh, little deforestation here? I mean, is that to die from or is that to die from?"

"I could die from ammonia inhalation is what I could die from," I complain. "Who'd you steal this formula from? Idi Amin?"

"Darling, you know you need a pre-bleach when you let it go this long. Now let's . . . just . . . *try* not to be testy until the timer goes off. I'm doing the very best I can."

"I know you are." I pat his hand as it brushes past my ear. "I'm just feeling cranky again. I wish I'd have that goddam birthday and get it over with. It's like waiting for your water to break."

"I was thinking of giving you a little party, Lil," he says gingerly.

"A party? *Never*."

"Come on, Lil. Everybody needs a little celebration sometime. I could make my crudités dip. Gwynneth could cut the vegetables. That much I trust her with. We could even get a low-calorie cake from somewhere."

"Yeah, but who would we get to pop out of it?"

"Oh, darling," he sighs. "Don't get me started. Don't get me started on that one . . ."

I let him talk me into it.

And so I'm driving now to Ronald's house above the Strip for whatever it is he's arranged. Sima sits beside me: placid, a casserole pot of stuffed grape leaves cradled in her belly, the fine hairs of her mustache catching the last fierce slants of the mid-April sun. I stop at the Russian roulette traffic circle at Beverly and Lomitas. The pink hotel looms beyond, buttressed by palms waving like the fey signal of a giant monarch. The cars at the five corners face each other head on, creep forward timidly. All these Porsches and Mercedes' in a strange exercise in humility. They never bothered to put up a stoplight here. No one has the right of way.

No one has the right of way. Should I, as I have been doing lately, blow up this silly metaphor for comfort? I have as good a chance as any. Why not? Fifty-four isn't eighty. There is more life left for me now: mine for the taking. Taking is a gesture of the young. I will have to make it mine.

Listen to this, will you? I have become my own goddam Hallmark card, my own Dale Carnegie, my own Daily Word from Lee's Summit, Missouri, for crying out loud! ("For crying out loud!" Morty's line. Who cares that he used it in anger; it seems tender to me now.) But really: Is it a sign of hope, or just absurdity, that these strident banalities aren't silly to me any more? That I find myself desperately repeating them—It's not too late. It's never too late. There is something out there for you. Take life. Seize life. Be happy. Have joy—as if, in the very thinking, my piety will be rewarded. *Then* will I get my tufted chintz sofa and organ music, my scrapbook, my peace, my *This Is Your Life*?

I keep thinking I should have been more reverent when I was younger; when such attitude wasn't a penitent, violent bribe but a gesture of volunteered goodness. I keep thinking of these little things. Inconsequential neglects. Like the way I used to go grocery shopping. The other women would wheel their carts like portable wombs. Brows knit, they fondled tomatoes like a doctor searching for lumps in the breast. I'd stand there, bemused, imagining stethoscopes circling their grave PTA faces, Steve Allen's voice coming out of their mouths: "Mmm, glandular." "Cyst!" "Ah, the swelling's receded." Last week, I watched Ronald making a salad niçoise for us. "You shop so carefully," I said, as he quartered the perfect tomato. "When I was married, I threw any farkokta tomato in. If it wasn't bruised already, it was when it hit the cart. I keep thinking I did something wrong."

"Wrong? Are you kidding?" He laughed. "There's nothing worse than a housewife who shops like a faygeleh. Darling, you were hip before they invented the word."

God knows what it is he sees in me. But God bless him for whatever the hell it is.

"Meester Rodol's house?" Sima asks as I turn my wheels in and set the emergency brake on the quiet canyon hill.

"Yes. Behind those bushes."

"The gang's all here, darling," Ronald calls gaily, stroking his cat on the front porch step. "And what a gang. I swear, if Noah had seen them on the pier, he'd have pulled up his ramp."

"Please," I whisper after he's kissed me, "don't let them sing 'Happy Birthday.' "

"Sing? Darling, they're all too busy dishing each other to get past the first bar."

He opens the door. Hesitantly, I step in. Sima follows, copiously wiping her feet. There, in various postures of mirth, atrophy and evasion are the ones who never made it to Ralph Edwards' couch. Three of Ronald's friends—looking like an Army-Navy store window—are draped on the wings of his love seat and resting their fannies on his armoire, their sherry glasses tinkling. Butting in on this khaki battalion is my friend Edith who, in her innocent, blathering way, feels she is a queen bee to every newly minted minority.

In her I. Magnin poncho, she looks like Arlene Dahl playing Pocahontas. Under its flapping wings, her charm bracelets clink as she swirls her arm, pollinating the flowers of
Sodom.

Sylvia sits on Ronald's Regency couch, sour-faced, volley-
ing a Salem back and forth to her lips and talking out of the
side of her mouth to (on her left) a young black man in a
riding habit and velvet waistcoat who is blowing smoke
rings and looking haughtily amused and (on her right) an
animated sombrero I can only identify as Gwynneth. A
skinny nymphet with hair as short as a shaved chick is rub-
bing Gwynneth's shoulders.

Clustered around the hors d'oeuvres table are Ronald's
next-door neighbor, Ralph Stein, a lawyer my age who, like
most lawyers my age in this town, looks like he is trying to
look like Lee Marvin; and his young, caftanned wife. Obviously skirting any displays of homophilia, they are left to
talk to (I almost didn't recognize her without her pink uniform) Clara Haupt: sharp-faced, shrill-voiced, red in the nose
from nights of bourbon and Sundays phlox-tending at her
tract house in Reseda. Clara Haupt is the only manicurist
on Rodeo Drive who still asks you if you want your moons
covered—and the only person in Ronald's salon who can ask
it without a titter.

"Happy birthday!" they call out, in jagged unison, as I
cross the festive threshold.

Lillian Resnick, this is your life.

Sylvia corners me first. "What is this already?" she snorts.
"I turn my head one way, I'm staring at the goose bumps on
what's-her-face's tits. I turn the other, I'm up the nostrils of
that phony-baloney shvartzer. You should've let me take
you to Chasen's instead."

"To tell you the truth, Syl, I'd rather be here." I say it to play against her crudity, but when Ronald's friend Leo slips his arm around me and says, "You look *fabulous,* birthday girl. Not a day over thirty-five," I realize I mean it.

Leo hugs me. Bert hugs me. Phil hugs me. "I feel like Judy Garland opening at the Palace," I say, and they curl their shoulders and fling their hands in laughter.

"Fel*lows,* lay your hands *off.*" It's Ronald, hugging me with a glass of freshly popped champagne. "She's *my* date for the Prom tonight."

"Do I get a wrist corsage?"

"Absolutely, darling. And we'll have our picture taken sitting on a cardboard moon."

"What a shame," I drawl. "I left my taffeta strapless at the cleaners."

"Oh, don't worry, darling," Leo chimes in, "Ronnie will lend you his organdy."

"Oh, aren't they wonderful!" Edith kvells, like the bride's mother at an overdue wedding. "Lil"—she pushes me aside and I see she is mildly plastered—"you're doing it the right way. For the first time I realize: You're doing it the right way."

"Doing what the right way?" I jut my head back from her spray of emotion.

"Maturing. Relating. I wish I had a Ronald."

"What's a Ronald?"

"You know. An interpersonal bond that transcends role playing."

"I never quite looked at it that way," I say, deadpan.

"Oh, but you should. Nothing is an accident. We are all the creators of our own realities. You *created* a Ronald in your life."

"Oh, Edith, please. Spare me that shyster encyclopedia

salesman. It was easier when you were just trying to be your own best friend."

"Li-ill!" Gwynneth's breathless cheer rescues me. "*This* is Edwin Henderson."

The black man in the riding habit nods over our handshake with great mock solemnity.

"I understand you're an actor," I say.

"By stage standards, reputedly. But for films—we shall see. At present I'm working on the wardrobe. The rap, as they say, shall come later."

"What's the wardrobe?" If they were casting a ghetto version of *Wuthering Heights*, he'd get it in a minute.

"Ah, the Hollywood soul brother suit. Denim pants, denim jacket, large, rakishly askew denim cap. All virtually encrusted with little metal studs and embroidery." I can't tell where his pretentiousness leaves off and his sarcasm starts. "It apparently bodes well to wear this kind of thing to auditions. They take one for the genuine article."

"I know," Edith says, shaking her head. "The exploitation, the stereotyping. It's terrible."

"On the contrary." He takes a drag of his French cigarette. "It rather cuts down on the variables."

"That's an interesting insight," Edith says.

"You see," he launches in tutorially, "there's always a formula. The college theater circuit called for an offstage persona of, shall we say, ponderous topical historicism? One did well taking tea with professors' wives and carrying on about one's father's whist games with Paul Robeson. Or Jesse Owens, depending on the college."

"Your father really knew Jesse Owens?" Edith is impressed.

"I know Jesse Owens," I say straightfaced. "He's a Malibu realtor."

"You're even better than Gwynneth said," Edwin whispers to me.

But Edith doesn't hear. "Jesse Owens," she corrects, righteously, "was the first black man in the Olympics."

"Oh, God," he mutters under his breath. "Where was this one before I went on the wagon?" Then he clears his throat. "At any rate, the formula here calls for a simple change of symbols. In name-dropping to one's peers, so to speak, the Quincy replaces the Roi in front of the Jones. One presumably goes to deaf-mute school to master all kinds of peculiar handshakes. One learns to like bagels and play tennis. Whereas, on the university circuit, tennis was avowedly gauche. Saying gauche was also gauche." He takes a drag. "One learns to science the market."

"Yeah?" I say. "And does one always talk like this? Because if you do, I'm leaving this piece of crap conversation."

"No, no, stay." He laughs, patting me on the shoulder. "It's all but a posture."

"Edwin's got the most far-out posture," Gwynneth pipes. "He's always kidding."

"I fail to see the point in it," I say. "Unless you were trying to con poor Edith. In which case, all you have to do is stand here looking fashionably oppressed."

"I'm hip," he says, with a wide sardonic grin. "No, but seriously, Lillian—if I may call you Lillian—I'm sorry for the overwrought irony, but one goes, or rather I go, a bit buggy selling plumbing equipment all day. One yearns for an audience."

"Selling what all day?"

"Plumbing appliances. Alas, I'm working at Sears while I find some brilliant way of marketing myself to Hollywood."

"That's right," I recall. "Ronald did mention something about that."

"Ronald," he laughs. "What did Ronald call me? The only straight black man he knows who talks like a middle-aged limey faggot?"

"Looove it," Gwynneth purrs, shaking her drug-sotted head. Then she leaves us to refill our champagne glasses.

Across the room, Sima sits alone, stuffing crudités into her mouth. Phil is hugging Clara Haupt and coaxing her to dance with him to the loud record that Bert and Leo are giggling and bumping their backsides to. Gwynneth's waif dangles from her neck, the zippers of her leather jacket glinting. She bites a grape leaf from between Gwynneth's fingers. She throws the grape leaf aside. She bites Gwynneth's finger. Sylvia stands moving her mouth passionately to Ralph Stein and his wife, rolling up her eyes and shaking her head with that hoary emphasis she uses when giving a dissertation on some mutual friend's ex. The Steins sneak off to the hors d'oeuvres table. Sylvia catches my eye, points to them, winks without smiling, contorts her noiseless mouth to tell me: "Talk. To. Them."

Edwin, meanwhile, is telling me he really did do *Othello* in summer stock. And a lot of other plays I never heard of. He keeps saying, "Marvelous! Marvelous!" when I say I never heard of them. He says he went to Princeton, "depressingly enough."

"Why depressingly?"

"Dispiritingly easy, those Ivy League girls. Why, they take all the art out of con artistry. All one had to do was hang one's head and nod cryptically to 'A Love Supreme.' Actually, I rather liked 'A Love Supreme.'" He flicks an ash. "Pity."

"What's so great about the Supremes? I always thought they were overrated, myself."

"Marvelous!" There he goes again. "You see? That's what I love about the West Coast."

"What do you love? And if you use the word refreshing, I'll kick you in your condescending shins."

"Oh, no, no, no. On the contrary, I've come here to get rid of all that. Do you *know* how bloody boring it is to be *constantly* prevailed upon to be condescending? My God, one is deprived of the challenge of being a genuine opportunist! I've had it with the Bullins plays, the Baraka monologues where everyone can't wait to gasp in the right places. Why, the last time I did a reading of Senghor in French, half the matrons in the audience were mouthing along in Swahili! But *here*—now here you have integrity. There's this wonderful innocence that comes with the worship of money. I would be abysmally happy to earn my grand-plus-residuals as the junkie on *Starsky and Hutch*. To run around in my encrusted denims all day, racquet aloft, blissfully vulgar. Jejeune. Self-made. An *honest* hustler." He sings: " 'Diamond in the back, sunroof top, diggin' the scene with the gangster lean . . .' Ah, and to sit at night and laugh with Langston, with him too dead to know the difference."

I smile at his theatrics. "My dear, I didn't understand a word of it. Except the part about *Starsky and Hutch*. I used to know somebody at the network."

"You *did*?"

"Wait a second. Hold your horses. I'm not sure he's still at the network."

"Lillian"—a slight bow—"whatever you know is something I think I can learn from. And it would be my privilege to learn."

Why do the misfits, the oddballs, the scavengers always love me? Aren't there any other people in my life?

"You know," I say, "I can't figure out just what kind of phony you are. I have this rule: Genuine phonies are one thing, but phony phonies are deplorable."

"I quite agree."

"You work at a plumbing store. Can you fix toilets and dishwashers and things like that?"

"I have, on occasion." He hands me his card.

"Well," I smile and shrug, "I guess I'll have to give you the benefit of the doubt."

He laughs heartily and steps into the shimmying arms of Gwynneth who has abandoned her young female James Dean to Ronald. Edith is circling Phil, flailing her arms in some dramatic rite she spent $200 learning at Esalen. Sylvia frowns. With more urgency, she points to Ralph Stein and wife, mouths again: "Talk. To. Them!" But I must get something in my stomach. I'm feeling dizzy. More than dizzy. Frightened. Unmoored.

"Okay, okay, you just overdid it a little," Morty's voice had comforted me, the first of the very few times I ever got drunk with him. "Here, *that*-a girl, just lean. You won't break me."

He steadied my hand on his shoulder and fastened his other arm tight around my waist as he hobbled me down the hall. "I feel like a scene out of *Boys Town*," I cracked, and he laughed.

We were at a party given by one of his clients—Sid somebody, a producer—and Morty was introducing me as his fiancée. Everybody laughed at my jokes, and in the churn of young, successful bodies I felt I had a circle, a crowd, a place. Flushed and eager to show me off, Morty kept retreating to the bar for drink after drink. We were so arrogant in our happiness. I glanced around the big early American living room, measuring my future against it, thinking:

"We'll have something like this, only *real* maple."

He banged open the kitchen door and sat me down at a breakfast table that was piled with silver trays of canapés; I could smell the cheese and damp bread through the wax paper. He stood, opening cupboard after painted wood cupboard. I smiled at his unexpected nurseliness, the seriousness with which he mixed his little potion together, squinted at the glass of odd-colored bubbly liquid he finally set in front of me. "What *is* it?"

"Seltzer, bitters, and baking soda," he said.

"Oh, *God*."

"Look, kid." Kissing the ear that my hairdo'd collapsed on. "They didn't call me Doc in college for nothing. Now drink it all down."

"Will you love me?" I hiccuped, satirically coy. "Will you love me even if I throw up?"

"Christ," he laughed. "Are we going to have to write that into the ceremony?"

He kissed me again—on my nose, I think. And I picked the two tiny white aspirin, like pearls, out of his moist, cushiony palm.

But the palm waving in front of my dizzy face now is Leo's. "Come dance, Lil!" he beckons, with undulating fingers, as he and Bert open their clasped hands for a threesome.

I smile a demurral.

"No?" His bright face almost hurt. "Just a birthday boogie? One little twirl?"

So I smile and take his eager hand and he directs me in an awkward little pirouette. Then he twirls, singing gaily along with the record. And Bert twirls. I feel the armpit of my pantsuit strain, feel so foolish making demure little back-and-forth steps with my self-conscious feet. "I really

must get something to eat," I whisper to Leo. He hugs me
hard, rocks me back and forth with some strange, huge
affection, releases me.

"How're you holding up?" Ronald's solicitous arm around
my shoulder now.

"By a thread," I find myself murmuring.

"Was this a mistake?" he asks, as he steers me into a
chair. "This *was* a mistake, wasn't it?"

"Oh, no," I rush to say, seeing the hurt in his face. "The
party's wonderful. And it was so sweet—"

"Lil, you know you don't have to lie to me."

"But I *mean* it."

"Oh, Lil, I wanted to give you a *nice* party."

"This *is* a nice party." He is unconsoled, so I frantically
call out: "Bert! Leo! Aren't you having fun?"

"I'm having a fabulous time," Leo gushes in the middle
of a shimmy, turning Bert under his arched arm. "Darling,
I feel like a deb!"

"See? Come on, Ronald." I give him a little push on his
shoulders but he doesn't budge. "Get up there and dance."

"This filly is hot—to—trot!" Bert vamps.

"Well bully for you, darling," Ronald chides, arms
akimbo, "but *this* old gray mare just ain't what she used to
be."

"May I remind you, my dear?" I turn to Ronald. "I'm
older than you are. And under the Clairol, grayer."

"That's different, Lil," he says quietly. "You just visit this
nonsense. You don't have to live in it."

Then where *do* I live?

The question must read on my face. "Darling, I'm sorry,"
he says, in a dither. "I've been a terrible party pooper." He
clutches my hand and stands me up. "Now let's get something in your tummy and let's go out there and *spar-kle!*"

"Lillian, so nice to see you again. And happy birthday."

"Thank you, Ralph," I say to the smug, robust face whose eyes I have been avoiding for the whole hour.

Once, men like Ralph Stein and I were contemporaries. Peers. Now they are as distantly, superiorly charming as maître d's—or priests.

"You've met my wife Jackie, haven't you, Lil?"

The chic young blonde nestled under his backhand elbow croons, "Of *course*. We met at Ronald's shop once. How are you, Lil?"

"Fine, just fine," I say, hoping to match their mellifluous good will.

"This was such a"—she casts about for an adjective— "*kicky* idea. Ronald *is* marvelous, isn't he? Whenever we come back from La Costa, I rush right over and knock on his door before we even unpack. Right, darling?"

Ralph smiles his husky assent.

"We scuba dive a lot," she goes on, "and the salt water just *wreaks havoc*. I always say, 'Ronald, this is better than having a doctor living next door. No wonder the property value's gone up.' "

Stein smiles at his wife's little joke. "Actually," he says, "the property value's gone up because the rattlesnakes just bought a condo down the road."

Stein's wife smiles at his little joke. "Really! When Ralph and I moved from Bellagio Drive, we thought we'd love the rustic quality of Benedict. But we didn't quite figure on the snakes."

"Oh, well." He smiles like a good sport. "At least they speed up my jogging every morning. I mean, there are enough *people* in this town who'd like to bite you in the ankle, right?"

We all smile at his little joke.

"Ralph does three miles every morning," Jackie says proudly.

"Nah. More like . . . two and a half."

"*Here* you do two and a half." She looks at his face for validation. "But in Palm Springs you do three. And *after* tennis."

"Well . . ." He shrugs, lavish with modesty. "In the Springs the ground is flat. And the air is much cleaner."

He takes a deep, illustrative breath, while Jackie confides: "I always told Ralph: Honey, if we have to live in a place as polluted as L.A., let's live high up. Of course it was hell getting him away from that pool on Bellagio." She shoots an adoring wink to hubby. "But we had a sauna built in, which is almost the same thing."

"*Sauna.*" He utters the word with much playful contempt. "What's a sauna? With a sauna, you just *sit.*"

She hugs her silver-haired Golden Boy and smiles proudly into his face.

What gets into these guys? They take a young bride and all of a sudden they're Mark Spitz? Whatever happened to their nice sedentary habits like poker and golf? The radiant, enlightened machismo in Stein's face tells me he doesn't even remember those days. He is a New Man.

And I?

Gwynneth dims the lights and Stein and his wife press my hand and mutter extravagant apologies and sneak out the door to their previous engagement.

Somberly, intent on not dropping it, Ronald carries in the lighted cake with tiny, mincing steps. *"Hap-py birth-day to you!"* the ragged chorus strikes up.

Bert and Phil and Leo hug me as they trill in operatic parody. Edwin winks. Edith shakes her head and smiles, desperate with joie de vivre. Sylvia shrugs: It could be worse.

"Oh, Lil." Ronald whispers, perturbed, drawing me close to the cake. "I'm so angry at the bakery! They spelled your name with one *l* instead of two!"

"That's okay, Ronald!" I cry out, loud in his ears over the drowning voices. "That's okay! It doesn't matter." I suddenly realize I am clutching his wrist.

"But it's mocha, darling!" And he is clutching mine. "*Mocha!* Your favorite!"

I smile my enthusiasm into his frantically hopeful face. I watch him read my smile, just as hopeful, just as frantic. *Hap-py birth-day dear Li-il . . .* We stand like this for a fearful, loving second while the innocent cheer washes over us. Then he releases my grip and puts both hands gently on my shoulders.

"Now take a deep breath, darling," he says, "and make a *fabulous, fabulous* wish."

"Ronald," I call into the kitchen after everyone's gone and Bert has driven Sima back to my house, "let me help you."

"No, no, no. You stay put."

But I gather the dirty plates anyway. He is standing at his kitchen counter, tucking foil over the leftovers, furtively nibbling at the cake.

"Take it home with you, darling." Aggravated, he pushes the plate away. "I don't want to be tempted."

"You think *I* do?"

"Well, then," he says testily, "let's throw it out." He picks up the plate, sighs, sets it down again. "Oh, I'll throw it out later."

"Now look, darling, don't get phobic. You lost a few pounds last month."

"Damn it, Lil, you're not supposed to say that! You're supposed to say: 'Throw out the fucking cake!' "

"And if I said, 'Throw out the fucking cake' "—my voice rises—"you'd bitch and whine and I'd never hear the end of it!"

"We're snapping at each other," he says softly.

"You're right. We are. Let's cut it out."

Wordlessly, we load the dishes in the sink, staring at our own separate hands. He picks up a sponge and wipes the counter.

"Ronald, come on." My hand on his arm. "I'll send my Spanish girl over in the morning to do this."

"No, Lil. I gave you the party. It's *my* job to tidy up."

I sigh and let it go at that. When he gets really fastidious like this I know he's upset about something.

"*Well*," I say resolutely, "I don't know about you, but I'm going in to watch TV."

I sit on his sofa in my usual spot and flick the remote control on. A special. Some Vegas type whipping around a microphone cord and contorting his jaw in front of a spangled curtain. I flick the sound on. "Darling," I call, "come watch Wayne Newton sing 'Danke Schoen' with me. It's very funny."

"Oh, God," he groans loudly, "I'd sooner watch a house tour of Pacoima."

"Aw, come on. Keep me company."

Dutifully he comes out and peers at the screen. "So that's who highjacked my last case of hairspray."

"Tammy Wynnette's on next," I say. "In case you're also missing your rollers."

But neither of us cracks a smile. He sits down, I click the sound off.

"Ronald, what's the matter?"

"Oh, nothing I haven't bored you with a hundred times already."

"No, I mean: What's the matter with *us*? Do we keep ourselves lonely on purpose? Are we doing something wrong with our lives?"

"I don't know," he says quietly.

"I felt so neutered tonight. I looked at Ralph and Jackie Stein and thought, God, they're almost a different species."

"Ralph and Jackie Stein are dipshits, darling. You know that. Everyone loved you tonight."

"Yes, but who's everyone? Aside from you, the people who seem to be making up my life these days are like the shmutz you shake out of the pockets when you're bringing a coat to the cleaners. People who don't *belong* anywhere. Ronald, I can do just so much Auntie Mame. I need someone *real*."

"You deserve it, darling. You deserve it, if anyone does."

"Is it so foolish to still want it? Should I be embarrassed to admit I still want sex? I see these women my age buying young men, parading them around like leashed pets. I can't do that. I have *some* pride."

"Even I have some pride," he says softly.

"But anyone who's interested is some dull old bore who doesn't even know when I'm being sarcastic. Or some toothpick-sucker in suede loafers who hasn't been the same since Milton F. Kreis closed, who you'd be embarrassed to bring to a cocktail party unless it was for the Pebble Beach Open. Should I settle for someone like that, just to have a body in bed with me? Just not to be lonely?"

He shakes his head emphatically. "Honey, you're just too hot. You're just too hot for them is all. You can't be with someone you can see through like that."

"Yes, but *why do I have to see through them*? How come I can't just accept? Me and my goddam cynicism, *that's* what's keeping me lonely. That's what's keeping us both lonely."

"No, darling," he says quietly. "It's just what's keeping the loneliness company."

"I don't know." I squint at his rug. "Sometimes I think we've fallen in love with our own complaints. Are we afraid to let anyone into our lives who doesn't have the password, who doesn't get our jokes? Are we so afraid of being boring?"

"Darling," he sighs, "I'd give anything to be that kind of boring. I'd sit home at night. I'd make the dinner. I'd darn the socks. I mean, look at my kitchen. All it needs is a china rooster to pass it off as an ad for the Pillsbury Bake-Off. I'm really as square as they come, darling. If only someone would give me a chance to be."

"Then how come in all these years since Damian—"

"Please. Don't mention Damian. God, I can't even bear thinking about that old apartment."

"I'm sorry, darling. But how come in all these years you haven't found anyone? Not someone boring, but not someone cruel either. Just some nice, sweet, funny person like yourself. There's *got* to be someone like that around. *You're* around."

"But that's the *whole thing*: I wouldn't want someone like me. And someone like me wouldn't want me, either. You made the rounds with me that night, Lil. You saw how absurd it is. Everyone trying to look twenty-five. So cool. So desperate. And those hot little numbers lording it over. Pulling the rings through the old aunties' noses."

"But I *keep* telling you: You don't have to fall for it."

"And *I* keep telling *you*: There's *nowhere* else to fall. It's like a private club, with rules and uniforms. So what

if I decided I wasn't going for looks any more. For style.
For edges. So what if . . . *Okay*," he says resolutely, "let's
say I decided to grow up and be healthy and find someone
compatible. *He* wouldn't want *me*! Don't you understand?
Only straight people get to grow up and be healthy. Only
straight people can be happy with being compatible because
you're *already* opposites. You're always looking for the person with the power to buy back your loathing. That kid you
never looked like in high school, wanted to look like, wanted
to have. Stared at one day and understood how awful and
agonizing and total that wanting was. And that kid—that hot
kid you followed with your eyes—he didn't have the slightest
idea. Didn't even look at you. And that arrogance was so
blinding, so gorgeous. God, there are nights, I swear, when
I see some pretty thing and I want to blurt out: 'I'll keep
you. I'll buy you anything. You can get it on the side.
I won't mind. Just be with me so I can look at you, so I can
look at you and pretend you accept me.' It's sick. I know.
It's terrible. But there it is."

"Oh, Ronald, let me make an appointment for you with
Dr. Fleischer. That shrink I was seeing? Please?"

"Darling," he smiles, as to a well-meaning daughter, "better you should make me an appointment with your plastic
surgeon. It's a meat rack, pet. And I'm an aged steak. No
one's cruising. No one's sniffing. And no one's eating."

"Will you stop talking like Methuselah already? You're
not *that* old."

"Younger than springtime am I . . ." he croons.

"And will you stop evading the issue?"

"God, Lil." He laughs, not quite bitterly. "When you
want to be serious, you want to be serious."

"I just want to talk, Ronald. And I know how you retreat,
is all."

"What do I always tell you?" He sighs. "Swishing isn't the best revenge. It's simply the only one left." He pats his lap. "Come here, Nureyev," he calls to his cat. "Come here, darling. Daddy loves you."

We are silent for a moment. On the soundless TV screen a woman is holding a pot roast up in nothing but a paper towel, smiling as if she had just given birth to it. STRONG! ABSORBENT! The words flash over her blissful face. I turn to Ronald, ready for a wisecrack, but he is squinting at his plant-laden window, concerned and paternal. Maybe it's not so funny, the things we make matter, the things we bribe comfort from.

"That wandering Jew," he muses. "I have *got* to cut it back." He walks over to the plant, pokes its leaves gently. "Are you ready for your summer haircut?" he asks it gaily.

Summer.

"You know what I wish I could do?" I say, feeling suddenly jaunty and wistful. "Take a little house at the beach for July. An apartment even. Give myself that as a present."

"That's a fabulous idea, Lil. You *should.*"

"Oh, but I'm just not strong enough to handle it alone out there."

"I'd visit you, darling. You know that."

"Yes, but what would I do in between? Write poems to the ocean all day? Marvel at the goddam seashells? Darling, Anne Morrow Lindbergh I am not."

"We could rent a house together. Wouldn't that be a scream?"

"Would it ever," I snort. "How would I introduce you to the neighbors? As my brother, my husband, or my nephew?"

"Why, your manservant, darling. Of course. The one who hauls in your steamer trunk."

"Yeah, and polishes my monocle. Not to mention the

wooden leg. Oh, *why* is it you even need a mate just to enjoy a lousy sunset?"

"I know, dear." He nods. "I know. I'd rent someone out for the day, if I could. I keep thinking about that line in *Sunday, Bloody Sunday* where Peter Finch is talking to his patient and says, 'People can manage on very little.' I don't want very little. I want *more!* But I'd take very little if I could just find it."

"You will," I say instinctively, the way I used to do with Andrea. "You'll find someone. We both will."

His smile is wan and ironic. "Do you give guarantees, mamale?"

"Sure, why not?" I smile back, tiredly. "With the kreplach soup." I stand up, stretch, reach for my pantsuit jacket. "Well, I guess it's past my bedtime."

"I'll follow you home in my car."

"Ronald, don't be silly. I'm not *that* bad a driver."

"The roads are so windy and dark up here, that's all."

"I'll make it. But thanks, dear."

"You sure you don't want the cake?"

I shake my head no. "All that fabulous mocha that you love?"

I shake it again, smiling this time.

I put on my jacket, pause at his bevel-edged mirror to fix up my hair.

"Darling," he whines, "you're not harvesting turnips, for God's sake. Don't *yank* at it. Just fluff it. Gently."

"Like this?" I obediently pat the hair over my ears.

He nods. Then, mouth pursed, he steps back and studies my face with arms crossed over his chest. "It wants to be just a tiny bit blonder in the front. Just four more streaks. I'll come by day after tomorrow at noon."

"You're a love." I smile, pat him on the cheek, go to

the sofa to gather my purse. He clicks off the television, turns on the radio. A black woman bleats out a warbly lament.

"I wish I had Aretha Franklin's voice," he sighs, fluffing up the pillows on the sofa. "I could sing the blues for days, darling. *For days.*"

"I wish I had—" Oh, never mind. "I wish I had a cigarette."

He hands me one of his. We peck each other on the cheek at his door, and he stands there in the soft pool of porch light while I monkey with the seat belt, the ignition, the high beams, figure out which way to turn the wheels.

"Remember, Lil: Don't pull it!" he calls out.

"The emergency brake?" I shout back.

"Your *hair,* darling. Your hair."

He is still smiling and shaking his head as I start off down the canyon.

3

"Look, Ronald! Did you read this part?" I squint over the letter as he wraps a strand of my hair around the gray plastic roller. *"We invite all Supporting Sponsors to submit short speeches (not more than five pages, typed, double-spaced) to the Program Committee (see Addresses You Should Know, inside back cover) at least three weeks prior to the retreat. We plan to schedule an afternoon of guidance talks to prospective sponsors, social agencies, and the press on the Santa Ynez Mountain inspirational hike and picnic (see*

61

*Schedule of Events, page 3). The address should deal with
the civic, inspirational, or interpersonal rewards of being a
Supporting Sponsor.* Darling, they're going to make you a
star!"

"Sure." He frowns. "Another Mary Pickford." Yet through
my bathroom mirror I see him leaning over my shoulder,
reading those same words with ill-disguised pride. "What
kind of speech could I make?" he asks. "Darling, I can't write
worth a damn."

"It'll be easy. I'll just sit at the typewriter and you just
stand next to me and tell me how you feel about Raulito
and I'll make it into something nice."

"Oh, you're a doll to offer, Lil, but—oh, I don't know.
It would be so presumptuous."

"Why presumptuous? You're paying your own money to
go to this thing. You *care.* This kid has mattered to you for
three years. Why not step up and take credit where it's due?"

"Oh, because they probably have all these civic leader types
who really know how to make speeches. What do they want
to hear from a silly old hairdresser for?"

"*There* you go again."

"Oh, but Lil, it's *true.*"

"Ronald, I'm not going to argue with you." I pass him
the letter over my shoulder. He wipes the conditioning gel
off his hands and prongs it carefully by the letterhead: the
words HAND TO HAND superimposed over a big hand touching
the fingers of a little hand, under which is printed Overseas
Mission Foster Children's Program, and under that, in italics,
Bringing Feelings and Funds, One to One.

He dangles the letter for a minute, searching for a dry
place to set it down. When he does, I repeat: "I'm not going
to argue with you, but I think you're being silly. You *have*
to stop putting yourself down, and this is as good a place

to start as any. I'm sure you have things to say about what it feels like to be somebody's, excuse me, guardian angel. To be supporting a child that isn't your own, a child you've never seen. The gratification. The poignancy. The—"

"Darling," he laughs, dabbing his fingers again into the jar of conditioner, "you've been watching *Search for To- morrow* too long."

"Well, *whatever*. It doesn't have to be corny. We'll just make it sound sincere."

"I don't even remember what that word means," he mutters softly.

"Oh yes you do." I hunt his eyes in the mirror. "As much as you'd like to pretend otherwise. When you opened that booklet, who was the one who laughed?"

"You did."

"Who was the one who said, 'You want to spend two hundred dollars to be shacked up in some Santa Barbara guest house with a bunch of old nuns?' "

"You did." He smiles. "And it was a *fabulous* line."

"Yeah, but who went and wrote out the check anyway? Who wouldn't miss that silly convention for the world because the people from the orphanage might be there?"

He shrugs. "I had four vacation days coming up."

"Ronald, come on. The thing matters to you a little more than you'd like to admit. Now we're going to sit down together, like Woodward and Bernstein, and write you a very nice little speech."

"*After* I plug you in and pluck your eyebrows."

"All right. After you plug me in and . . . why the eyebrows?" I move the magnifying mirror in front of me. "What's wrong with my eyebrows?"

"They're getting a bit shaggy, that's all," he says gingerly. "We need just a tiny bit more arch under here. See?" His finger lifts the crepey skin. "Won't that look better?"

"Yes, but I'm afraid it's not the plucking that's going to do it."

"It's the plucking," he says, coronating me with that iridescent hairnet and tying it at the nape of my neck. "It's the plucking, darling. Leave it to me."

He turns on the stand-up dryer that he got for me at cost, tucks two wads of cotton in at my ears. "We could start it," I say excitedly, "with something like: 'As a Beverly Hills hairdresser, I'm always in contact with vanity. Being an overseas foster parent—getting letters every month from a child who depends on me for the smallest favors of life, such as food and clothing, helps me keep my perspective.'" I dip my head under the dome of the dryer and louden my voice against its hum. "'Makes me know that I'm doing something else besides making wealthy women beautiful, makes me feel that I'm—*Ronald*, why are you shaking your head and smiling like that? Damn it, you're making fun of me!"

"No I'm not." He tries to stop smirking. "I'm just touched at how much you care about this. I'm honestly touched."

"Well, don't just stand there being touched, for Christ's sake. Get out the tweezers and lift up my face!"

So now, three weeks later, he is off in Santa Barbara. Two nights ago, we sat sipping sherry in his bedroom. I watched him pack, solemnly dismissing most of his wardrobe.

"Relax, darling," I said. "You don't have to dress like a banker to prove to them you're a serious person."

"It's not that," he said, plumping his overnight case with toiletries. "I just don't want to look like your typical childless fruit."

"Come on." I raised my sherry glass, and my chin. "To thinking good things about ourselves from now on."

"To finding love," he amended, raising his.

"To first things first."

"My God, Lil," he laughed. "You don't let me get away with anything these days."

I nodded to the Instamatic lying next to the cardboarded shirts on his bed. "You're getting away with my camera, aren't you?"

"Leave it to a Jew," he smiled, shaking his head as he zipped up his case. "Just leave it to a Jew . . ."

And now I find myself missing him. I know, I know, it's only a couple more days, but I miss dressing up the small, banal events of my day for company. Your jokes are only as good as your audience, and the audience I make for myself is no good at all. Without Ronald as my sounding board, my monitor, my thoughts go sneaking back to the past the way a man calls his mistress the minute his wife's back is turned.

Today, for instance. It's hot for June, and I awake with perspiration under my chin, in the crooks of my elbows, with a certain terror for the brazen yellow streaming in through my French curtains. Sima makes breakfast sounds. and as soon as I hear the front door close behind her I do what I rarely have done since I took her in as a boarder: I go into her room, the room that used to be my daughter's.

Here is Andi's quilted bedspread, her white rattan chair and desk, even her high school bulletin board. Sima keeps it officiously neat, almost vacant. It has little character, this room. None but the most listless, impersonal memory, for we moved here from the big family house on Oakhurst the summer before Andrea started college and she made a great show of indifference as to how it would be furnished. I wanted to give her a dazzling room—modern, antiques, new stereo, anything she wanted—but she saw the presumption and the bribe, and said, in a tone as crisp as umbilical scissors, "Mom, I'll be here like twenty days a year. My life is in Berkeley now. Why spend the money?"

She'd come home from Berkeley two, three times a year. Each time I opened the door at her ring (she had a key, of course, but ringing signified adulthood: *It is your house, Mother; I am just visiting*), I was rushed with her newness. Somehow they never get past twelve in your memory; and the face I carried around in my head during her absences was chubby, trusting, distended in a laughter that I didn't have to *earn*. But her face at the door now was fixed in an attempt to spank away all its girlishness: the nostrils slightly flared; the chin cocked; her light brown hair, proudly untended and frizzled, hiding the bulbs of her cheeks and drifting past the shoulders of her parka. For an instant before we embraced I always wanted to laugh and say, "Andi, darling, don't work so hard to look arrogant," so much did her stubborn innocence touch me. But, instead, I'd simply open my arms to hug her and she'd fall into them more eagerly than she'd planned. Her cheek would be chilly under that downy ripple of hair.

"Cold?" I'd ask.

"Kind of." Carting in that interminable mangle of canvas knapsacks. "We put the top down after Ventura."

She'd walk the two steps down into the living room, eyeing it all with the quiet, critical authority of a prospective renter. I'd be careful not to stand too close, not to ask too many times how the semester went, how it felt to be home, if she were tired, whom she drove down with. My antique hall mirror threw back the face of a beckoned, expectant French maid.

"Yich!" she'd say, picking a framed photograph off the piano. "I hate this picture."

"Oh, Andi, come on. It's a mother's privilege."

"But I was fat then. And I'm wearing that dumb uniform."

"So you were a cheerleader once. That's nothing to be ashamed of. It was just a phase."

But when you are young there are no phases. You have the privilege of feeling that every new year exquisitely cancels the past—because, of course, the past is not the bulk of it.

"Mo-om, *please.*" She would turn to me. "Respect my right as a person. Throw it away."

"Darling," I'd smile, "if I didn't respect your right as a person I'd say let me get your hair cut and buy you some eyeliner. But I re—"

"You always manage to sneak that in, don't you?"

"I didn't mean it that way, Andi. I was just drawing an analogy. All I was saying was: *I* respect *your* right as a person, so I have my own rights as a person. And a person who happens to be your shmaltzy Jewish mother, that's all, that's all." I'd smile, bright with appeasement. "Listen, enough pictures on top of that piano and the stains don't show. I won't have to have it refinished."

But she'd only pout at my anxious levity.

"Okay, okay," I'd say. "I'll get rid of the picture. But send me another to replace it. I *know* you're grown up now. You're anti-establishment. You're—"

"Oh, God, Mom. You got that word out of *Time* magazine."

"Well, whatever. Whatever the new word is. All I'm saying is: I like keeping your picture here. Send me any picture you want."

"Mom, I'm not *into* pictures. You know, there happen

to be more important things in life than smiling in front of a camera for a silver frame on your mother's piano."

"Yes, darling, I completely agree. And one of them is food. Are you hungry?"

"Mmm, kind of." And she'd leave her flaccid gray bags in a heap in the hall and head for the kitchen. I'd hear the refrigerator door open, then her sheepish penitence: "I'm sorry, Mom. I'll unpack later. "

Don't unpack and ferret your things away! I wanted to shout. Leave them here. Litter this whole antiseptic house with your presence. Drag those gray knapsacks from room to room. Leave your notebooks around. Drop your jeans and kurtas over my antique chairs. Brush your hair wildly from room to room and let the split ends fly. I *want* that disorder, darling. Don't let me know I'm alone!

But instead, with much sardonic tolerance, I would say: "Yes, Countess."

Then I'd stand in the living room, consoled by those eager kitchen noises and leave her alone for the five minutes she needed to reclaim my succorance: bang open familiar drawers for polished matched silver, check for cookies and tuna fish, comfort herself in the lined shelves, the rows of superfluous cans the maid had unpacked: the gleaming, consuming provision of it all.

And then I'd walk into the kitchen, and, after I replied to her obligatory lecture about my Kraft American cheese ("What does having a lousy cheeseburger have to do with napalming Hanoi?") or my Gallo Chablis ("Of course I'm for Cesar Chavez, dear, but it's the only kind you can get at Safeway") or my cocktail oysters ("They happened to be on sale at Akron. What's so 'decadent' about that?"), we would sit down at the round Formica table. And as she raised that unwieldy sandwich to her lips, her soft, wild hair would fall with sweet clumsiness into her face again and again. And again and again she'd brush it over first one ear, then the other, her eyes darting away self-consciously. In this simplest and most unintended of acts, she gave me back my motherhood.

"Why don't I get you a rubber band for your hair?" I'd ask.

"Mmm." Pushing it back again. "I have a clip in my knapsack."

I would bring in her knapsack and she would say, "Maybe tomorrow night I'll do this really neat vegetable casserole I make," and the barricade would fall. I'd put up the coffee, and out would rush the earnest details of her classes, her boyfriends, her endlessly shifting but ever-specific politics: the sentences arranged to allow for no questions, synopsized for an alien. There was always so much effort in her voice, the effort to believe her own beliefs. I would contain my smile as I nodded at each Truth. And as she talked—so bright and touching and anxious in her certainty—I heard her double plea: *Let me believe all this now, Mother; don't make fun of it!,* and also, at the same time: *Take it off my shoulders, Mommy. I don't really have to be this grim, do I?*

"What's People's Park?" I'd asked her after one such exegesis that left tuna fish droplets all over her plate.

"This park on Haste the cops are trying to close because the people took it over from the University."

"You mean they just took it over, these, uh, The People? They don't have any mortgage or rent?"

"Mmm hmm." Proudly through a mouthful of sandwich. "*Expropriated* it. The People's Park Liberation Army."

"Jesus," I mused, "could they send me a mercenary unit? There's some property on Spalding I've had my eye on for a year."

"Oh, *Mom.*" But her wince contained mirth.

"Come on, Andi. You can be idealistic and still have a sense of humor. I mean, I always laugh whenever you call my powder-blue Mustang a Jew canoe, don't I?"

And in her smirk, more mirth.

And as she cleared the table, my eyes would fix on her graceful, small-wristed hands, the hint of her shape under that workshirt, those dungarees. And I knew that that room into which she would soon cart her canvas bags would be just a comfort station—and never acknowledged even as that much. That I could stock it with her favorite flowers and records and posters but she would never herself do the same, would never really live here. We would sit then, cradling our coffee cups, reaching for cookies off the plate, talking words so banally intimate that for weeks after I would not be able to watch those suburban mother-and-daughter TV ads for dish soap without my heart filling with an unnamed regret. Already, just sitting like this, that clumsy emotion would build in me.

And she'd see it. "I'm going into my room now, Mom," she'd announce.

"So soon? We've hardly had a visit."

"I'm really bushed," she'd apologize.

But I knew what she really meant. She'd pull the hall phone in and close the door, and it would take all my self-control not to lean my ear against her door as she gushed into the receiver: "Hi, Daddy! Yes! Just half an hour ago . . ."

Remarried, he had so much more to give her than I. His invulnerability, his healthy indifference. Not so with him the sharp sadness in the old eyes, the hundred awkward begging gestures. She was not responsible for loneliness with him, never had to shrink from that awful debt. During those brief college visits, I would see (or was I just imagining?)

her face fall as she walked back into my house after an overnight visit with him. Stubbornly, sentimentally, I had kept the furniture from the old house: evidence, to her, of my stagnancy, my defeat.

"Andi," I said once, coming upon her reading her sociology book sprawled on the living room sofa, "please take your shoes off, my dear."

"Why? For this old couch?"

"But you're the one who's always accusing me of being a compulsive consumer. What's wrong with it being old?"

"What's wrong is that you're living in the past, Mom." She sat up abruptly. "These pictures. This old Ciro's ashtray. Everything. It's *pathetic*."

I snapped my eyes shut for a long several seconds. (Was I angry at her or merely assenting?) "That's a cruel word, Andi," I said, when I opened them.

"I just meant it to help you, Mom. You're always saying, 'Let's be honest with each other.' Well, I'm being honest. Every time I come home I get this creepy feeling that I'm all you have. You ask how come I'm arrogant? How come I cut you off? Well, that's how come. You should make a new life for yourself instead of just going shopping with Sylvia all day long. The two ex-wives, licking your wounds and buying clothes you don't need and talking about the past. Really, *it's not good!*"

And almost inaudibly I replied: "You don't think I know that?"

She moved to New York after her last year at college and I banged around this house, living off the stocks and real estate I got in the settlement. Except for the old furniture, my moorings seemed to have been knocked out. Morty died of a sudden heart attack, five years the husband of another woman, and for a whole year after I would put myself to sleep with a willed dream: I was standing at his hospital bedside. I lifted up the oxygen tent that curtained him like florist's flowers and asked: "Weren't there good times? Despite the end, didn't we have feelings for each other?" And true to any hackneyed deathbed scene, he clasped my hand and whispered, "Yes."

"Look," I would have myself say then, "I *know* what happens. I felt it at the end, too. Your chafing at the bit, my getting more and more neurotic. Listen," I'd shrug, and smile, and say, like a favorite Jewish uncle, "if I were you and I had an Alana, I'd probably have done the same thing. I mean, all you can hope for these days is twelve good years, and we had eighteen. Which means two poor shmucks out there got cut off at seven, before they even finished the second mortgage." And I would have him smiling. "Look, Morty, let's forget the end. Let's cut the film with, say, with you and me sitting with the Ah Fong's cartons, watching Steve Allen. The nervous one. Don Knotts? Remember? What did I used to say?"

"You used to say . . . something about him pulling on his right ear all the time. Something about . . . the way he kept it up, the part in his hair was turning into the San Andreas Fault. *Something* like that, only funnier."

And I would have us groping around trying to remember that line together. And as we did, all those petty animosities over stocks and money disappeared. All the awful, polite civility of living apart in the same city crumbled. There was *more* than atonement in that imagined bedside laughter of ours; there was reclamation. And I'd put myself to sleep trying to remember what it was I used to say about Don Knotts pulling his ear while we ate egg roll and why, *why* it seemed so funny at the time.

But that silly scenario did little to relieve. It is a dreadful thing when death comes too suddenly for you to forgive. For the next year I saw a very patient psychiatrist, Dr. Abram Fleischer. I started each session with the words "If only" and ended them the same way. My bookends, he called them. My theme song. He gave me pills for sleep. Half unwittingly, I overused them. I was zombied as a sleepwalker, chaining Phenos and Nembutal, lighting cigarette butts and sucking on them till I coughed.

Once a month, I drove to the Fairfax district apartment building I owned to collect the rents from Hilda Schlesinger, who managed the depressing lot of elderly Jewish tenants.

"Ach, Lillian!" Hilda whispered, as she undid the chain on her door that particular Sunday. "Tank God you come! Tank God tank God tank God. I vas going to call the police, you shouldn't come." She pushed me by the shoulders into the only overstuffed chair in the room that wasn't piled with old clothes she altered and ironed for Israel. Every other available surface was crammed with framed photographs of her grandchildren, glass-jarred candles, fetid plants that miraculously survived despite the fact that the curtains were never opened.

"What's wrong, Hilda?" I asked, after the inevitable inhalation of musty chintz and gefilte fish.

"Dose new tenants. Dose *boice* in 3-B? A regular demolition crew! You never see so much plaster. And the fixtures dey remove. The vall dey saw in half! I tole tem: You vait. The landlady vill come vit a varrant you should be arrested. *Listen.*" She pointed ceilingward; the faint sound of hammering brought a righteous smile to her lips. "Dey vant to tear down effrytink. Better you should go see." With that, Hilda grasped me by the wrist and lumbered us both out the door.

"Relax, Hilda," I begged, as we approached the steps. "Just relax."

"Relax, vat? Vile the roof iss fallink down? Vile ve get buried in dis Holocaust dey make?"

Hilda barreled up the stairs with a speed my drugged body couldn't rival.

"Boice!" she trumpeted from the third floor landing. "The landlady's here to see vit her very own ice, her very own ice."

The younger one, a blond T-shirted Adonis, gripped his hammer at the doorway. The older one crouched, as if for shelter, behind a freshly shellacked bookshelf.

"You see, vat I tell you?" Hilda huffed proudly. "Vat I tell you?"

I stood at the doorway and stared in. My musty little hovel was transformed into a decorator's showcase. "It's gorgeous," I whispered.

Hilda stared from Adonis to the croucher to me. Then she shook her head at the incomprehensible conspiracy and muttered Yiddish all the way down to the ground floor.

The older one broke into nervous, effusive laughter. "I swear, that biddy was just croaking. Just positively fit to have her tits tied. I mean, God," he drawled, "she threatened to turn off the heat, the lights, the water, the gas."

Adonis shut him up with a stern glance. "Ronald," he ordered calmly, "get the sherry and the good crystal. We're having a drink with our landlady."

Adonis—whose name, it turned out, was Damian—moved out three months later. Ronald bought a cat, and when I came to collect the rent, I'd knock on his door and we'd sit by his massangeana tree, staring out the window and sipping Pernod.

"I don't care that he stole my crystal," he sang, "but why oh why did he steal my heart, darling?"

"Morty just took his office chair," I said. "I kept my lousy crystal."

"The better to smash at the window, darling. The better to break on your wrists."

"God, Ronald." I laughed in spite of myself. "Where did you get that deadly humor?"

"It comes with the affliction, darling. It comes with the affliction. Feel blessed."

The first time Ronald saw this house he rolled up his eyes. "Who was the decorator? Charles Dickens?"

True, true. Morty thought Old English looked masculine and established. Yacht club smug, East Coast refined. Anything not to be anxiously nouveau, rootlessly Jewish. ("I don't want a house where you smell empty Nate 'n' Al's containers the minute you walk in the door," he used to say.) So I'd stuffed it with oak and brocade and heavy drapes.

Ronald fingered the two china beagles guarding my fireplace. "Really, did you have to go loot an old *Father Knows Best* set? Good God, Lil, what kind of old stiff were you married to, anyway?"

In weeks the house was transformed, and I had my new life. Louis XIV, French Regency, gold striped wallpaper, witty little touches like naked cherubs. White wicker and sinewy green plants. "Sometimes style can keep you from sticking your dear little head in the stove," Ronald sighed.

But that was just his hobby. With his trade, he remodeled my head. "Did your old colorist use a paint-by-number set?" he asked me, separating my hair into a dozen little ponytails. Then he ceremonially flapped a plastic smock in the air and fitted it around me, working it gently under my collar like a parent tucking a child in for the night. "Clairol twenty-

eight plus my special formula," he snapped to his assistant.
And to me, "Darling, now we are going to *make you shine*."

The phone on Sima's bedstand rings, jarring me out of
the past. It rings again. As if fearing the caller might see me
prying here, I rush into my own bedroom before answering
it.

"Hello?"

"Hey foxy mama in yo blue pajama, The Groove Merchant callin' you. Hey foxy mama with yo wig hat on ya,
he hot an' bothered too."

"Dear," I groan into the receiver, "I left a simple message
with your service. I did not ask for a wake-up call from Iceberg Slim. To what do I owe the pleasure?"

"The immersion method." Edwin's voice returns to its
suave, laughing alto. "Total Sensibility Empathics. Grotow-
ski, love, by way of Stagolee."

"I don't keep a Thesaurus by my night lamp. Would you
mind giving me a translation?"

"I am *becoming* my character. Willy Gee, a.k.a. The
Groove Merchant. Thanks to whom we are both going to
soon be rolling in the green."

"Yeah? Well, darling, go ahead and roll without me." For
the past two months I have been sending Edwin's glossy
and bio to every casting office in town, and not one callback.

"But this one is foolproof, Lillian. I promise you. And it's
going to be outrageously amusing. I can't wait to see your
face when we walk into that radio station together."

"*Radio?* So soon they give up."

"No, there's money in this one. The Black Millennium In
Sound, 99.4 on your FM dial. 'Fifty thousand watts of peace,
roots, warm vibrations, and cosmic tranquillity.' Darling,
I've been barking up the wrong tree with those television

gigs. They're just walk-ons, one-shots. This is compleat personality merchandising. And, I hear, six hundred a week for anyone whose gimmick is good enough to replace Funky Rashid."

"Who the hell is Funky Rashid?"

"I'll explain it all when I see you, love. Which will be in about twenty minutes. What is it this time, the garbage disposal?"

"The dishwasher. I think I put a fork in upside down."

"Again?"

"What do you mean 'again'? The last time it was a spoon."

"Love," he says before hanging up, "be chic. Buy chopsticks."

I only blink once when I open the front door. I am used to Edwin's denim-on-denim by now, but all those little chrome studs still take their toll on my retinas. "Don't ever fly up to Frisco like that," I say, by way of hello. "You'll never get past the metal detector."

He steps in. "Mama Gee's homemade shortnin' bread," he announces, handing me a box of croissants. Then, following me into the kitchen he croons, "I'll always love my mama, she's my fav-rit girl. I'll always love my mama, she brought me in this world . . ."

"Okay, okay." I cup my hands over my ears, then bend to open the dishwasher hatch. "See? It isn't draining right."

He gets down on his hands and knees, squints through the flooded plastic gridwork. "Have I known rivers," he mumbles, shaking his head.

"Every time I push ON it just fills up more."

"Ancient as the world."

"No, it's new! I just bought it last year."

"Older than the blood."

"Huh?"

"The San Bernadino or the Niger, baby, they all the same."

"I don't get it."

"You're not supposed to," he says, taking a wrench out of his tool bag. "Ah, if Arna Bontemps could see me now . . ."

"Oh, Edwin, you're always muttering about these people nobody ever heard of."

"My cloak, love." His voice echoes out of the dishwasher cavity. "My proverbial ace in the hole."

"My proverbial ass," I say, and I hear him chuckling as I measure out the coffee.

Just as I'm plugging the pot in, the phone rings.

"Hello? Yes, dear. What key? No, he only gave me his front door, why? What do you mean 'got away'?" I shake my head, annoyed. He never should've entrusted it to her. I *told* him I'd drive up and do it. *"What?* Whose tree? Well, of course people are going to think you're crazy if you run up and down the canyon shouting Nur-ey-ev! at four in the morning! Darling, I can't say I blame them. People just *do not* go around feeding cats at four in the—Did what? *Overnight?* Well, how come—Oh, *honestly.* Honestly, honestly. A glove compartment is not a medicine chest, for Christ's sake!" I sigh copiously. "Yes, he's fixing my dishwasher. Hold on a minute." Covering the mouthpiece with my hand. *"Edwin.* It's Gwynneth."

"Tell her," his voice resounds, "that I'm embroiled in the bowels of a Westinghouse at the moment. Which is far kinkier than anything she's ever done."

"You wanna bet?"

The ominousness of my voice hastens his head out.

"We'll be right over," I say into the phone again, and when I hang up, I calmly hand Edwin his denim jacket, take a deep breath and recite: "We are now going to drive over to Crescent, dear, to bail Gwynneth and that girl friend of hers out of jail. The cops picked them up climbing somebody's tree on Westwanda looking for Ronald's cat and after the girl friend spat at the cop, they found drugs in her car and—oh, Edwin, how the hell do I get into the middle of these things?"

"Well, as my daddy, Preacher Amos Gee used to say: Them that's got git, them that's jive scam, or else grits ain't groceries, eggs ain't poultry, and Mona Lisa was a man."

"Do me a favor?" I hand him his car keys. "Leave the Apollo Act at home?"

"Of course, love," he says, as I make sure my checkbook and identification are in my purse. "There are occasions where dialect is supremely ill-auguring. And of those occasions, meeting BHPD's finest is paramount, not to say archetypal."

"Good." I pat his shoulder as I lock the front door behind us. "Stick to the syllables. Just stick to the syllables."

God knows what the poor cop with the clipboard is thinking as we all march out of the bail room together, Gwynneth's car keys in my custodial grip. The happy foursome: your standard middle-aged north-of-Olympic matron (the kind of broad who calls for fire trucks whenever her steak fat smokes up the oven; who has her typewriter ribbons delivered; who asked for police escort to Westwood the last time the Bel Air fire displaced half the Veterans Hospital mental ward); that tall shvartzer on her left who talks like a nineteenth-century barrister and looks like a thumbtack convention sponsored by Levi Strauss; and the two defendants, the Brontë sisters here.

"Lil, you're a doll," Gwynneth murmurs under her crimson fedora.

"Yeah, thanks," James Dean unglues her head from Gwynneth's shoulder to mumble. Then she sneers, to no one in particular: "That creep. Those pigs. This town. Face like a potato."

"The creep, the pigs, or the town?" I inquire, as we walk down the high-ceilinged City Hall corridor.

"Spuds and everything," she hisses on. "Shit, you can't even walk down the street after eight o'clock without their big dildo flashlights glomming in your eyes. 'Pardon me, miss. We just wondered what you were doing on the street.' Pardon *me*, spudface, it's none of your jerkoff business. 'Pardon me, miss, can we give you a lift home?' Pardon me, fart face, but you get your limp dick any closer to me, you'll have a bite on your neck'll make Dracula look like—"

"Dear." I pat her leather-jacketed arm. "I think we get the point."

"Nikki's real dramatic." Gwynneth smiles proudly, drawing the pouting, kohl-eyed face closer.

"Ah yes," Edwin mutters under his breath. "Pinteresque irony, Chekhovian pith. Eliza Doolittle crossbreeds with Sal Mineo and lives to tell."

"She knew Kenneth Anger when she was eleven," Gwynneth goes on. "She held up a dead bird in one of his films."

"Ah, Lester! Prez, baby," Edwin pleads, *sotto voce*, "just give me four clean notes . . ."

And we walk out into the glaring sunlight and stand on the precipice of the parking lot as if on the White Cliffs of Dover.

"Gwynneth." I notice scratches on her bare arms as I hand her her keys. "These better not be what I think they are."

"You kidding, Lil?" She laughs. "Needles? Nev-errr. It's

just trees have like twigs that you can't see too well at night."

"Yeah? Then why weren't you wearing this?" I point to the cardigan knotted around her waist.

"It's from Theodore!" Her tone is proprietary. "I didn't want to get a Theodore filthy in some tree. Anyway, I was going to return it."

"You can't return it now," Nicki sneers. "The fucking cops put a staple in it."

"Langston," Edwin sighs, exhaling a dramatic billow of smoke from his Gauloise, "where are you now that I need you?"

Ronald, where are *you*?

As Edwin starts the motor of his car, I notice the two of them across the lot, licking skinny cigarettes behind Gwynneth's windshield. "*See?* What did I tell you!" I slap my handbag for emphasis.

"Relax, Lil, relax," Edwin says, "*I'll* spring them the next time."

"But you don't have any money."

"I will next month." He steers us out of the lot while I watch their huddled faces suck in the smoke, as if jelly through straws. "As I was saying—before we were so *rudely* interrupted—there's this deejay job open at one of the progressive soul stations. And I am packaging myself as precisely the kind of jocular back-alley number-runner cum ebony Will Rogers that will make their cornrows stand out on end. And you, Lillian, as my—well, let's call you my agent for purposes thereof—you, my dear—"

"Just tell me I don't have to row the corns," I mutter, closing my weary eyes.

"You don't have to row any corns. You just have to—"

"Can you fix the dishwasher?"

"—call the station for an appointment and—"
"Just tell me: Is the dishwasher fixable?"
"Relax, Lil." Turning onto my street. "The dishwasher is going to be just fine."

The phone rings. I pick it up immediately. "Hello?" Gwynneth. Nureyev is alive and well, crouched under Ronald's bed. Thank God.

I go into my television room, kick off my shoes, lift my feet atop the glass coffee table. Sipping my scotch, I turn on the six o'clock news. Long-distance rates are lower after six. I feel pleasantly expectant.

The phone rings. "Hello?" Sylvia. Do I want to meet her at the Hamlet on Beverly and then go to the sale at Ohrbach's? "Sylvia," I reply, "my entire day was an Ohrbach's sale."

The phone rings. "Hello?" Some unintelligible young man. (I thought they all bowed to the East at this hour.) "No, Sima isn't home."

The phone rings. "Hello?"

"Well, *greetings* from The Queen of the Missions, darling! In both senses of the word."

"Darling! I've been waiting to hear your voice! How *are* you? How *is* it?"

"It's a scream. Darling, Santa Barbara is a Lawrence Welk fan's idea of a wet dream. They gave us these positively spinsterly rooms in this golf tournament hotel and we walk around wearing plastic nametags all day, watching films of how they build basketball courts in Bangladesh and health centers in Uruguay, with Peter, Paul and Mary singing 'If I Had a Hammer' for the soundtrack! Fabulously camp, darling. In fact, I think I saw your last maid in yesterday's double feature."

"That must not have been hard to spot. Was she wearing my cashmere sweater?"

"Wearing it? Don't be gauche. She was using it to wrap her cornhusks."

We laugh, and then I ask: "What are the other people like?"

"Oh, the predictable," he says gaily, but with none of the usual whine in his voice. "Schoolteachers, widowers, ladies' club types. Darling, this convention must have evacuated Pasadena. The parking lot looks like a Ranchwagon showroom."

"Ronald, you sound so 'up.'"

"Listen, it's a goof. I'm giving our little speech tomorrow."

"Oh, good luck, darling. Are you nervous?"

"No, not really."

"You *do* sound up. And calm. You're not on anything, are you?"

"How can I be? You took the last of my Vallies."

"I guess I'm just not used to talking to you when you don't sigh."

"Well, you know how it is: Put on a happy face and all that. But never mind me, darling. What's been happening with you?"

"Well." And I lean back, ceremonially light a Salem, and launch in. He laughs madly at all of it: Edwin, Gwynneth, Nikki, jail.

"Can't you just see them in that tree, Ronald? Descending on Ralph and Jackie Stein in the middle of his fiftieth pushup?"

"Oh, darling, I love it!"

"You're not angry that Nureyev went without food all night?"

"Listen, that cat eats better than I do."

"Gwynneth really didn't mean anything by it."

"Of course not. Look, if she *didn't* fuck up, *then* I'd worry."

"My," I hum, perplexed, "aren't we becoming the forgiving one all of a sudden. Here I leave you alone with a bunch of charity types for three days and you turn into a regular Pollyanna."

"Gingham skirt and all, darling. Gingham skirt and all."

"No, but really, you sound very . . . mellow, to use Gwynneth's word. Almost curiously so."

"I needed a vacation is all."

"You did. Definitely."

"I did. Absolutely."

"Well, darling," I say, to cut through the sudden awkwardness, "it better be just a vacation. If my hair goes one more day, it's going to smell like Hilda Schlesinger's living room."

"Oh, call Leo, darling. He'll tide you over."

"Nah, Leo doesn't have your touch. It can wait two more days."

He hears my dependency. "Darling," he clucks, "the *minute* I get back, before I even check my mail, I am coming right over with my little black bag. And when I get through, I swear, Betsy Bloomingdale won't want to be in the same room with you."

"You promise?"

"Boy Scout's honor."

"Listen, you stay up there with those do-goods much longer, you won't be kidding about that. I expect you to walk in my door in a blue uniform peddling those farkokta cookies."

"Oh, but darling, I'm stopping off first in San Diego, and

if anything knocks the piety out of you, it's those walking tattoos."

"*San Diego?*"

"I'm giving someone a lift home."

"Five hours out of your way? That's some lift."

"Well, why not do a favor?"

"Jesus, you *are* turning into a saint. Will your seatmate appreciate your disco station? Or are you going to have to placate her with Andre Kostelanetz?"

"Um, it's a he. My seatmate." After a pause, the words rush out in nervous, cautious gulps. "Lil, I didn't want to go into it on the phone because I didn't want to jinx it. But I'll tell you *all* about it when I see you, *I promise.* It's good. And he's different from the others. *Really* different. A graduate student, can you believe? Bright. Decent. All those things you were always hammering into my head. You'll approve. Believe me, you'll approve."

"My God, Ronald." I almost whisper. "You've met someone."

"Lil, I'm a little scared."

"Scared? Come on! This is what you've been waiting for! This is what we've both been waiting for." It's not jealousy that I feel, but it's *something.* "It's fabulous! Mazel tov! Go for it! as Gwynneth would say."

"I know, but I can't help it, Lil," he says, before we blow lavish kisses. "I *am* a little scared."

And when I hang up the phone, I am a little scared, too.

4

"THE FUNNY THING IS, LIL"—RONALD'S VOICE DRIFTS IN FROM the breakfast room—"the first time I saw him, I thought he was a real nothing. Just some skinny, straight kid standing up there—"

"One second, darling," I call to him. "I don't want to miss a word."

I push open the kitchen door with my back, set his cup of coffee in front of where he sits: his mouth anxiously half-opened, an unlit cigarette poised in his fingers, his suitcase and Vuitton bag of hair supplies on the floor by his crossed ankles.

"Now," I smile, passing him a packet of Sweet 'n Low, "I'm all ears."

"Well, he was just this kid on this podium-type thing in the conference room, giving this talk about the orphans in Baja California. I mean, God, by that point, gimme a *break* with the orphans already. I would've given anything for a couple of poppers and an old Howard Duff movie instead. And here was this kid: a little mustache, a Pendleton shirt. He looked like someone who collects John Denver albums and married his high school sweetheart.

"Anyway, there was this scream of a woman who latched on to me. A fat Gardena schoolteacher. Fern. You would have loved her. Lil. One hundred percent trailer park. She started drinking at noon and had this bracelet with all these little painted enamel charms of her five Chihuahuas. Oh, darling"—he shakes his head—"the loonies that thing pulled out of the woodwork. But I guess I was one of them.

"Anyway, Fern kept raising her hand and asking him all these idiotic questions. But there was something kind of . . . *cute* in the way he answered her. He leaned over and squinted and called her Ma'am. *Ma'am.* Don't you love it? I thought, this poor kid: he's afraid if he doesn't take her seriously, she'll come up there and sit on him.

"And then later I'm walking into the coffee shop in the motel. And there she is, waving me over to her table. Darling, I was *so tired.* The last thing I wanted was to be stuck there with that motor-mouth. And I walk over, and he's sitting there with her. I say, 'Fern, dear, I can just stay five minutes,' and he gives me this look like, 'Do I ever know what you mean.'

"His nametag says *Gary Price, Assistant Administrator,*

Las Floras De La something or other. He shakes my hand. And then he says, very bright-eyed, 'I think I saw you on the hike yesterday. Do you hike a lot?' Darling, I could have *died*, he was so earnest. I felt like saying, 'My dear, if you piled all the bars I've trucked through on top of each other, I'd be starting the second stretch to Kilimanjaro by now.'"

I laugh.

"But I just said," he goes on eagerly, " 'No, I don't do much hiking.' With *my* flabby old bod? Is he blind or what? But I was flattered. I have to admit, I was flattered. And there was something very sweet about him, very warm. Every time Fern started going on about her damn dogs, he'd smile at me, like we had a private joke. I thought, *Is* he? But then I thought: No, not on your life. This one looks as straight as they come. And besides, he's much too open, and that is *not* the way to cruise.

"Then Fern says something about how she wants to take a trip to Guadalajara to visit the orphanage, but she's heard about how sick you get from the water. So he says, 'I never got sick, but I had a *roommate* who did.' And then he says, very fast, very nervous: 'Uh, a *college* roommate,' like he wanted to tell me he was covering tracks. He said that for *me*. Darling, this kid was hoisting up his flag for dear life.

"Part of me was thinking, God, I need this? Some desperate kid passing me notes under the table? Honey, if you don't know how to wear it, keep it in the trunk. But the other part of me was . . . touched. I mean, here's this really sweet kid—a little clumsy, maybe, but a sweetheart—and *he wants me*. How did this land in my lap? It was so off the wall, Lil!"

I smile.

"It was *so* off the wall that I didn't know what to do with it! He'd look at me hesitantly—like he had all his cards on the table but he didn't know what to do next? And I just kind of looked away. It was my move. He'd laid himself bare. He was waiting for some sign from me, and *I just couldn't give it to him.* I don't know, did I want to have the upper hand? Was I being cruel? Or was it just all too sudden?" He looks dazed and puzzled, as if it was all happening as we talk.

"Anyway, then Fern gets up to leave and he stands up with her. Right away. And then she goes to pay the cashier and he says, very firmly, very proudly, 'Look, I'm not very good at this. And I know what you're thinking. So let's just forget it.' And, Lil, *I don't know why.* I don't know if it was the tone of his voice or what, but I didn't want to let him go. I *couldn't* let him go! I said, 'No, you're wrong. That's *not* what I was thinking!' And he could see my anxiousness. And I could see him seeing my anxiousness. So I just laughed and said"—he leans back and sighs grandly— "'Sweetheart, there is none so green as he who's been over the hill. You get used to looking under the wrong rocks so long, you just . . . you just . . . Oh, hell. Is my face red? Are my hands shaking? Let's go.' "

"Oh, Ronald, I love it."

"Anyway, we went back to his room and—what can I say, darling? We ended up spending a fabulous night together. It was so *easy,* Lil. We talked for hours. And we could laugh. Like at one point he brought out a couple of joints. Honey, he had them so elaborately hidden, you'd think he was going through an Interpol checkpoint. And I looked around the room, with his guitar in the corner and his jeans on the chairs and his papers all scattered around—and I couldn't help laughing. And *he* started laughing, too. He said, 'Do you get the feeling you're at a fraternity mixer?' And I said: 'What *I* want to know is, when do they start playing "The Sweetheart of Sigma Chi?" ' And he turned on the radio and said: 'Maybe we can at least get The Carpenters? I mean, this *is* Santa Barbara.'

"He's really *very funny.* I mean, to look at him, you wouldn't expect it, but these off-the-wall things would pop out of his mouth. Like, the motel room had these plastic lamps? The kind that—" He stops himself. "Oh, here I go babbling."

"That's okay, darling. I'm kind of tickled to see you this way."

"No, I mean, it wouldn't sound funny unless you were there. Unless you saw the lamp." He swallows his embarrassed smile: then he laughs, with sadness or relief, I can't tell. "God, Lil, it's been such a long time, it's hard for me to even talk about it without feeling ridiculous."

"Why? Because you think it'll go away?"

"Oh, because of a lot of things, I guess. It's funny," he muses, "I said to him the next day, I said, 'I never used to trust myself to like anyone as vulnerable as I am. I always knew the day would come—day? the next morning, even— when I'd look at his face with this horrible contempt and think, What am I doing with this? *He's* got all *my* weaknesses.' I said that to Gary." He stops for a second to hurriedly, finally light his cigarette. "I said that to Gary and he looked at me very calmly and said, 'Maybe you *will* think that about me. Maybe you *will* leave me.' And I was terrified! I said, 'What do you mean? Do you *want* me to say that? Do *you* want to say that to me?' And then I caught myself, and I said, 'I'm sorry, honey. It's just that this old fairy's wings have been singed so much, he feels like Joan of Arc.'

"He doesn't mind it when I talk that way, but it's like a foreign language to him. God, he's so different. He takes guitar lessons, he's a student, he hitchhikes through Mexico with a backpack. The amyl nitrate pansy patch *I* live in? Can you believe I'm with someone like that?" He laughs—embarrassed, or delighted, or maybe both. "But I love that about him."

"I believe it. He sounds darling. How old is he?"

"Twenty-seven." He looks at me questioningly. "But it's not an age thing. Honest."

"Twenty-seven isn't cradle-robbing," I reassure him.

"And he doesn't *seem* that young. I'm so used to old screamers acting like their own idea of twenty-five, and nineteen-year-olds who've been tricking so hard and so long, they might as well be fifty—that I don't even know *what* age Gary seems. I mean, he's innocent in a lot of ways. He's even a hick in a lot of ways. I swear, if he got cruised by some butch with forty-three keys on his belt, he'd probably take him for a locksmith. But there's also something very serious about him—dignified, even. He'd never do the parks. He'd never do the baths. He hates the bars. I mean, we all hate the bars, but he hates them the real way. He was in therapy for two years before he could come all the way out. He said he 'went into hiding' as a social worker. That way he—how did he put it?—that way he was *allowed* to be celibate. All he did for two years was go to work and go to his shrink. He said, 'That was my little-old-man period. I lived like a priest.'

"After he came out he went to some campus activist group for counseling sessions. He said he didn't mind their marches but he could never get used to dancing with another man while people were watching. He said, 'I didn't feel liberated. I didn't feel gay. I just felt self-conscious.' Lil, I loved him for saying that! It was just so . . . *honest.* He's like that. He has this way of being honest about his awkwardness without making a fool of himself, without putting himself down. He said, 'I spent the first twenty-three years of my life

learning how to have girl friends before I realized why I
could never get it right. And then I had to start all over
again, learning a whole new thing. Except I wasn't fifteen
any more.' He became less and less of a kid as I got to know
him, do you know what I mean?"

I nod.

"Anyway, then he went back to graduate school at San
Diego State and—" He looks at me. "Am I boring you?" I
shake my head. "Then he went back to graduate school and
he met someone, and they were together for a year, and then
it broke up. He said, 'One thing you learn is you don't sign
on for fairness.' Amen to that, darling, amen to that. So
when it was over with his lover, he went and did field work
with that orphanage in Baja. I never thought about it, but
he says places like that are full of people who want to escape
whatever's inevitable in their lives. He said, 'You should see
my friends in Vista. Vista's even worse. Vista's just one big
closet.' Did you ever know that, Lil?"

I smile at the funny, sudden innocence in his face, at how
swept up he is. "No, I never knew that," I say.

"He's only been back in San Diego a few weeks," he goes
on. "He said I was the first person in months. That when he
went up to Santa Barbara for the conference he was going
to make up his mind about how he was going to deal with it
when he got back. If he should withdraw again, or if he
should force himself to go to the bars. He said, 'If I jumped
on you, if I seemed anxious, it was because I didn't want to
do either.' He said he felt I was someone who would accept
him, someone who wouldn't make it hard. Lil, he said everything you're not supposed to say, and *I still wanted him.* It
was okay. It was finally okay to hear someone else saying it!"

"Ronald," I say, as he takes the first sip of his cold coffee, "it sounds so sweet. And he sounds very sensitive, very bright."

"Oh he is, he is. I kept waiting for him to find out I'm not."

"Oh, Ronald, come on."

"But I *did*, Lil. I'd say things that made him laugh and I kept wondering: How long can I do this until he figures out it's all the same joke?"

I laugh at the truth in that. Then I say: "Why is it so hard for us to trust the good things?"

"Oh, I don't know, darling," he sighs. "Is it really so hard for us to trust them, or is it just so embarrassing to be caught? I mean, look at me. This old auntie has turned into a blathering schoolgirl. And I'm probably going to go on like this *for days*."

"I don't mind."

"For *weeks*."

"That's all right."

"And if I start making an ass out of myself, you'll be gentle in telling me?"

"I'll be gentle." I reach across the table and touch his hand. "Do you believe that I want this to work out as much as you do?"

He nods. He squeezes my hand. Then he cranes his neck to peer at my kitchen clock. "My God, it's five-thirty already. We'll have to get you right into the sink if we want to keep our reservation."

"What reservation?"

"I'm taking you to dinner at La Scala tonight. To celebrate."

"Oh, Ronald, no. It's much too expensive."

"Darling," he sighs felicitously, "if you've got it, flaunt it.

And this old doll has got . . . it . . . *bad*."

I smile as I follow him into the bathroom.

An hour and a half later, he gives me the hand mirror and turns me gently around by my shoulders so I can see the back of my hair.

"Well, darling . . ." he says.

"Oh, I like it. I like it." Except it doesn't look that much different.

"Don't you just love this bias?" With his finger, he traces an invisible arc under my skull. "It won't even be in New York for another three months. I saw it in Italian *Vogue* and I said to myself, 'Lil has *got* to have this.' "

"I really like it," I say again, moving my head admiringly.

"Do you *really*?"

"Oh, absolutely. I love it." Now all I need is a man of my own to use it on.

He turns me around again, then carefully untucks the towel from under the collar of my bathrobe.

"I shouldn't call him tomorrow, should I?" he asks.

"Well, how did you leave it?"

"That he would call when he found out his exam schedule."

"Then, no, you shouldn't call."

"I was afraid you were going to say that," he sighs.

"Well, I mean, you *could* call him, just to see—"

"No. You're right. I shouldn't call."

Lips pursed, he throws the towel into my hamper, tidies up the brushes, sponges the sink. "Now," he says, with gentle authority, "let's close our eyes." And make a wish?

I feel his hand shielding my brow as the strong-smelling lacquer hisses all over my head.

And I wish for it to work out for him, so then maybe it can work out for me.

A few minutes later, I call him into the bedroom to help zip me up. I suck in my stomach and press down on my hips as he pulls to the waist. "I've got to go back on that diet," I mutter.

"Nonsense, darling."

"No. No. I do. And, damn it, I was doing so well before last week."

"Lil, you look fine. I'd tell you if you didn't."

"No, I can tell. It's not much, but I've gained."

I step back from the mirror to get a better line. I look sharply at my hips. Avoiding my eyes, I turn slowly right, then left, then right again, then left again. I feel like someone taking lessons at Arthur Murray's so I stop.

The room is half shadowed now. Miles away, the sun is setting on the ocean; half in, half out. ("Like dunking a big candied apple," I used to say to Andi, when she was five years old and sat on my lap, with Morty next to us, during those warm, sandy dusks at Ocean House.) It sends a last fierce stream of light into my west window. Through the mirror I see Ronald, in the shadowed half of the room, sitting on the edge of my bed. His back to me, he is dialing the telephone softly.

"Anything on 802?" he asks. "Ronald Halvorsen?"

Silent, he drums my bedspread with his fingers; they've put him on Hold.

"Just Miss Coburn-Coxe? Thank you," he says, hanging up.

I fumble with putting my makeup in my purse while he arranges his face into cheer.

"Well, darling," he says, with much bravado, "shall we?"

I walk around the room, flicking off lights. I pause at the

last one. "Ronald," I say. "You can tell me the truth." He looks at me expectantly. "Do I look a little . . . chunky in this dress?"

"Oh, God, no, darling," he says, in a preoccupied voice. "You look elegant."

I snap off the light and we grope through the dark room, the dark hall, like children through the forest in Andi's old favorite bedtime story.

"God, Lil, after sundown, this house turns into the crypt of the Dead Sea Scrolls. Don't you even supply Chanukah candles?"

"Darling, if you could have seen my last electric bill, you wouldn't be bitching."

I turn off the light in the breakfast room.

"Separate cars?" I ask.

"No. Let's take yours. I'll come back and pick up my bags after."

"You want to drive?"

"I'll drive."

I hand him my car keys. We walk to the front door. Before turning off the last light, I pause, as I always do, and fluff up my hair in the hall mirror.

"Ronald, I really do like it."

"Oh, I'm glad. I didn't think you did."

"No, I do, I do. What do they call it?"

"Oh, God knows. Tortellini? Marinara? Bocce ball? I have enough trouble with Spanish."

I turn off the light and open the front door. As I'm locking it behind us he says: "Now don't you let me call my service again from the restaurant, okay, darling? If I get the urge, just spank my hand."

The convertible top collapses behind me in big accordion pleats. Looking in the rearview mirror, I shift into reverse and steer out of my space in the Canon Drive parking lot across the street from the cleaners. The plastic clothing bags flap in the late September breeze.

I wave to the cute young attendant in the snappy red jacket. We have an arrangement; he lets me park in this private office building lot, and I give him a dollar. Smiling (he's up for an Ultra-Brite commercial, he tells me), he comes jogging over.

"You're a sweetheart, Ricky," I say, slipping him his tip.

"Rocky," he amends, still smiling. "Any time, Mrs. Resnick."

He pats the hood of my car affectionately, then goes jogging off to the next one. He sticks one of his tickets in the metal time-punch, opens the door for the driver, then, with a little hop, jumps in and careens the car to a space clear around the lot without even closing the door.

I like days like these—when I have an excuse to be out of the house. I stretch my errands out, sometimes driving around the same four-block radius two or three times because I've forgotten how close one shop is to another and what lots validate for which. It would probably be more efficient to park in a half-day lot and walk, but going back to the car is a nice delaying ritual, like having a cigarette after every course of a five-course meal. I look forward to the small talk of these days, the contact I make with the world. And then when I come home later the house feels new again, and I call my answering service and usually there's a message or two.

I drive slowly down Canon, signaling with my hand for the impatient driver behind me to pass. I am trying to decide where to go next. If this were an ordinary Saturday, I'd drop in on Ronald at the shop, but he's in San Diego again. He's so cute about this love affair of his. "Darling," he sighed last night, standing in front of his open closet, "I feel like a Wellesley girl going to visit her Harvard beau. Now *what* shall I take for the homecoming dance? My basic black with pearls?"

But his flippancies don't quite cover his nervousness. By Thursday night, every phone conversation he's had with Gary over the week has been turned upside down for signs of waning interest. By Friday night, he tries not to act expectant, excited—but only manages to seem more so. He drops things packing. He chatters. He frowns at his face in the mirror, jutting his chin, fluffing and flattening his hair. When he comes back on Monday, he's buoyant and happy and calm. But Tuesday the cycle starts up again. I can walk into the shop at three and tell by how his lips are pursed whether Gary has called.

"Come on, don't work yourself up again," I say. "It's been two months already. You *know* he'll call."

"You're right, Lil, you're right," he says, "I'm just being neurotic."

"Listen, thank God you're still that. What I love about you, darling, is that you don't leave me to suffer alone."

I turn right on Wilshire now and right again into the drive-in-teller window of City National Bank. I slip my passbook and withdrawal slip into the chrome drawer. I lean out the window and say into the microphone: "Tens and fives, please."

"Thank you," a very polished and amplified male voice returns.

"Uh, make one of those fives five ones instead," I amend.

"Thank you," the voice says again.

The drawer springs open with my passbook, my machine-stamped receipt, my money in a little packet. Printed on it: *Please count before exiting.*

I count the fresh bills.

"It's all here," I say into the microphone. "Thank you."

"Thank *you,*" the voice returns heartily. "And have a nice day."

I make a right on Little Santa Monica, drive four blocks, pull in under the big winged roof of the Union station on Crescent. I love this station. It's so dramatic, so futuristic. It makes buying gas an Event, like going to the Greek Theater.

"Half a tank of supreme," I say to the bright-faced young man with the ponytail. The front of his T-shirt says JACKSON BROWNE.

"Couldja back her up a coupla feet?" he asks.

I shift into reverse. He directs me grandly, like Zubin Mehta conducting the Philharmonic. "Thaaat's good. Right there."

I park and pull the gas tank release. He jumps around, sticking the long hose in. The back of his T-shirt says *On Asylum Records and Tapes.*

"You got the right idea," he says now, smiling approvingly through the blue liquid he's squirting on my windshield. "Top down."

"Why not?" I smile back. "It's a beautiful day."

"Lotsa people are really out of it." He frowns as he wipes. "Windows up, tops up, air conditioners goin'. Man, a day like today? Crazy."

"Mmm." I nod, like a compatriot.

"I had this one, about an hour ago," he goes on, moving to squirt the other windshield. "Real stuck-up chick. Seventy-five Porsche, plates say P-H-U-K-O-F. Thinks she's Greta Garbo or something, cigarette holder an' everything.

Wouldn't roll down her window more'n an inch to pay me. Whaz'she think? I wanna make it with her?" He shakes his head, working the chamois vigorously. "But then I had this other one. Fifty-nine Jeep? Quad tapedeck? Plates say JONI 24. Now she was awwright. Her I liked." His smile suddenly fades. "Hey, you could use new rubber on these wipers. I bet they're squeaking."

"I hadn't noticed. It hasn't rained lately."

"Well, bring her back next week if you want and I'll fix her right up. Check your oil and water?"

"Please," I say. And I lean back and pull the hood release.

"It must be a"—I choose my word carefully—"drag for you. Working on Saturday."

"Yeah, no, not really," he hums through the hood of my car. "It's slower. We close up at five. I can take off for Zuma against the traffic. Thirty minutes, flaaat out." He slaps the hood down. "Cash or charge?"

"Charge," I say, pulling out my credit card.

He slides it through his little metal machine. I sign my name. "Thanks now," he says, handing me the receipt. "And come again." Patting the car hood. "Have a nice day now."

I drive back down Canon and pull into the Food King lot. Inside the market, I buy several cartons of yogurt, cottage cheese, a tomato, a steak. The items knock around like pebbles in the bottom of the huge metal cart (everyone else looks like they're hoarding for an earthquake) and there is no Express line today anyway, so I anchor the bottom with three six-packs of Fresca.

There. *Now* I look like a serious shopper.

I wheel myself into line.

Over the large brown bag he's stuffing with items that come rolling down the black conveyor belt to the chime of the register, Tony lifts up his eyes in happy recognition.

"Hey, Mrs. R. Long time no see."

Tony used to do deliveries for the typewriter shop. But he changed jobs because this one gives him more time to create.

"How are you, Tony?" I ask. "How's it going?"

"Pretty good," he says, lifting the plumped bag into the customer's cart. "I think I've got a winner this time. Me and my partner are just typing it up. It's called *Planet of the Saints.* It's about"—punching open another large brown bag—"a couple of fundamentalists who find this UFO and go live in another reality zone on the lost planet of Pre-Time. Kind of like *Dune* only more metaphysical, you know?" I don't know, but I nod anyway. "The girl fundamentalist has these supernatural powers," he goes on, plunking my groceries in, one by one, "like defying gravity and making ashtrays vibrate and everything? She can get men to dig her with extra-sensate mind vectors. Kind of a Scarlett O'Hara type. Except she's married to this oil rigger in Galveston and what she really wants is to get liberated and be a nightclub singer instead.

"And the guy fundamentalist has this pre-B.C. karma range. He used to be Pontius Pilot's adviser but all he ever did with it in this life was work on a cashew farm in Jackson, Mississippi. Just poor white trash, you know? And no one would listen to his apocalyptic visions, not even after he went to work as a handyman for this commune in Taos. They were all into this chauvinistic cosmic thing and they thought he was just a dumb cracker. But *little did they know.*" He grins portentously while I pay the cashier.

"Anyway"—hefting my grocery bag to his chest—"they both end up on top of this desert cliff in New Mexico called Point Destiny. Did you ever see *Zabriskie Point?*" I hadn't, but I nod anyway, as we walk to the parking lot. "Kind of a similar visual. He's there gathering dry hemp for the commune and she's trying to fix her car that broke down while she's on her way to Phoenix to be a cocktail waitress. And then the sands kind of shimmer—the two of them are doing molecular telepathy, but you get the effect just by shooting through Vaseline with a hand-held—and there's this UFO, right in the middle. And they both *run* for it from opposite ends of the canyon and take over the knobs from a bunch of CIA-backed right-wing NASA Mission Controllers who had the thing built on the sly right before Kennedy was killed and tested it out in the Yukon with Arab oil highjacked over the Aleutians." I tap him on the shoulder and point to where my car is parked. "Anyway, they kill off the Mission Controllers infrapsychically and then they ascend together and break the ozone layer and restore the ozone layer and will themselves into orbit around the lost planet of Pre-Time. And then they land and start a religious colony there. You want this in the trunk?"

"No, the front seat's okay."

"I'm thinking of Tuesday Weld and Waylon Jennings if it goes." He opens my car door and sets the bags down. "And maybe someone heavy like Carlos Santana for the soundtrack."

"Well, Tony, it certainly sounds like you didn't miss a thing."

"I sure *hope* so," he says, shaking his head as if after a long labor.

"Just make sure I get invited to the premiere," I say, with a wink, as I press a dollar bill into his hand.

"Sure thing, Mrs. R." He flashes a triumphant smile. "Thanks a lot."

He pockets the dollar and goes jogging back to the market. "Oh," he calls out, jogging backwards now, "and if you ever need someone to come over and change your typewriter ribbon, just give me a ring here."

I drive down Canon again, turn right again on Wilshire, stop for a red light in front of the Brown Derby. Years ago, I used to meet Morty and his clients here for lunch. I'd wear my plaid silk Don Loper shirtwaist. Its skirt billowed out from under a tightly cinched waist and I'd turn up the collar and tie a beige silk scarf around my neck. Sometimes, if Morty's client was from the East, I'd wear my Mr. John pillbox, too. People always told me I looked like Ann Sothern in that outfit.

"Ah, Mrs. Resnick," the maître d' at the Derby would say, bowing slightly as my eyes blinked to get used to the dark, "so nice to see you again."

And at the end of the string of faces lined up against the wall under the framed caricatures, Morty nodded proudly from his corner booth. We'd smile at each other—almost sheepishly—as I walked down the row of banquettes. There was something urbane and romantic in dressing up to meet your husband for lunch, and we were still young enough to play at it, yet finally successful enough to play at it *right*.

"Sam—my wife, Lillian," he'd say, squeezing my hand. "Whom I wouldn't recognize if she ever showed up on time."

"It's just a foil, Sam." I'd wink, shaking the client's hand. "So I'll think his third martini was his first."

And they'd both be chuckling as I slid past Morty—the silk of my skirt grazing his thigh—to take my seat between them in the soft, tufted booth.

The light turns green. I pull the visor down and squint against the sun. Up ahead, Wilson's House of Suede and Leather and the Beverly Hilton shiver through my narrowed eyes, fanned by lazy palms. I imagine them Miami Beach hotels. I see a woman faintly resembling myself, but ten years older, lumbering down the sand. A bright-faced young man props up her chaise; she tips him; he says, "Thanks, Mrs. R. Have a nice day now." Another comes with a pillow and newspaper; she tips him; he says, "Thanks, Mrs. R. Have a nice day now." A third with a cold, sweating drink on a tray. She tips him; he says, "Thanks, Mrs. R. Have a nice day now."

She wants to keep him there for a moment's banter—keep *somebody* there, anyway. So she takes a sip of her drink, then grimaces. "Listen," she says, "I know they love Arthur Godfrey so much in this town they named a freeway after him, but do they *have* to make their scotch sours out of Lipton's iced tea?" (On a business trip here years ago, Morty had loved that line.) She turns now to see if the bright-faced young man is laughing. But he is already jogging back to the hotel.

With a familiar bump, I make the left turn into my alley; a right and I'm in my garage.

Monday afternoon at four, I drive to meet Edwin at the radio station on Sunset. After a letter and three phone calls (Sima acted as my secretary on two of them, so it wasn't so bad), I managed to get him this appointment. I still don't understand this new deejay fetish of his: the four-week course in radio engineering he just took at Santa Monica City night school, the incessant talking in those dopey rhymes. "Everything's irony, love," he says, "so why not just shoot for the ultimate?" I don't understand that either.

But then what *do* I understand these days? Gwynneth's

traipsing around with that female juvenile delinquent of hers? Edith and her meditation classes with that phony fifty-year-old monk in Venice? Sylvia making like Louella Parsons on every second divorce of the men who got their *first* ones from the women *we* knew ten, fifteen years ago? ("You know, Sylvia," I said to her, "not everyone has your mummified sense of revenge. Some women close a chapter on their lives and simply move on." What I didn't add is that I wonder who those women are.) Only Ronald's life makes any sense to me. He seems to have found love—as much as he thinks it's a jinx for me to say so. "You're next, darling," he keeps telling me, as if in the four years we've spent leaning on each other's shoulders and nodding to each other's laments we've become yoked oxen, hobbling to the water trough after a long, grueling plod. "You're next, darling," he keeps saying. "If it could happen to me, it's *got* to happen to you."

And I'm ashamed to admit I let myself hope that he's right.

As I walk through the glass doors of KNNT-FM, my ears are assaulted by a gospel chorus wailing: "Posner's custom-blend cosmetics keep you-ou in mi-ind . . . "

"Ronald should be here," I whisper to Edwin when I find him. "He loved Mahalia Jackson."

"See?" Edwin says as we sit down in two chairs in the corner of the large studio, "I told you it would be fun." Then he gestures to the tall, lean black man in the cream-colored silk suit who enters the glassed-in booth. "That's him. Larry Monroe. The guy you sent the letter to."

Monroe removes his straw boater; his straightened Prince Valiant pageboy gleams in the blinking control lights. Then he flips up the vents of his suit and sits down between the two microphones, making hand signs to the blond earphoned hippie across the glass.

"Smart sonuvabitch," Edwin goes on. "Owns half of the action by now. But he really paid his dues, I guess. Worked every major black station across the country. He was Stuff in Philly, Sly in Boston, Spiff in D.C., Spats in New York, Slick in Chicago, and Sport in Frisco. Here he's SunSsset."

"What was he doing?" I ask. "Overcoming a lisp?"

"He just got attached to his monogrammed bath towels. Love, if mine were sable, I would be, too."

The speakers blare out another commercial: "Say Akadama, Mama. Pure plum wine. Modesto, California."

"Mo-*des*-to, of course," Monroe chuckles suavely into the mike. "Yeah, I was drinking some Akadama in my chopper the other day, cruising above the land I'm buying in Big Bear. Mmm, it was nice. See all that fine earth laid out under you like a patchwork quilt. So I pulled out my bottle and my two crystal goblets . . . "

"He sounds like Billy Eckstine," I say to Edwin, "trying to sound like the chairman of the board of AT&T."

". . . and I turned to the lovely lady on my left and said, 'Have some Akadama, Mama.' And she just said . . . "

"Awww, SunSsset," a tape-recorded woman's voice cuts in, "you ride so smooth, my engine's just lubed up and purr-*rrrrin'*."

Then one of those bouncy, thumping records that Ronald's always listening to comes on. Monroe swivels around in his chair, opens the booth's glass door, calls sternly: "Seretha! Where's my Perrier? Where's my Ojays-at-the-Bowl spot? Where are my next three commercials? What is this, your day off?"

A young black girl in a shoulder-padded dress comes hobbling in nervously on platform heels. She wears her hair the way I did in 1945. She hands him a sheaf of papers and a decanter of water.

"And get his goddam *rake* off my desk!"

The girl hurriedly picks up an Afro comb.

"The dude wants to take a walk around the block to another station, he takes his noserings with him," Monroe mutters. "Funky Rashid, my ass. Levon Prendegast from Dorsey High. He knows as much about jazz as he does about astrophysics. But let *them* find out." He swivels his seat around and cocks his chin in the direction of Edwin and me. "Who are they?" he seems to be asking, none too impressed. The girl whispers a reply in his ear.

"He sounds perfectly charming, Edwin," I mutter. "No wonder you wanted to pay me for this."

"It'll be okay," Edwin says. But he's nervous. I can tell from the way he keeps picking lint off his jeans.

A few minutes later, the girl ushers us into Monroe's private office to wait. Everything is chrome and glass. "I feel like I just walked into a microwave oven," I whisper to Edwin.

"Monroe likes to catch his reflection, love," Edwin whispers back. "To make sure the bridge in his nose stays where the plastic surgeon put it."

In an entrance he must have memorized from *Executive Suite* (or—who the hell knows—maybe *Henry the Eighth*), Monroe strides into the room now without deigning to look at either of us, stands behind his desk, picks up and sets down several thick stacks of paper, lowers himself into his swivel chair, pushes an intercom button and says: "Hold all calls for five minutes."

Then he leans forward, snaps open a silver cigarette case, and, by way of silent introduction, gestures we might have one if we wish. We shake our heads politely. He leans back, rocks magnanimously in his leather chair, his long fingers making a little chocolate dome in his vanilla lap.

"See those transmitters?" He nods outside the huge plate-glass windows to the girders with the sign that says KNNT-FM. "When I came to this station, you could've hung laundry on them and they'd collapse. Could've played badminton over them, they were so low. Could've folded them up and packed them in a Parker Brothers box and given them to a ten-year-old for Christmas. And *he'd* sneak around the block to a Chinese restaurant and sell 'em as chopsticks!"

"This station," he goes on coolly, "had the kind of frequency, you could clap two tin cans to your ear with a string between them and get a better reception. Ten thousand watts of pure *dreck*. No stereo, no class, an I.D. that sounded like an old Stax studio band sloshed on Gallo with gum in their trumpets in a wind tunnel. And the ads. Hey, nigger, wanna buy yoself a used Cadeeelac? Pssst, nigger, wanna get ridda them ants and roaches? Wasn't anyone west of Avalon or north of Slausen caught dead listening to KNNT. Then, in '72"—he pauses to secure a Tiparillo in a teak holder— "I came out here and hired the best talent and cleaned it all up. Renamed it The Black Millennium In Sound. Upped the transmission, upped the demographics on the industry sheets, screened the ads for relevance to an upwardly mobile audience. Made the format so*phist*icated. Mellow. Kind of sound you could pipe into your tennis courts and not be embarrassed. Dig out by your swimming pool, you know?"

"I hear you, brother." Edwin nods obligingly.

"Okay," Monroe says, "I've done my spiel. Now what have you got for me?"

"My client has an act called Willy Gee, The Groove Merchant," I say. "Perfect, we think, for the time slot vacated by, uh, Funky Rashid. I believe you got our press release and explanatory letter?"

"I got the letter. What's the package?"

"Kind of middle-period Rosko but without the shmaltz," Edwin explains. "Or early Magnificent Montague but without the Watts Riot." Is this what Edwin meant when he said he did enough research on black radio in L.A. to qualify for a Ph.D.? "There seems to be a hunger in the community to get back to basics. Affluence breeds confidence, leading to a kind of second-generation wistfulness for—well, *roots* in a word."

"Or *jive*," Monroe says, "in another word."

"But stylized," Edwin is quick to say. "Tongue-in-cheek. A sort of affectionate period piece, if you will. A Dolphins of Hollywood of the mind for all those who've made the great leap forward across LaBrea."

Monroe leans back, considering. "I *have* been thinking about putting on an oldies segment," he muses. "To compete with AM. That seems to be the only hole in the format. LeeAnn DeFarr, our Vibes Goddess, is doing the jazz now. I do the disco, which takes care of eighty percent of the record company ads. I put on a Kiwanza Hour from midnight to one, and a Bilalian Hour after that." He takes a long puff of his Tiparillo. "That takes care of the social obligations. I upped Natty Rudeboy's Reggae Explosion to four hours in the afternoon to sew up the white audience. And Hector Rodriguez is doing salsa on Sundays, which also takes care of the white audience, plus San Pedro. And gives us spot ads for every burrito stand between Western and Alvarado." He rocks in his chair, pensively squeezing the knuckles of his clasped hands. "It just might be time to go after Compton again. Sort of smooth a few ruffled feathers down there." He sits up challengingly. "Okay, give me a fifteen-second rap that can be used as a sign-in, a pre-spot, a trademark, and a wrap-up. No bleed-in. No echoes."

Edwin takes a deep breath. Then, in a voice like snapping fingers: "Hey, all you bad johnsons and sweet young sparrows, thiz the Groooove Merchant: wheelin' you the wax gonna crack yo' backs, hustlin' out the hits gonna juice yo' grits, rollin' out the gold's gonna soothe yo' souls. You jess lay back, hey, and turn yo' box up to ten, and let Willy Gee grease yo' grooves and heat yo' hooves, and fill yo' crib with pure, un-ay-dul-terated *soul!*"

Jesus, if I had known Edwin had this talent, I would have used him to auction off my old rugs, instead of giving them to Goodwill.

"All right." Monroe slaps the desk and leans forward. "You're taking call-ins, but the phone mike's out. You've gotta pad a three-and-a-half minute B. B. King twenty seconds upfront to segue it into the news. You can't find your fade tape, you've run out of commercials, and the engineer's in the john. How do you fill it?"

Another deep breath, and this time even more staccato: "Thiz the Groove Merchant at dedication time, and we gonna testify in rhythm 'n' rhyme. Scrapple in the Apple and ease to the tease, and I got a Soul Sistah on my knees. Sistah, she sweet like a young parakeet. Mmm, fluffy feather and ver-y to-ge-ther. And she the saw in the jailbird's pie. She sharp and shiny and *su*perfly. And Sistah requestin' that B. B. King get on with his bad self and *shake that thing.*"

Monroe leans back in his chair a few silent seconds. Then, contemplatively rolling a chrome pencil between the tufts of his fingers, he drawls: "Not bad." He picks up his telephone, signaling that we may go now. "Leave your phone number with my secretary and she'll call you for an audition at the controls," he says.

"Mazel tov, dear," I say as we walk back out to the main studio. "He seemed very impressed."

"He should be," Edwin mutters. "I dropped enough g's to supply a whole Scrabble board. And to think, five years of *Othello* led to this. Ah, well. My choice, my laughter." Except he's not laughing.

A stunning black woman comes rushing through the studio and into the control booth. She sets down a tennis racquet and takes the seat between the two microphones. With that tropical fabric wrapped all around her head like some kind of exotic bandage, she reminds me a little of one of the Katherine Dunham Dancers. They used to play Ciro's around Christmas time every year. God, they were marvelous. Bongo drums, coconut trees, great leaps on bare feet across the stage with spotlights on the perfect muscles of their arched backs: they made Xavier Cugat look Presbyterian.

"Got my waterfall, Fred?" the woman in the headdress asks in a snappy, all-business voice. "Got my flutes? Got my congas?" To each question, the engineer across the glass makes a little circle with his thumb and index finger. "Got my birds? Got my whimper? The ten-second whimper, not the five."

"Got it, LeeAnn," he says.

"Okay," she says, "I want to try a new mix today. Double-track the waterfall over the congas, echo the flutes, jump in with the birds, trail with the whimper. Read me?"

"Loud and clear." Then he clamps one hand on his earphones and diddles with all kinds of dials with the other. "Ten, nine, eight," he counts while she closes her eyes, takes a deep breath through theatrically flared nostrils, throws back her head and hugs her arms across her chest like a woman about to leave her husband on a soap opera.

". . . three, two, one. Rolling, LeeAnn."

"Good vi-bray-shunzzzz, Los Angeles," she coos into the mike, over what sounds like a waterbed demonstration in

the middle of the Nairobi game preserve. "Are you feelin'
'em, too? Mmmm, I *bet* you are, Gemini." A sexy chuckle.
"You, too, Capricorn. Yeeeaaaah, layin' out on that bear-
skin rug with your patchouli lit and your mojo workin'.
Mmmm, that's what I'm doin' right now at this fiiine six
o'clock hour in the City of the Angels. Virgo-cusp-of-Libra.
Which means"—she exhales the words like some extrava-
gantly enunciated secret, every *s* pronounced *sh*—"the ele-
ments . . . are in celestial harmony . . . with the inner
essences. It's LeeAnn DeFarr, the Vibes Goddess, here on
The Black Millennium In Sound: fifty thousand watts of
peace, roots, good vibrations and cosmic tranquillity. And I'm
endeavoring to take you on a mellow spiritual journey down
the valleys of your mind . . . the rivers of your soul . . .
the summits of your inspiration."

"What is this?" I ask Edwin. "A geography class led by
Kahlil Gibran?"

"Whatever it is," he answers, "she makes about eighty
grand a year with it."

"Just for mouthing this crap and playing records?"

"That's just the tip of the iceberg, love. She does bit parts
in movies, discotheque openings, concert emceeing, product
endorsements. Some cosmetics company came out with something called Ebony Rainbow last year. She did one thirty-
second syndicated TV spot and bought herself a house in
Trancas."

"My God, there *is* money in this." I shrug. "Life is certainly full of surprises."

"Isn't it, though?" Edwin says. We sit down; he lights another one of his French cigarettes as a swill of flutes and
saxophones fills the darkening studio. "Five years ago, if
anybody told me I'd be dressed in this hardware, talking
that nonsense, I'd have laughed them out of the room. And

what a room it was. A little book-lined cell in Princeton, New Jersey. I'd sit there drinking my Spanish rotgut, reading my Rilke and Dunbar, studying the lines of those Angry Arts plays. Once a month, I'd do your standard pilgrimage to the 125th Street Y. I'd stand around outside with my hands in my pockets, quaffing up Langston's essence along with a dozen other outrageous phonies and shivering naifs. Then I'd head downtown to a little bar where Charles Gordone sat polishing his Pulitzer, and walk down to the Lower East Side past the building the old Umbra offices used to be in. I'd drop in at Slug's for a set. Then I'd walk all the way back uptown to Yorkville, stopping to pick up some Brie and Swedish flatbread, and ring the doorbell of these four SAS stewardesses I knew.

"Then one day I realized I was putting all my energy into the wrong hustle. You couldn't *get* anywhere with that game any more, even—*especially*—if you were foolish enough to believe it. My life wasn't sublime irony; it was second-rate farce. So the logical question became: How do I turn second-rate farce into bankable farce?" He takes a puff. "And that question, love, brought me out here."

"You make it all sound so distant, so calculated—whatever it is you're saying."

"What else is there to do? Take it seriously? Love, earnestness isn't tax deductible. You spend a lifetime cultivating the art of affectation, you better damn well find the cartoon that gives you the best mileage. Or, as Willy Gee would say: Shake yo' moneymaker, but make sure the box ain't coins, but paper. Amen, and can I get a witness."

"Edwin," I suddenly wonder, "do you like yourself this way? Are you happy?"

"Who knows? That isn't even a priority right now. Ain't

got mind to deal on pastry when the beans hasn't got off the stove."

"I wish I thought money would solve *my* problems."

"Lil." He turns toward me comfortingly. "If this thing works out, you're getting twenty percent."

"Oh, Edwin, I don't want that. I've got my real estate, my stocks. You don't have anything. Besides, I didn't even earn it."

"Of course you did. Listen, if you hadn't written that letter on that stationery of yours, I'd never have—"

"That stationery," I scoff. "I never even use it. Lillian Resnick, Public Relations—that's a joke. Some women my age do charity work for Cedars of Lebanon? I had stationery printed instead. That's not a career; that's an alibi."

"Lillian, you're a fine woman. And a very funny woman. And, on top of that, a sport."

Why do they all say that? "Thanks, Edwin," I say with what is probably a wan smile.

"Let me buy you dinner at Joe Allen's," he says.

"Okay. As long as we don't sit on top of the jukebox."

"Love, I wouldn't have it any other way."

He stands up.

"Wait," I say, tugging on his huge shoulder bag. "I just want to hear this song."

"Ah, Coltrane," he says, half closing his eyes. " 'Just Friends.' "

"Lovers no more," I sing, under my breath, along to the music. "Just friends, not like before. We laughed, we loved, we cried. Then suddenly love died, the story ends . . .' "

"Now *there* was a man," Edwin muses. "Turned the soprano sax into the human condition, you know?"

No, I don't know. I don't even know who's playing it

now. I just remember dancing to it, on an evening in 1956. Morty had just become a full partner. We celebrated at the Mocambo. Ella Fitzgerald was singing it. She wore a dress—a blue dress, I think—with sequins, and they dimmed the lights on the dance floor but you could still see the sequins, like tiny fish underwater, as you danced. I had my head on Morty's shoulder. One thing we could do was dance well together, really well. He used to say the secret was that my knees locked him in the right places ("but in the arm-lock, kid, I've got it all over you"). I had my head on his shoulder and he hummed into my neck, tickling me there, and I closed my eyes and wondered why I deserved to be so happy.

"Ready?" Edwin asks, as the final notes fade. "I don't want Monroe to see us hanging around."

I stand up. "Despite it all," I say, nodding to the woman in the booth as we leave, "she really does look like one of the Katherine Dunham Dancers."

"Who are the Katherine Dunham Dancers?" he asks.

"Oh, you're such a baby." I pat his cheek. "So young."

We walk out to the parking lot and get in our separate cars. By the dim dashboard lights I check to see if I have a dime or two nickels in my change purse. I want to call Ronald when we get to the restaurant. He said he'd be back sometime Monday night.

Edwin's car leads, I follow. He turns right on Sunset, I turn right. The Mutual of Omaha light flashes like a beacon through the dusk from Wilshire as we take Cahuenga down-hill to Third. It will probably be seven by the time we get to the restaurant. Seven is night, isn't it? What did she say? "The valleys of your imagination, the summits of your mind"? What did I say? "A geography class led by Kahlil Gibran"? Oh, he'll love it. Ronald will just love it.

5

JESUS, RONALD HAS BEEN REARRANGING HIS LIVING ROOM furniture for almost an hour now. I put down my magazine, take another sip of my scotch. "Ten more minutes of this and you'll qualify for retirement benefits from Bekin's."

"Either that or a hernia," he sighs, lifting up the Chippendale again.

"So *stop* already. It looked fine the first way, it looked fine the second way, it looks fine this way. I thought I was invited over for dinner. If I wanted this kind of evening, I would've picked up a sandwich and set up a camp chair at the loading zone at Sloane's."

"I'm sorry, darling," he says fretfully, setting the chair down in another corner. "But I just have to get rid of the *busyness*. That prissy, overdecorated look."

"Ronald, the room is *not* overdecorated."

"Not for us it isn't. But for someone who sleeps on a mattress on the floor with a *Viva La Huelga* poster taped to his wall? Darling, if it screamed any louder, he'd have to stuff cotton in his ears." He frowns. "Oh, I should have redecorated months ago."

"In what? Burlap and packing crates?" Against my better judgment, I pour myself some more scotch. "Come on, darling. Gary *knows* you've got taste."

"Oh, he'll walk in here and think he's in Billy Baldwin's attic."

"Listen, we should all be so lucky."

But he's not listening. He's thinking hard and drumming his fingernails against his teeth. "Let me just try it out in the hall," he says, moving the chair again.

"Ronald," I call out, "I'm about to faint from hunger."

"I told you, darling," he calls back. "There's some cheese in the refrigerator. And some pâté."

"You know as well as I do, the best way to ruin a diet is with hors d'oeuvres."

"I'm sorry, Lil." His penitent face appears in the doorway. "I'm being selfish."

"Oh, for God's sake, you know I don't care about *that*. It's just that I hate to see you working up anxiety again—and for no reason." He sits down across the coffee table from me and pours himself another scotch. "Now, look," I go on. "Gary's excited about coming tomorrow. You're excited. *I'm* even excited."

"He's excited to meet you, too, darling."

"Okay. *See?* You're going to have a marvelous weekend together. You've been having marvelous weekends from the beginning."

"At *his* place we have."

"His place, your place, what's the difference? I don't know why you feel you have to make an impression all of a sudden." I frown at the brand-new art and anthropology books he's scattered on his coffee table. *"Pre-Historic Art of Australia,* really. What's wrong with the magazines you usually keep here?"

"Vogue? Women's Wear? Please, Lil. He knows I soak my hands in peroxide all day. I don't want him to think I soak my brain in it, too." He looks at me pleadingly. "I want him to see I have *substance.*"

"Hey, come on," I say softly. "He's not blind. He saw that from the beginning. Why do you think he's been with you so long?"

He swallows the reassurance along with the scotch. "Thanks." Then, with a little ironic smile: "And I used to think *you* relied on *my* flattery."

"I *do.*" I take another sip. "I'm not too proud to admit it."

"I guess that's why I asked you over tonight: to hold my hand. I swear, you couldn't *fit* another butterfly in my poor little stomach, pet, unless you removed a rib."

"So what else is new?"

He laughs lightly. Then he says: "It's just that it's so *easy* when I'm there with him, Lil—at *his* place. It's like a vacation somehow. I don't feel like the silly old hairdresser who has to be on. Oh, I get campy and dishy with him, but it's not the same thing. It's . . . innocent, in a funny way. We do things I never do here. We go biking together. I mean, can you just see this old fruit peddling down Coldwater on a ten-speed? With a *knapsack?*" I smile at the image. "We drive to Tijuana. And then we come back to his little dump. Oh, it *is* a dump, darling." He shakes his head, smiling fondly. "The books all over the place, the lopsided Mexican wall hangings. You'd *die* if you saw it. But I *love* it. All that schoolboy wholesomeness, that absolute imperviousness to style. It's like a breath of fresh air I want to hold down in my lungs forever."

He leans forward, urgently. "I'm *afraid* of what he'll think of this faggot museum I live in. I don't want to bring him to the shop, to the clubs. I don't want him to see me swish with Phil and Leo. When I'm with him in San Diego, I'm just me. I'm afraid when he puts it in context, he'll think: So *that's* what he is—just another piss-elegant old fairy, just another old boy in the band. Lil, we're talking about *living* together—here—when he finishes the semester. *Do you know how much I want that?*"

"Of course I do," I whisper as he refills both our glasses.

"God, the stupid fantasies I let myself have. I walk around the house and figure where he'll put his desk, his bike, his guitar. I drive home from work and imagine what it'll feel like to find him here. I picture us talking on the phone in the middle of the day, both of us with our *Herald-Examiners* opened to the movie page. Deciding what show to see, where to meet for dinner. God, David and Julie Eisenhower should be so square."

"We all should be," I say softly.

"I feel like an old spinster whose dowry is up for inspection. And, darling, this old doll does *not* want to blow it."

I smile like a mother through the blur the scotch has brought on. "Ronald, did I ever tell you about Ed Loeb?

The man I was going with in New York before I came out here?"

"Of Leopold *and?* Why, darling, how fabulous! I mean, I knew your past was a killer, but I never took it literally."

"No." I laugh. "I'm afraid Ed Loeb wasn't nearly that interesting. He was a bore, as a matter of fact. But a very rich, handsome bore. A Wall Street broker from one of those stuffy Jewish families who like to think they're Episcopalian. I met him when I was working for the *Telegram.* At a party at the Copa given for . . . who was it? Abel Green of *Variety,* I think. God, that seems like a million years ago." I take a sip. "It *was* a million years ago. Anyway, he fell for me. God knows why. He thought I was racy or independent, or some such nonsense."

"That's not nonsense, darling. He just knew a hot lady when he saw one."

"Well, anyway, back then it was the big thing to go slumming. To pretend you hung out at the clubs in Harlem, to know the first names of a couple of the hoods who took out the Earl Carroll girls. I guess Ed Loeb thought I was his ticket to that world. I mean, I could tell him the Bugsy Siegel stories I heard. I knew the producer of *Shadow and Substance.* I'd even dated one of the Gershwin brothers. Leave it to me to pick the only unmusical one."

"Oh, darling, don't *tell* me you flunked as a groupie."

"With flying colors, darling. With flying colors." We both laugh. "But I couldn't keep up that novelty forever. I wasn't *that* well-connected. I mean, God forbid he should scratch the surface and find a nice Jewish girl whose father was an insurance man on Bradford Street in Brooklyn. So I knew if I wanted to marry Ed Loeb, I'd have to fit in with his stuffy crowd. Change the way I dressed, the way I talked.

Even get a job away from Broadway. I tried, Ronald, I really tried. But I didn't make the grade. He dropped me and got engaged to someone else. That's when I left for the Coast. God, was I miserable. The entire train ride out— and, believe me, they were long in those days—the entire train ride out I kept thinking: If *only* I'd made myself into the right kind of woman for him. If *only* I'd earned him. If only, if only, if only. Darling, you *know* how I can hit myself over the head with regret."

He nods.

"Well, to make a long story short, about ten years later, Morty and I were at some party at Ciro's. A Maurice Chevalier opening, I think. And who should we run into but Ed Loeb and his wife, Marjorie. They were out here on some business of his. She hated it, of course. You know those smug, phony women. They do a whole Sarah Bern-hardt over what a wasteland it is out here, how *famished* they are for culture. She knew I was in movie publicity, which was of course so far beneath her she was amused. So she asked me—in that ridiculous voice they freeze-dry the minute they learn it at Vassar—she asked me: 'Uh, tell me, Lillian, who is this, uh, *Dabbie* Reynolds I keep hearing about?' Well, I knew damn well she knew who Debbie Reynolds was, so I just looked at her very straightfaced and said: 'Oh, Dabbie Reynolds. Don't you know? She's a well-known opera singer.' "

"Fabulous, Lil!" He laughs, clapping his hands.

"But I realized, Ronald, I realized in that instant why I never could have married that man. There was no way I could have made myself stuffy enough for him. And if I *had* somehow managed to change into that kind of woman, wouldn't *that* have been awful?" I take a sip. Then, gently: "Look, darling, all I'm saying is: You can't sweep your life under the rug to make someone love you. You can't change into the person you think they want. From everything you've told me about Gary, he *doesn't* sound critical, he *doesn't* sound judgmental. He sounds lovely. But if he can't take who you are, if your life *does* threaten him, then he's just not for you." I pause. "It's as simple as that."

"Oh, I wish it really were," he sighs. "As simple as that."

We look at each other for a minute. Then I admit: "I know. So do I." I stare at his rug. "Why *is* it that the older you get, the less you can afford even your own advice? They tell you the years bring grace? Bring dignity?" I smile wearily. "I'd love to believe it. Boy, would I love to believe it."

"I believe it, darling. Just by knowing you."

"*You* say that. But why doesn't some marvelous man ever say that?"

"Because there aren't many. There aren't many, and the ones that are are all with the wrong women."

"*Should* I have settled for someone after Morty left? There were men around me then. There always are, at the beginning. Murray Roth. Sam Lerner. Even Len Kornbluth, my accountant."

"That godawful drip in the plaid pants? *Come on*, darling. You'd have made out better cruising the Corningware salesmen at Zody's."

"It's true. At least then I'd have somewhere to put my leftover tuna fish. But I lose my perspective, you know? I begin to wonder if my loneliness isn't a punishment for my snobbery. What right do I have any more to be choosy?"

"Every right, darling. More right than any other woman I know."

"That's why I think about Morty so much, I guess. To remind myself of how simple it used to be—how natural it felt—to care for someone without *trying* to. And to be cared for the same way back. Jesus, did I ever take it for granted—that whole period of my life. I still think about him. I'm embarrassed to tell you how much. Little moments we had together—the best moments, damn it.

"But everything's changed so much," I go on, pouring us a little more scotch. "The way they do it these days. In my day, we just fell in love. Blindly, maybe. Ignorantly. But who cared? It was buoyant, it was fun. So you made a mistake? You cleaned the egg off your face later. I talk to my daughter on the phone and I'm amazed at what a *project* they make it into now. They're so somber, so skeptical, these young girls in New York. 'That one plays games.' 'This one can't face his emotions.' 'This one is too insecure.' I love her desperately, Ronald, but to listen to her talk about romance is like being trapped in a closet with Joyce Brothers' dictaphone. Sometimes I just want to beg her: 'Andi, *please,* let yourself be light while you still can. You think all that analyzing will save you from being hurt? It won't, darling. It won't.' It won't."

I must be getting drunk; I'm repeating myself. But I take another sip anyway. "But then I think: She's just being arrogant the new way. When I was her age, I was arrogant the old way. We all liked to pretend we were Katie Hepburn." I smile, thinking back. "God, the bravado I used to have. The flourish. The style."

"You still have it, darling."

"Of course when you were twenty-five, you could pull it off. You just held up the hoop and they jumped. You didn't have to keep inventing your pride. You were always bumping up against it."

"When *I* was twenty-five, all I ever bumped up against was the hot little locker attendant at the Olympic steambaths. Ten months of bliss," he sighs, "and he *still* made me pay for my towel. Pride? Honey, this little trucker didn't even know the word until they came out with the furniture wax."

I laugh, despite myself. He laughs, too.

"Well, my dear," I say, setting down my glass, "I don't know about you, but I'm stewed."

"You're stewed? Darling, I am *pickled*." He holds up the three-quarters-empty Chivas bottle. "God, did we drink all this?"

"Well, I don't exactly remember you watering the plants with it."

"Speaking of the plants . . ." He turns to his window.

"*No.*" I pull him up gently by the collar. "Speaking of *dinner*."

"Oh, darling," he camps, making his way into the kitchen, "you just love me because I can cook."

"That's right," I hum from the couch. "I'm only after you for your recipes."

"Goldbricker!" he calls back. "Hussy!"

"Keep flattering me," I laugh, picking up the *TV Guide*. I turn to Thursday, November 18. I look up the shows under "Evening." I put it down. In the corner of the coffee table is a gift-wrapped book. It must be that *Five Families* by Oscar Lewis, the book Ronald ordered weeks ago from Campbell's, right after Gary first mentioned wanting to find it. God, he must have called that bookstore every day for two weeks to see if it came in. I hear him humming in the kitchen now over the sound of something sizzling in a pan, so I gingerly flip open the fold of the little gift card. *To G.*, he's written. *From R. Because.*

"Ronald," I call out, "you're going to have a *marvelous* weekend. I can just feel it."

"Oh, I hope so, Lil. But who knows? *Qué será será.*"

"Jesus, leave you in Tijuana one more weekend," I say, walking into the kitchen, "and you'll come back as Fernando Lamas."

"Oh, would that I could, darling. Would that I could."

He shakes a colander of Boston lettuce under the tap water.

I dip my pinkie in the saucepan, lick it. "Mmm, this is delicious. What is it?"

"Béarnaise," he says, patting the wet lettuce with a paper towel. "For the sirloin tips."

"Béarnaise. That's butter and eggs and—"

"Don't worry, darling. I'm rationing your portion. And I won't let you cheat."

"I just asked a simple question, dear. I did *not* request a prison warden."

"I'm sorry, darling. I thought you wanted me to help you with your diet."

"I do. You're right. I do."

"*Any*way," he says, breaking the lettuce leaves over a bowl, "I want you to save your appetite for tomorrow night. I'm making my special veal scallopine with escarole."

"Sounds divine." I lean over the saucepan again, inhaling. "And this *is* divine."

"Move just one inch, darling." He maneuvers in nervously with the wooden spoon. "I have to keep stirring it or it gets all congealed."

"Do you want me to slice the mushrooms?"

"Okay, but be *gentle.* Don't—"

"I know, I know. 'Don't let them break at the stems.'" I pick up a small knife. "I'm not *that* clumsy a cook, you know."

"Did I ever accuse you of that, darling?" He gasps. "*You?* The Julia Child of Van de Kamp's frozen dinners?"

I laugh. I slice. He stirs. Nureyev rests on the tile ledge above the sink, arching his back slowly against the handle of a copper kettle full of violets. What does he think of the two of us—that fat, petulant cat? What would anyone think, looking in?

I glance at Ronald's kitchen clock. "There's some special with Carol Burnett at nine."

"Spare me, Lil," he groans, leaning to open the broiler. "Haven't I been seeing enough hyenas at the San Diego Zoo?"

"And that Farrah Fawcett show is on at ten."

"Darling, if *you* spent five days a week duplicating every curl of her ridiculous hairdo for every little chippie between here and Pico . . ."

"All right, all right." I shrug as he lifts out the pan of sputtering steak. "I just thought TV might relax you."

"I'm relaxed now."

"Like hell you are."

"Okay, so I'm a little jittery. What can I say? It's like the night before Christmas."

"In that case," I say cautiously, "if you want, Santa has a little present for you."

"Librium?" His eyes light up as I nod. "Oh, Lil, you're a godsend! How did you know Gwynneth took the last of my stash?"

"Just one, darling. And *after* dinner."

"*One?* Darling, one doesn't even give me a buzz."

"*Just one,*" I repeat sternly, as we carry the plates to the table. "You've had a lot to drink tonight."

"But you *know* I need my beauty sleep."

"Count sheep, then. Or read that book on Australia."

"Oh, Lil." He pouts tenderly as we lay out the silverware together. "And you're calling me a prison warden? *You're* calling *me* . . . ?"

ᴬᴮ

My service calls me at nine sharp the next morning. I get out of bed, hurriedly pull the black tights and leotard out of their cellophane package and slip them on. I haven't even taken a class yet and already I'm cheating. Last week, when I went for my complimentary session, the director of the Body Awareness Workshop told me I should stand naked in front of my mirror for five to ten minutes each morning. "To take a visual inventory of your body expressiveness," she explained in her peppy voice.

"You mean to see where I'm the fattest?" I asked. "The flabbiest?"

"Well, no," she said. "We don't like to make value judgments like that. We feel bodily self-*knowledge*—not self-criticism—is the key to a lifelong program of firming and trimming. We want you to think of your body as your friend for life—a friend you want to keep getting to know better."

Briefly I imagined her—this brightly smiling young woman whose nameplate said *Penny Babst, Dir.*—waking up each morning and singing "Getting To Know You" to her naked self in the mirror, like Gertrude Lawrence to the Siamese schoolchildren in *The King and I.* More briefly, I imagined myself doing the same thing. Then I put my cynicism aside and impulsively (desperately?) signed up for the ten-week course that promised all kinds of bizarre rituals, starred and indented on the program card like Stardust Hotel coming attractions:

* BREATHASTHENICS
* DANCERCISE
* KINETICONTOURING
* SLIMNASTICS

Of course it's silly. But there comes a point when you just can't laugh at silliness any more. God knows, I should have joined an exercise class long ago, but with each year I didn't it became harder and harder to start. Oh, I'd get up in the morning and try to touch my toes ten times in my nightgown. I'd treat myself to massages at Elizabeth Arden several times a year. I even took two or three beginners' tennis lessons. But who was I kidding? I had let myself go, and dieting alone wouldn't make up for all the years of neglect. The tranquilizers Dr. Fleischer had me on three years ago made me overeat. So did boredom and self-pity. Then, after my hysterectomy last year, I guess I threw in the towel. My body became simply a thing I wrapped up each morning and tolerated. Now, perhaps, I could learn to look at it again.

So I drive down Santa Monica now and park in the lot next to the pink one-story building. At five of ten, I walk in the door, studying the faces of the other women who enter with coats over their leotards. Last week, the class was flat on their backs and all I saw were four dozen kicking legs. Now I see the faces, and most of those faces are a hell of a lot younger than mine. Oh, well, what does it matter? What does it matter, right?

"Good morning, Mrs. Resnick." It's *Penny Babst, Dir.* again, clipboard clasped to her bosom like a perky stewardess. "Well, it certainly looks like you're raring to go."

"Really?" Her calm enthusiasm disarms me. "I hope so. I made a mistake and had too many scotches last night."

She giggles good-naturedly, like someone enjoying an off-color joke. "Oh, we'll fix you up in no time," she says, leading me down the hall. "There's nothing like some good cardiovascular work to re-equalize the metabolism and get the blood rushing again."

Cardiovascular work? Are they going to give me an EKG?

But no, I realize, as she slides open the glass door. She is referring to this circle of leotarded women prancing around the mirrored room, slapping their knees as the instructress calls out: "Feet high! Feet high! *In*hale! Feet high! Feet high! *Ex*hale!" They look like overaged Santa's reindeer in a fourth-grade Christmas play.

"Once you start doing this for ten minutes every morning," Ms. Babst assures me, "you'll actually wean yourself of the need for caffeine as a pick-me-up." She cocks her head jauntily. "Well. How about giving it a try?"

So I enter the ring of trotting, knee-slapping women. "Feet high! Feet high! *Ex*hale!" Around and around I go: breathless, anxious, awkward: my eyes fixed on the small-fannied, flapping-maned colt of a girl in front of me in order not to find myself in the mirrors. But there I am, all right— "Feet high! Feet high! *In*hale!"—reflected back at every turn: panting, chunky, hunched over to slap the knees that barely come up to my crotch, much less my waist. And now—Oh, God!—the instructress is jogging next to me, like a trainer. "If you straighten your back," she says, putting one hand on my stomach and forcing my shoulders back with the other without breaking stride, "you'll find it's much easier."

"But then," I manage between huffs, "I can't . . . reach my knees . . . with my hands."

"You will," she smiles. "You just keep at it and you will."

Will I? *Will* I?

After another minute she jogs to the center of the circle.

"Okay, ladies, let's stop where we are now and just run in place to keep the rhythm. Good. *Very* good. Now we'll go right into twenty jumping jacks. Ready? One! . . . two! . . . three! . . ."

I stand, glancing around bewildered, while everyone else starts. How do you coordinate this? Do the arms go out when the legs go out? Oh, no, I've got it wrong. The arms go *in* when the legs go out. The arms go *in* when the legs go out, the arms go . . .

"Eighteen! . . . nineteen! . . . twenty! *Good.* Now, ladies let's space ourselves out into four rows for the tensing-detensing."

I find a nice anonymous space in the middle of the third row, as far from the mirrors as I can get.

"For those of you who are new," she continues, "we're going to be discovering just how rigid our bodies can be. And just how limp and relaxed they can be. Now everybody lie down. Eyes closed. Hands by the sides. Feet about a foot apart."

Good. Now this is the kind of exercise I can deal with.

"*Now,* I want you to contract *every* muscle in your body. Tense them up just as tight as you can. I want you to feel, really feel, that tightness. In the buttocks . . . the arms . . . the hands . . . " She purrs, like a hypnotist, as she strolls between the rows. "The upper thighs . . . the abdomen . . . the facial muscles. Make your whole body into a *fist,*" she whispers dramatically. "Say to yourself: I am a sphincter. I am a wound-up coil. I am absolutely as tense, as tight, as compact as I can possibly get."

I am a sphincter. I am a wound-up coil. I am absolutely as tense, as tight, as—

"Now!" Clapping her hands. "*Release.* Relax. Go limp. Let every single muscle just col-*lapse.* Say to yourself: I am a noodle. I am a rag doll. I am a cup of Jell-O. I am going to just . . . float . . . away . . . on a cloud."

I am a noodle. I am a rag doll. I am a cup of Jell-O. I am going to just . . . get nauseous from her metaphors, is what I am going to do.

"And just enjoy," she coos, "the deep relaxation of the moment. Say to yourself: I enjoy every muscle in my body."

I enjoy every muscle in my body? I don't even know where most of them are.

"I want to understand my body. To experience my body to its fullest. To empathize with and respect and be *at one* with my body."

I want to understand my body. To experience my body. To—Jesus Christ, is she a gym instructor or a justice of the peace?

"Now stand," she says in a reverential tone.

We clamber to our feet.

"Felt good, didn't it?" Everyone nods her head eagerly. The instructress beams. "Now, ladies, we're going to do a series of what we call stretching-elongating exercises." She demonstrates: "Stretch up with the right arm on one, up with the left arm on two, the right arm, the left arm, the right arm, the left arm. Then flat back, arms extended: bounce, bounce, bounce. Touch your toes on the count of ten and up again with the right arm on one. Okay? Now let's tighten our buttocks, tuck down with the small of the back, lift up our thorax, center our energy in the abdomen . . . " I glance around again, bewildered. ". . . and take a deep breath. Now ex-hale *slow*-ly and one! . . . two! . . . three! . . . let's *really* get a stretch there, four! . . . five! . . ."

To the right of me, a woman my own age stretches as gingerly as I do. Lumpy in her leotard like me, she leans forward—"flat back and seven! . . . eight! . . . nine!"—her arms outstretched, like mine, as if for mercy. I turn my head toward her in the middle of our breathless bounces. Flush-faced, we catch each other's eyes.

"Do you think this really does any good?" I whisper, over the strident "and one! . . . two! . . . three! . . ."

"Well," she says weakly, "I figure it can't do any harm."

"I guess that's the most we can ask."

". . . five! . . . six! . . . flat back seven! . . . eight! . . . nine!"

And as our hands strain down toward our knees, she smiles tiredly back at my own tired smile.

When I arrive home, Sylvia is sitting at my breakfast table, talking on the phone. Sima must have let her in. She waves me over urgently. "Quick," she says, her hand clasped over the mouthpiece. "I have to bring one of them back before noon." She nods to the two open Saks boxes she's laid on my breakfast table. "Which one should I wear to the SHARE party tonight?" Then, back into the phone: "Edith, for Christ's sake, don't be so naive. Of course she's leaving him. Why else would they be selling the house? Sure I'm sure. I drove past it *twice*. Yeah, a big sign: Stan Herman Realty."

Sima sticks her head out from the kitchen and hands me a piece of paper. In her childlike handwriting: *Mester Rodol call. say is going fabaless. he to see you at PM 8. with bell on.*

I smile at the message. "Thanks, Sima."

"Look, Ede," Sylvia goes on. "If you heard what I heard about his stock losses, you wouldn't say, 'Maybe they're just moving.' She's like all the rest of them. God forbid she should wait for him to lose his whole shirt. He loses *one button,* she wants out. And to think he left Vivian for that . . ."

She must be talking about Herb Glazer and his second wife, the Harrah's showgirl he married ten years ago.

"Give them a shiksa with a basket of bananas on top of

her head and all of a sudden they're Aly Khan."

Before I met Ronald, I was Sylvia's partner in this neurotic floating crap game. Ten minutes after leaving each other's house we'd be on the phone with each other. Did someone we know have a new car in their driveway? A FOR SALE sign up? A different pool cleaner's truck parked in front of their house? Sylvia would call. Was the dress she just bought at Magnin's marked down 20 percent at the Broadway? Was Akron advertising Nepalese wicker flyswatters? I would call Sylvia. We bought two or three of everything just so we could kill an extra hour returning things to the store. No event was too small to warrant our fingers on the dial. We would have done better, in fact, with walkie-talkies. But now she has Edith for that and, thank God, these unannounced visits of hers are rare. Is it cruel of me to be repulsed by the two of them now? Do I feel above it all only because I can't bear to admit how narrowly, how indefinitely, how concertedly I've escaped?

"Poor Vivian," Sylvia clucks on, as I lift a black scoopneck jersey out of one of the boxes. "I told her ten years ago: Pride, shmide. Get the shtupper for another twenty grand, go to the Golden Door and get your jaws done. So it's a little extra chozzarai with the lawyers? So what. It'll save you in the long run."

I fold the black jersey back into the box and lift a chocolate-brown silk shirt out of the other one.

"So which one?" Sylvia asks me.

"The black."

"Lil says the black, too," Sylvia reports to Edith. "Huh? I don't know, I'll ask her. Lil, do you want to come with us to the SHARE party tonight?"

"Thanks," I say, "but I've already got plans."

I walk into the kitchen for a cup of coffee. Through the

door I hear her humming sourly into the phone: "This one with the plans. Huh? I don't know. She just walked in wearing a leotard." Loudly now: "What's with the leotard? You joining the Russian ballet so you can do arabesques with your hairdresser's cat?"

"Don't get smart," I say, walking back in. "I just came from an exercise class."

"She just came from an exercise class," she tells Edith. "What? Oh, Edith, stop with that already." She taps me on the arm and shakes her head in exasperation. "Okay, Ede, okay. I'll ask her. Lil, Edith says maybe you'd also like to go with her to her meditation class."

"Tell Edith," I say, taking a sip of my coffee, "that if spiritual awareness is anything like body awareness, I know what they mean now by Ignorance Is Bliss."

"Lil says if spiritual awareness is anything like body awareness she knows what they mean by bliss."

"By *ignorance* is bliss."

"By ignorance is—Hey, what am I, a U.N. translator? Talk to her yourself." She thrusts the receiver in my hand.

"Come with me today, Lil," Edith cajoles. "It's really marvelous. They teach you how to breathe."

"I know how to breathe."

"They teach you how to sit."

"I know how to sit."

"They teach you to relate."

"That," I sigh, "I may not know."

"*Edith.*" Sylvia shakes her head disparagingly after we've hung up. "Give her an inch, she takes a mile. You really like the black?"

"I like the black."

"Better than the brown?"

"Better than the brown."

She folds the tissue paper over the shirts and closes the boxes. Sima walks in timidly, holding a plate of food.

"Oh, I'm sorry, Sima," I say. "We'll just clear this off the table so you can have lunch."

"So why can't she eat in the kitchen?" Sylvia whispers as we move into the den.

"Because she pays me money to live here. This is her house, too."

" 'This is her house, too.' Lil, why don't you stop with this refugee camp already?"

"Sylvia, we've gone through this a dozen times. I don't like rattling around in the house alone."

"So don't rattle. Get a smaller place, I keep telling you."

"I happen to like this apartment." I sit down. "And it's a pain in the neck to move."

"What's to move? *I* moved. Was it so painful? You call the movers, you call Mike Silverman, you move."

"I just can't do it now, Syl," I say, wearily. "I just moved to this place, which is half the size of the house on Oakhurst. Now you're telling me to move to a place half the size of this? Where do I finally end up, in a broom closet?"

"Oh, Lil," she says, lighting a cigarette. "I worry about you sometimes."

"Please, Sylvia, spare me the worry. The way we cope is different, that's all. We just happen to disagree on the lesser of evils."

"Come on," she coaxes now. "Come with Edith and me to the SHARE thing tonight."

"I can't."

"Why not?"

"I'm going to Ronald's for dinner."

"So break it."

"I don't want to break it."

"Why not? You see him three times a week as it is. This isn't a bunch of faygelehs. It's people like you and me."

"People like you and me. Oh, Sylvia, how you delude yourself. It's young married charity dames who get dressed up in eight-hundred-dollar cowgirl suits twice a year to get their names in the columns. It's a glorified Hadassah brunch is what it is, and it's dreary as hell."

"Do what you want," she says, flapping her hand in frustration. "But I'll tell you something, Lil. I'll tell you something that only a long and trusted friend can tell you, and I hope for your sake you take it the right way. Because I know you with your stubbornness, Lil. You take things the wrong way, even if they're meant to be constructive."

"You can be constructive by shortening your drumroll. What *is* it?"

"I am *trying* to tell you, I have been trying to tell you for months now: You *lean* on him too much. Okay, be friendly with your hairdresser. I'm friendly with my Wally. I give him nice tips, little presents once in a while. But I mean, for Christ's sake, he's not my *gigolo* already. He's not my crutch. He's not my whole goddam social life!"

"I resent that, Sylvia," I say, after a deep breath.

"*See?* There you go again, taking it the wrong way! A friend tries to help. A friend who knew you when we were both—may yours rest in peace and may mine rot in his mishegoss—when we were both in happier times. A friend tries to tell you how she sees you ruining your life and you resent it!"

"Don't get yourself so worked up, for God's sake. I heard you. I disagree. I resent it. But I'll let it pass." You don't bother arguing with Sylvia. You just pretend her bludgeoning is affection and leave it at that.

"I'm only saying it for your own good, Lil. What's *with* you and all these weirdos lately? That doped-up dyke receptionist? What is she, growing a marijuana tree under those hats of hers? That shvartzer plumber? I tell you, ten years ago you would've laughed him out of your house if he came over to visit your maid. And Ronald. Okay, he's your hairdresser. All of a sudden you have to make like the Bobbsey Twins? I mean, Christ, I like my Japanese gardener, too. But he comes over to trim my hedges, not to take me to Jack's At The Beach."

"And your life, Sylvia? Is it so full? So marvelous?"

"Of course not," she says bitterly. "But whose is? Joanne Carson's maybe? Her looks? Her youth? Her settlement? If her life isn't marvelous, she's a damn ingrate."

She slips on her jacket, puts the two Saks boxes back in their shopping bag. I walk her to the front door. "No," she says, as I open it, "my life isn't so full. My life isn't so marvelous. But I'll tell you one thing, Lil. At least it's appropriate."

I close the door behind her, collapse against it for a long minute. "Sometimes," I sigh, "I wish I could trade in all my women friends for one good dog."

"You ask something to me, Meeses Resunk?"

"No, Sima. I was just thinking out loud."

⁜

I ring Ronald's bell, excited.

He opens the door: a big smirk on his face, a potholder mitt on his left hand.

"Darby and Joan, who used to be Jack and Jill . . ." he croons under his breath as he steps outside to hug me.

"Oh, I love it already!" I whisper, handing him the bottle of wine.

He ushers me in. I smile at the darling, sandy-haired young man who stands up from the couch so anxiously he almost bumps his corduroy knees on the coffee table. Leaning over to extend his right hand to me, he smiles back—a wonderfully open, boyish smile.

"Lil, this is Gary. Gary, Lil."

"I've heard *so* much about you," I say, shaking his hand.

"*I've* heard so much about *you*."

"Just leave it to me to be a blabbermouth," Ronald says. He stands beaming and awkward for a few seconds, looking from Gary's face to mine and back. Then he pulls the bottle of wine out of the paper bag. "Oh, fabulous, Lil. Margaux sixty-six."

"Is that what it is?" I set my purse down. "You know me with wines, darling. I just told the guy at the liquor store: Anything that won't clash with veal scallopine, as long as it's not Mogen David. Ronald can tell you," I explain to Gary, "I'm hopeless as a connoisseur."

"Me, too," Gary says, laughing eagerly. "Of course, in my situation you kind of get used to always buying the cheapest."

"See?" Ronald clasps my shoulder. "I *knew* you two would have a lot in common."

"Oh, *you*." I elbow him.

Gary smiles at him affectionately, then continues, to me: "But now they've got all those candy wines. Annie Greensprings. Boone's Farm. They're really . . . *awful*." I smile at his earnest grimace. "But at least they make me feel sophisticated buying Almadén."

I laugh. He smiles, gratified by the laughter. I start to unbutton my coat.

"Oh, here"—he lunges politely—"let me help you off with that."

"Thank you, Gary." And he shuffles behind me respectfully, holding the shoulders as I slip my arms out.

"I'll just . . . hang it in the hall closet?" he asks Ronald.

Ronald nods, uncorking the wine. I tuck my skirt under me and sit down. From the corner of my eye I glimpse them conferring about the vegetables, the silverware, the fire: their blond heads close together, their voices soft and serious. I leaf through the Australia book and try not to smile.

The minute Gary goes into the hall with my coat, Ronald reels around. "Adorable," I mouth from the couch. "Adorable." He nods his head up and down, smiling.

Gary comes back with a stack of old newspapers. "Do people ever tell you you look a little bit like Patty Hearst's boyfriend?" I ask.

"Do I?" He stops in his tracks, slightly embarrassed but smiling.

"The nice one, I mean. The first one."

"The one she dumped on," Ronald says.

"Oh, *Ronald.*" I look at Gary. "This one with the jokes. Couldn't you just kill him sometimes?"

"Yeah," Gary says, feigning toughness. "Especially when he makes cracks about my chili."

"*Me?*" Ronald gasps. "Why, Gary, I never make cracks about your chili. Offering it to the dachshund down the hall is a compliment to the chef."

We all laugh, and I look discreetly away from their tender chiding glances.

"Well," Gary says, stopping by the fireplace and crumbling the newspapers, "I guess it's Boy Scout time." (He *does* have a cute little sense of self-parody.)

"And I guess I'll start on the veal," Ronald says.

"Can I do anything?" I ask. "Set the table or something?"

"No, darling," Ronald insists, on cue. "You just sit and relax."

I wink at him as he turns to walk into the kitchen.

Gary sips his wine. I sip my wine. I cross and recross my

legs, searching for a good way to open a conversation. It looks like Gary is doing the same thing. Self-consciously, he arranges the logs and kindling, then cranes his neck in the opening.

"It's a narrow flue," he says, turning around to me. "Canyon building regulations, I guess. Ron says there's something like a dozen fires up here a winter?"

Ron says: Oh I love it, I love it!

"Yes," I say. "Farther up, you can get fined just for smoking in your car."

"Wow, really? Just for smoking in your car?"

"That's the Beverly Hills Police for you. On a really slow day, they'll get you for a crooked antenna."

He laughs. Such a warm, easy, wonderfully wholesome laugh. I smile. We sip our wine. Then, together:

"So how do you like Los Ang—"

"Ron tells me you're a publici—"

We laugh at the collision.

"I'm sorry," he says. "You go first."

"I was just going to ask you how you like our fair city of freeways and smog."

"Oh, I really like L.A." He shakes his head enthusiastically as he sits back on his heels. "I really do. I know it's . . . *hip* . . . or whatever, to put L.A. down, but every time I've been up here I've really enjoyed it. Like we were in Westwood today, just sort of walking around and browsing in the bookstores and I thought: This is really charming. It's built on a human scale. I don't know why people say L.A. is so plastic."

I smile to myself. (Of course Ronald would take him to the most collegiate part of town.) Then I say: "I've never understood that adjective myself. 'Plastic.' It seems so outdated. I mean, why don't they say polyester? Or Formica. Christ, even Naugahyde."

He laughs again. (God, I wish I could always get such good audiences.) "I know what you mean," he says, turning to stuff more paper in the fireplace. "Of course, San Diego is so nondescript, you can't even put it down with any . . . colorfulness."

"Have you always lived there?"

"Just about." He wheels around anxiously, as if thinking it impolite to talk to me and make the fire at the same time. "My folks moved to La Habra when I was five. My dad was an engineer for the Navy." He's silent for a few seconds. "I'd kind of like to move—after I finish my master's this term. I'm sending my résumé to different places. San Francisco. Oakland. Here." He looks into the fireplace as he says those last words; my stomach tightens a little for Ronald.

I try to think of something to say for Los Angeles that won't sound too obvious. But his match in the fireplace spares me. "Bravo!" I applaud as the flames burst on the little pyramid of logs and paper.

"Oh, thank you," he says, blushing.

"Ronald said you did a lot of camping. Is that how you learned to make such a good fire?"

"Yeah, although basically the kind of camping I do is day hikes. Digs."

"Digs?"

"Archaeological digs," he explains. "I spent a couple of years outside of Guadalajara, co-administrating an orphanage."

"That's right," I say, as casually as I can. "I think Ronald mentioned that. It must have been fascinating. Oh, what am I saying? I mean, it must have been very rewarding, very personally gratifying."

"Actually, it was pretty boring." He smiles wryly to set me at ease. "The work itself."

"Really?"

"Well, most of it was paperwork. People who aren't in the social services tend to think it's all human interest and progressive reform and all that, but on certain levels it's just like any other bureaucracy. Your hands are really tied by the fund raisers."

"Mmm, that must be frustrating."

"It is. And then you've got your sponsoring organization to deal with. And are *they* ever conservative. And surface-oriented." He shakes his head. I shake mine. "Really, all they care about is the window-dressing. Like that the main building gets repainted in time for the visit from the UNICEF honchos and that the kids all get clean clothes and ribbons in their hair that day." He frowns. I frown. "One of the reasons I'm getting my master's is so maybe, hopefully, one day I can be in a position where I can change that a little."

"That's a wonderful goal," I say.

"Well, I mean . . ." He shrugs, embarrassed at his grandiosity. Then he squints. "I forgot how I got on to that."

"We were talking about archaeological digs."

"Oh, *right*. Well, anyway, my hands were really tied in that job and there were like two or three days a week when I had nothing to do. So my co-administrator and I got to know these anthro students from the U. of Mexico who were doing research at the ruins, and we worked up a program for the older kids at the Mission to help them out. Shoveling, classifying relics, *everything*."

"How interesting," I say as he sips his wine.

"It was. It really was." His eyes are wide. "We'd go on these all-days. From five A.M. to midnight."

"My God, what energy!"

He smiles another flustered thank-you. "But it was really great. The kids learned about their history and culture, and I learned. It was *fantastic*. The U. of Mexico people gave us practically a whole course for nothing We learned to take microscopic specimens, to do age-dating. You could take a three-by-four-inch sandstone chip and mineral-process it and in twenty minutes date it within fifty years of Aztec history."

"That *is* amazing," I say. "Oh, you know where you should go this weekend if you have time? The LaBrea Tar Pits."

"Oh, right, that fossil bed. By the art museum, isn't it?"

I nod. "On that part of Wilshire they call the Miracle Mile. Named because the May Company and Ohrbach's are across the street from one another, if you can believe it."

He smiles. "In Guadalajara they had something called the Miracle Mile. The Via de Milagros, actually. Named because some saint in the fifteenth century made the land fertile. I wish there had been a department store *there*."

I laugh.

"Would you like some more wine?" he asks.

"Please."

"I'm sorry," he says, refilling our glasses. "I've been talking so much about myself."

"*No*, don't be silly. It's been fascinating."

"Ron tells me you're a publicist," he says brightly. "Now *that* must be fascinating."

"Well, 'publicist' is a generous description at this point. I *was* one, more or less. I'm trying to start it up again."

"All I know about the profession is from *The Days of Wine and Roses*. That's what Jack Lemmon was, I think. But doing it for movie stars: I guess that's a whole different thing."

"Well, it's a lot of, excuse the expression, b.s."

He laughs. "Yeah, I can imagine. I mean, wheeling and

dealing and stuff. But I think that's exciting. All the ins and outs of who gets on the cover of what magazine. Is that kind of what it is?"

"Exactly," I say. He smiles, like a student just praised by the teacher. "But I've been away from the mainstream for a while. I'm easing back in with a client—a friend of Ronald's and mine—who's trying to establish himself as a disc jockey."

"Wow, that's interesting. I read *Rolling Stone* once in a while and I really think . . . I mean, it may just be my own generation, but it seems to me that music has kind of replaced movies. Not totally, but in terms of heroes. So disc jockeys must have the same power the old studio executives had."

"That's an intriguing point," I say, trying not to laugh at the image of Edwin sitting behind Irving Thalberg's desk. "You may be right."

Again he smiles that delightfully abashed smile. I consider telling him that my daughter feels the same way about music, but it seems . . . what?: inappropriate? impolitic? . . . to mention a daughter who's closer to his age and sensibility than Ronald is. So I simply say: "Actually, I must confess I don't know that much about the record industry. But if the deal goes through, maybe I'll call on you as a kind of adviser."

"Oh, well, I don't really know anything about it, either," he's quick to say. "Especially now. My own taste is kind of . . . hopelessly stuck in 1968. Joni Mitchell, Paul McCartney, Paul Simon. Ron and I are going to the Paul Simon concert at the Bowl tomorrow night. I'm really excited about that."

Oh, I love it, darling! You didn't leave a stone unturned.

"*Well,*" Ronald says, coming out of the kitchen now, "it

sounds like the two of you could just chatter away until dawn."

"Oh, we could, we could," I say. "Gary's been giving me a whole course in archaeology."

"Well, I hate to break it up, kids, but: dinner . . . is . . . served."

"You'd make a marvelous butler, darling." I hug him as I stand up. "Wouldn't he, Gary? We could just rent a tuxedo. Get a little napkin for over his arm."

"Oh, if only they were casting a remake of *Dinner at Eight*," Ronald sighs.

Gary laughs. (I guess these kinds of lines are new to him.) Then he picks up the near-empty bottle of wine. "Let me get the other bottle," he says softly to Ronald. "The one I brought."

Again, their heads are close together as they whisper about who should bring in what from the kitchen. I precede them to the dining room, the honored guest. The candles flicker in the darkened space. The warm is wine in my stomach. I watch Gary take Ronald's half-smoked cigarette from between his fingers. Frowning tenderly, he stamps it out in the ashtray. I am so happy for Ronald I could burst.

"What a beautiful cactus." I finger the centerpiece. "And with flowers!"

"Gary brought it from San Diego," Ronald says, setting down the serving tray.

"I figured," Gary says, smiling as he uncorks the new bottle of wine, "the cat could always use it as a scratching post."

I laugh. "Aha," I say, as Ronald pulls out my chair for me, "so you were prepared for the infamous Nureyev."

"Well, I heard about what happened that weekend when we were in Santa Barbara."

"Well, in all fairness to Nureyev," I say, "that was more the fault of our mutual friend, Gwynneth."

"I've warned Gary about Gwynneth," Ronald says.

"She sounds kind of neat," Gary says, pouring the wine. "She sounds like a real character."

"Oh, that she is, that she is. You're not the only one who's run an orphanage, Gary. Ronald's been sheltering Gwynneth off and on for a year now."

"If only I could just get a tax deduction," he sighs. "I'd even take food stamps."

"Hey, that's an idea!" I say. "Gary, there must be some way, with your influence, that Ronald can work out an official adoption."

"Hmm, let's see," he says. "Does she speak Spanish?"

"Well, I think she can manage 'Mañana ees good enough for me.' It's kind of the leitmotif of her life."

"That's it!" Ronald exclaims, almost knocking over his wine in all the corny mirth. "With that sombrero of hers, darling, all we have to do is dress her in sackcloth and give her a couple of Ludes and take a picture of her by the banana tree outside Ralph's and I'll have a monthly stipend."

We all laugh—loose, happy, high laughter.

I raise my wineglass. They raise theirs. "To . . . health," I say judiciously. "And"—catching Ronald's eye for a brief, bright second—"to happiness."

"To meeting you, Lil," Gary says.

"To . . ." Ronald begins, his face filling with emotion.

"Why, darling," I chide, "it's not like you to be tongue-tied."

"Oh, I'll think of something funny later," he says.

And we clink our glasses and sip.

"Ronald," I say, lifting up my fork, "this salad looks almost too gorgeous to eat."

"Oh, the garlic bread!" He whisks the napkin off his lap. "It's probably burnt to a crisp."

"*I'll* get it," Gary says, touching Ronald's hand briefly. He stands and goes into the kitchen.

"As my mother used to say," I whisper across the table, "I could just *kvell*."

"You could kvell? Darling, just call *me* Molly Goldberg."

"Should I turn off the oven?" Gary calls from the kitchen.

"Better leave it on low," Ronald calls back. "For the dessert."

"Dessert?" I groan loudly. "Ronald, if my clothes don't fit me tomorrow, I'll sue."

"Oh, sue me, darling, sue me," he whispers rhapsodically. "Get F. Lee Bailey. Get Louis Nizer. I'll be so high tomorrow, I won't know the difference."

Gary comes out with the basket of steaming, pungent bread. Ronald stands to ladle out the scallopine. Gary hands him one plate at a time. Their shoulders touch, their wrists graze lightly.

"Mmm," I hum, biting into the veal. "It's wonderful." Oh, it is. It is, it is.

THE HOLIDAYS TIPTOED MERCIFULLY PAST, BUT I MISSED MY co-conspirator. "Maybe if we just close our eyes and count to ten, they'll be over with," I'd said to Ronald last year. "We could always revive hibernation as part of the human potential movement."

"Oh, would that we could, darling. Would that we could."

We sat around his house a lot that week last year, getting angry at ourselves for nibbling at the fruitcake and candy and cheese his customers kept giving him, drinking the gift-wrapped champagne and inventing Good Samaritan missions for ourselves.

"I've got it," he said, unpeeling the gold wrapper from an Almond Roca as he sprawled on his living-room couch. "I'll dress in a Santa suit and pop down Robert Redford's chimney."

"Sorry, dear. He's got solar heating."

"Foiled again."

"Come on, think like an altruist. You could donate your used fermodyl vials to a methadone program."

"And my heat lamp, too. 'Give this slum child a winter tan.'"

"Darling, they already have them."

"*You* didn't grow up in Minnesota, pet. Some of the *hottest* little Svens on those street corners," he sighed. "Zip knives and everything. Oh, blue-eyed soul, darling. Blue. Eyed. Soul."

"We could turn on the television," I suggested.

"*Miracle on Thirty-fourth Street? The Bing Crosby Special?* Gimme a break."

"You expected maybe some Joe Dallesandro movie instead?"

"I can dream, can't I?" Then he sat up. "*I* know. Let's play Scrabble."

"God, I haven't played Scrabble in years."

"Oh, *let's*, Lil." He jumped up and dug the set out of his cabinet. "Unnatural acts count."

"Yeah? Well then Yiddish counts, too."

"Brand names for French depilatories count."

"Now, Ronald, come on. That's not fair."

"Neither is life, darling. Neither is life."

And, laughing and pouring ourselves another glass each of Dom Perignon, we unfolded the board and began.

But it wasn't the same this year. Ronald had Gary, and his visits to my house were always breathless and hurried; his manner, over-solicitous, moist with apology, full of transparently phony gloom. "Damn it, don't patronize me!" I wanted to say. "Don't feel so goddam sorry for me!" But I didn't, of course. And I'm glad I didn't. (For God's sake, I can't resent him for being happy.) Now, with the tinsel cleared, maybe I can snap myself out of this martyred mood.

I stuff my unopened mail in my jacket pocket, pull open the big Deco doors of his shop, rush in guiltily: as usual, late.

"Hey, Lil! Ever whiffed this up close? Outraaaaageous."

My eyes shoot up to Gwynneth, who is atop a footladder by the big white Christmas tree, making like Juan Valdez on his coffee plantation.

"Are you taking the ornaments off," I ask as she beatifically inhales the pine needles, "or molesting it?"

"Trip and a half," she drawls, slowly twirling one of the iridescent balls in front of her eyes. "Trip. And. A. *Half.* I could just get off on these things for *hours.*"

"I bet you could. Listen, just be careful you don't fall and sprain something."

"No hassle," she says, smiling down at the young woman with the corkscrew curls and Clara Bow lips who is sitting on the floor, packing the balls in a corrugated box. "Sasha's a nurse."

The Kewpie doll smiles. "I do alternate healing. You know, acupuncture? High colonics?"

"High *what?*"

"Colonics." Gwynneth smiles proudly. "Kind of like an enema, except you get a rush from it. Totally mellows your whole intestinal track."

I squint from the Kewpie doll to Gwynneth. "What is

this?" I whisper. "You go from James Dean to Florence Nightingale inside of a week?"

"Huh?"

"Whatever happened to Nikki?"

"*That* little butch thief? After all I did for her, she went out and totaled my car. And then she had the *nerve* to strip it down and sell the parts to some hood in Torrance."

"You're surprised?"

"Tried to rip off my charge cards, too. Except"—a triumphant smile—"the stores already canceled those from when I bummed out on them last year."

"Yeah? Well, be grateful for small favors." And I walk past the two of them into the back room.

Leo puts down his hand dryer, rushes over to hug me.

"Happy New Year, darling," he gushes.

"Happy New Year to you," I say. "Are you sad to see the holidays over?"

"Over?" Ronald sidles up. "With the two of them out there? Darling, we'll be tripping over that smelly old tree in July."

We kiss. "I'm sorry I'm late," I say.

"Don't be silly, darling. You're early. By Honolulu time."

"You know me with the mailman," I explain.

"Oooo." Leo shimmies. "What's the dirt on you and the mailman?"

"The postman always rings twice, darling," Ronald camps. "And this doll gets *handled . . . with . . . care.*"

"Oh, how fabulous!" Leo giggles. "I thought that only happened with milkmen."

"No." I laugh. "Seriously, I have this crazy habit. Somehow I can't leave the house until after my mail comes."

"Funny." Ronald sighs euphorically. "When *mine* comes, I can't leave the *bedroom.*"

"*Show-off.*" Leo slaps his hand. "Oh, love in bloom. Isn't he disgusting, Lil?"

"Isn't he, though?"

I wink at Ronald, then walk over the hair-littered harlequin tiles into the dressing room. I set down my purse and the clump of unpromising envelopes. I unzip, unbutton, unhook, and hoist. Off with my clothes, on with the navy-blue smock. I slide open the curtain, stop at the Mr. Coffee tray. "How was your New Year's, Lil?" "Have a Happy New Year?" Clara Haupt, Phil, even Marcus the janitor: why must they all ask? "Yes, yes, marvelous," I lie, pouring the coffee in the styrofoam cup. I spoon in some Cremora and tear open two little packets of Sweet 'n Low.

"Want some, darling?" I call to Ronald, who is standing by the empty chair, shaking my plastic bottle of formula.

"Just some hot water, love," he calls back. "I'm de-caffing, remember?"

Oh, that's right. That damn herbal-tea kick he's on. "Listen," I say, taking mincing little steps so the cups of hot liquid won't spill, "just do me a favor, okay? Promise you won't start reading Adelle Davis. At least"—I sit down—"not out loud."

"Well," he sighs, tucking the plastic bib around me, "we've all got to start getting healthy *some*time."

"Ah, what a lovely new lover will inspire." I set down my purse, my mail. "Does he still stamp out your cigarettes after two puffs?"

"Only when he thinks I've had too many." He dips his tea bag in the hot water. "But I think I'm on my way to quitting on my own."

"Mazel tov!"

"Now if *only* I can just keep my weight down."

"Well, they say you have to expect to gain a little. At first, anyway."

"Oh, *God*." He sighs lavishly as he parts my hair with his comb. "I would die if I gained. I would *die*. Then Gary'd never move in with me."

"Of course he will. What does he have left? Three more weeks down there?"

"That's just for his courses." He squirts the dark, gummy liquid down the center of my scalp. "Then he takes his finals, and then some state qualifying thing. And *then*"— holding up crossed fingers—"*then*, darling, if this old fairy still has a godmother kicking around somewhere, you may be looking at one half of the future Ma and Pa Kettle."

"Fabulous, darling. Will you invite me over to watch your parsnips ripen?"

"Absolutely." He laughs. "And I'll feed you some of my home-pickled corn."

"I think you already are."

"I know, I know." He shakes his head blissfully as he makes another part in my hair. "Isn't it *awful*? And to think: I used to be so witty, so bitchy, so hip."

"Don't worry, darling. You're still bitchy."

We laugh, and he squirts, and the cold, gluey Clairol tickles my bare scalp again.

I lean over and leaf through my mail. A bill from Saks. A white-sale catalogue from Ohrbach's. A bill from the Auto Club. The *Reporter*, which I'll save for under the dryer. *TV Guide*. A January Clearance notice from Pixie Town, where I haven't shopped since Andrea was eight. A fat window-envelope packet of 5¢-Off! coupons for family-size sacks of barbecue briquets and obscure detergents—Crystal this, Bubbles that, something-or-other Dawn—apparently named after strippers. A . . . what is *this*? I tear open the small,

square, hand-addressed envelope and pull out an embossed
card.

BENNY CHIU CORDIALLY INVITES
YOU AND A GUEST FOR COCKTAILS
TO CELEBRATE THE OPENING OF
CHIU'S-AT-THE-MARINA
SATURDAY, JANUARY 29 / 5–7 P.M.

"Look." I hold it up to Ronald.

"My, my. That little Chink just keeps on trucking, doesn't
he?"

"Come with me. And if Gary's here that weekend, both
of you come."

"Fabulous, darling. You're on. No . . . wait a minute."
He leans over and squints at the invitation. "Damn it, darling, I can't. That's the night of the Golden Globes. Those
female giraffes that hand out the trophies? Wouldn't you
know, I have comb-outs on three of them."

"Aw, come on. Can't you give them to Leo or Phil?"

"I wish," he sighs. "They each have four. And split ends?
Dry? Oh, *why* do they always pick the ones who shampoo
with Borax?"

"I could take Sylvia." I'm thinking out loud. "Or Edith."

"Puhleeese, Lil. Talk about cramping your style . . ."

"Or Edwin. Poor Edwin. That radio station is still making
him jump through hoops for that job."

"Lil, you *could* go alone, you know."

"Sure. And stand in the corner alone all night, munching
on egg rolls till the cows come home."

"Lil," he says impatiently. "Now stop being so self-pitying."

"*I'm* self-pitying?"

"Yes," he says gingerly, "you are. Look, how did I meet Gary? By going out somewhere new, *alone*, right? Lil, time *isn't standing still*. You can't just keep hiding behind people for the rest of your life. You've got to go out and take some risks."

The words are like lye in my open wound. "Since when have you become such a pious sadist, Ronald?" Since your own wound closed? "I want that kind of crappy condescension, I'll write to Ann Landers."

"Oh, Lil, why can't you just *listen* to me for a change instead of snapping? All I'm saying is: If you have someone to hang on to all night, you don't circulate."

" 'Someone to hang on to.' You're beginning to sound like Sylvia."

"Darling, how would you like chartreuse spitcurls?"

"Don't joke with me, Ronald; I mean it!" I order, suddenly furious. "Sylvia says I lean on you too much. Now you're saying the same goddam thing. And with all the subtlety of a bulldozer, thank you. These smug little edicts all of a sudden. I shouldn't hang on to somebody. I should *circ*ulate. You think I'm tugging on your sleeve now? I'm dragging you down with my neediness? *Okay, I get the hint.*" I pause for a breath; then softly, bitterly: "What's happened to your memory, Ronald? Has it *really* been so long? Have you been with Gary so goddam long you've forgotten how it feels to be where I am? And is it so *goddam beneath you* to be reminded?"

"Jesus, Lil." He looks terrified. "You're really mad at me."

"No, I'm not mad," I grumble. "I'm just . . . it's just . . . oh, forget it."

"Lil, I'll break those appointments! I'll go with you to Benny's!"

"Don't do me any favors."

"Listen, they all need wigs anyway."

"I said, *Don't do me any favors!*" My God, I've shouted. Through the mirror I see him clutching his squeegee bottle timorously; his face stricken, bewildered.

I snap my *Hollywood Reporter* open and bury my face in Hank Grant's column: reading nothing, just seething. Silently, with what I hope are intimidated fingers, Ronald resumes parting my hair and squirting the formula on the roots. I turn the page. He leans forward, pours the rest of the formula into a plastic bowl, puts on his rubber gloves and dabs it on my head, working it through with his fingers. I turn another page. "Am I pulling?" he asks. "No," I say tersely. He leans forward again and prongs a small square of aluminum foil in his fingers, then crunches it around the clump of hair he's just bleached. I turn another page of the *Reporter*, then another. He takes another square of foil, then another, then another. I put down the *Reporter* and pick up *TV Guide*. "Now you're pulling," I say tersely. "Sorry," he says tersely.

He takes the last square of tin foil. Finally, slowly, I lift my eyes to the mirror. Tiny silver geysers spark out all over my head.

"Christ, are you doing a frosting job, or a remake of *Journey to Mars?*"

"Actually, I'm preparing you for Safeway's frozen steak locker."

"Well, as a very funny hairdresser I used to know once said: Darling, meat is meat. And hard up as *I* am, I'm ready to cruise county morgue."

And slyly, slowly, we smile.

"I'm sorry," he says softly.

"*I'm* sorry."

"Look," he says gently, "what's the silly Golden Globes? I'd rather go to Benny's with you."

"No, Ronald, your work is your work. It was unfair of me to make such a thing of it."

"But will you go anyway?"

"I don't know. Go, not go—what's the big deal?"

"Come on, Lil," he says tenderly. "You haven't been to a party in a long time. A few drinks, a few laughs: what do you have to lose?" He shrugs and smiles and his eyes are as desperately hopeful as mine always were, years ago, when I'd say the same thing to Andi. Or as his always were, months ago, when I'd say the same thing to him. "Give yourself that much?" he pleads. And I don't know whether to burst out laughing or hug him for the Jewishness he's so earnestly trying to affect. Oh, he *is* my friend.

I nod, grateful. Then I look away and confess: "You know, I guess I'm a little . . . jealous . . . of your relationship with Gary. Not that I don't want you to have it. *I do.* You know I do!"

"I know," he whispers reassuringly.

"But it's just that, I don't know, the less vulnerable you get, the more vulnerable *I* feel." He nods. "I know it's crazy, but . . ."

"It's not crazy."

"Oh, Ronald, why do things always get so complicated between us?"

"Oh, I don't know, darling," he sighs as he moistens a cotton ball. "It must be because we're two *fabulously* complicated people."

"Neurotic, you mean."

"I'll settle for complicated. Now lean back so I can get the bleach off your face."

"Yeah." I shrug and lean back and close my eyes as he gently dabs the wet cotton around my forehead and ears. "I'll settle for complicated, too."

So here I am, three weeks later, holding on to this rope banister, making my way up a slatted wood ramp over a fake canal full of lily pads, ducking the bamboo shoots as I go. Benny should have supplied machetes, for God's sake.

"Welcome." The smiling woman in the coolie hat and silk pajamas bows as she takes my invitation. I walk through the pagoda-shaped doorway and wade through the crowd of bodies.

"Lil!" It's Eloise Kreske, whom I've known for twenty years from the Hollywood Women's Press Club.

"How are you, Eloise?"

"Hot." She fans herself wearily. "Why do they always have these damn openings before the air conditioning comes?"

"Who says it's coming? Did General Electric ever make it to the Bridge on the River Kwai?"

"Well at *least* he dispensed with the mosquitoes."

"I'll drink to that."

I lift a fruit-laden glass off the tray that is floating in front of my eyes. I nod thank-you to the obsequious young Chinaman whose palm appears to be attached to the tray. I pick the toy parasol out of the drink, then the little plastic spear with the three maraschino cherries on it. "Is there any liquor at all in this?" I ask, after a sip.

"God, no," Eloise says. "Unless they injected it into the pineapple spears." She grimaces. "These things make you gaseous."

"I know."

"Remember when they used to have *real* drinks at press parties?"

"Remember when they used to have real *press parties?*"

And we smile the old-veterans smile. Okay, so we're reduced to doing Martha Raye and Joan Davis snickering in the wings. But it could be worse, right?

"Well," I say, "I think I'll go find something to munch on."

"Try the rumaki," she says. "It's better than the Luau's. Which isn't saying a hell of a lot, but . . ."

"Thanks." I smile. "I think I will." And I continue into the jammed room.

None of these people look familiar to me, but they all greet each other with laughter and fey smiles and kisses blown into the air behind their ears. I guess I will track down an hors d'oeuvres waiter, nibble a few things at a leisurely pace, admire the teak, admire the bamboo, stare at the sailboats out the window, and make a foray into the ladies' room. Eloise and I will bump into each other at uncomfortably frequent intervals, make bright, arch remarks about whatever it is we're ingesting at the moment, then push on through the din of joviality as if we have someplace to go. Damn it, why couldn't Ronald be here with me now?

"Lillian!" I turn around. "You *did* come."

It's Benny in the corner there, merrily pumping hands. He beckons me into his arms.

"Of course I came," I say, after we embrace. "I wouldn't have missed it for the world."

"This woman," he announces to the small crowd of people gathered around, "practically started me out in this business. Then she had the nerve to disappear from my life for fifteen

years. Now"—a showmanly wink—"*now* the only way I get
to see her is by opening new restaurants. How do you like
that?"

"Well, Benny," I say, "if I can get you to proliferate, I'm
delighted."

"Listen, don't give him any ideas," cracks the frizzy-
headed young guy with the mezuzah shining through the
chest hair of his open cowboy shirt. "He's already working
on his third."

"*Are* you?" I ask.

"By the Music Center." Benny smiles proudly. "Good
shoes may come in pairs, but good restaurants come in
threes."

"God, Benny," I groan, "if Confucius were alive today,
you'd outsell him in paperback."

"Don't give him any ideas about *that*, either."

"Nah." Benny winks. "I'm just happy to be outselling
Ah Fong's." Then he tightens his arm around me and
starts the introductions. "Lillian, this is Seth Silverman, my
business manager." I nod to the hairy-chested cowboy. "Alice
Reiner, from *Sunset* magazine." I nod to the woman next
to him. "Joyce Wong, the best banquet director a man could
ask for." I nod. "And . . . I'm sorry, I didn't get your
names?"

"Lou Cochran," the man says, smiling at me warmly. He
is about five or six years older than I—and not at all the
kind of man you expect to find at a press party. Square-
jawed, suburban, a little corny in that white turtleneck and
checked jacket. (Do people really take Johnny Carson's wardrobe seriously?) But he's kindly looking—*very* kindly looking. Who was that actor in *The Defenders* years ago? He
does commercials now? E. G. Marshall. Yes, that's who he
looks like. His eyes twinkle pleasantly behind his tortoise-

shell glasses. Could that be a look of interest—or am I just imagining it?

"Gail Cochran," the young blonde standing next to him says. Is she his wife or his daughter?

"The Cochrans are our first private party customers," Benny says proudly. "They'll be christening the Flower Drum Room next month. A reception for eighty."

"We're really pleased about that," the man says. "It's a lovely restaurant."

"It certainly is," I say, meeting his smile. "Benny knows how to run them."

"I learned, you might say, by managing this lady's bars at private parties."

"Really?" The man asks—eager, it seems, to converse.

"He learned to improvise, he means. When we ran out of grenadine, I'd slip him a packet of Kool-Aid."

"Sssh, Lil." Benny winks. "Don't give away my secrets." The man laughs. "No, but really," Benny goes on, "Lil gave the most wonderful parties. By the end of the evening, she'd be sitting on the piano, singing Ethel Merman songs."

I shrug. "How else was I going to clear everybody out?"

He laughs again. And as Benny and I reminisce about the old days and the young woman flips through Joyce Wong's loose-leaf notebook full of photographs of elaborate tropical cocktails, he keeps smiling: warmly, almost appreciatively. *Yes,* appreciatively. *Is* he . . . ? He certainly doesn't seem the type that would marry such a young woman. But then these days they all do.

"Well." Joyce Wong hugs the notebook to her chest and puckers her face up expectantly. "Shall we go back into the office and talk menu?"

The young woman nods eagerly.

"Listen," Benny says, "when you're finished, come back out for another drink."

"Thanks, I think I will." The man smiles wryly. "Signing checks always makes me thirsty."

The young woman hugs him. "But just think," she says playfully, "this will be the last one you'll ever have to sign."

"I know." He smiles again. "And *that* makes me even thirstier."

She laughs. "Aw, come on," she says tenderly. "I'm not leaving the country, Dad. I'm just getting married."

So. There it is. Suddenly—involuntarily—my eyes lift up to meet his.

"My youngest," he explains, with weight on the singular pronoun. "The other two left home while their mother was still alive," he adds, after a pause, "which made it a little easier on them." He smiles. "Now poor Gail's got this old sentimentalist here on her hands."

"I know what you mean." I smile. "I have a daughter who's three thousand miles away. I get a little twinge every time we talk on the phone long-distance. You do everything in the world to keep it out of your voice but"—I shrug—"it just sneaks through."

We laugh a little. Benny and the others have dispersed; the jumble of voices all around form a cushion to his attention as he asks, "Is she in college, your daughter?"

"No. She's out of college and working at a publishing house in New York. She'll be . . . my God, twenty-six next month."

"I know it's not the most original thing in the world to say, but you don't look old enough to have a daughter that age."

"Listen," I say delightedly, "sometimes the unoriginal things are the best. Thank you."

"You're quite welcome."

"Dad?" His daughter cuts in gingerly. "Excuse me." She smiles at me. "Dad? We're going back to the office. You want to meet us there?" She pauses. *"Whenever,"* she assures him. "No hurry."

"Fine," he says. "I'll give you a little head start to order up a storm of caviar."

"Caviar? Dad, at a Chinese restaurant?"

"Well, lobster then. Whatever they have that's expensive."

"I'll find it, all right," she teases.

"I bet you will." He winks at me. "Never a problem with that."

"It was nice meeting you," she says.

"Nice meeting *you*," I say, as she turns to leave with the banquet director.

"I tease her a lot about the money," he explains, "but it's all just a joke. I'm really tickled to death to be doing this."

"I bet you are," I say. "I can tell."

"Don't tell me I've given myself away," he says kiddingly.

"Well"—I smile—"what's it between strangers?"

"Fathers are supposed to be hard-headed about these things. Grumble about the expense. That the fellow isn't good enough for his daughter. But I'm really an awful softie in that department." He pauses to sip his drink. "It's funny how times change. My older daughter was married in a church. Reception at the country club. My son had the same. Now Gail and her young man are having the ceremony in the apartment they're already living in. And they're writing their own vows, and having the reception at a Chinese restaurant. About the only thing traditional's the cake." He smiles. "And *that's* just because it tastes good."

"Listen, I can't think of a better reason."

"But you know something?" He smiles sheepishly. "They

don't fool me with any of it. The way they talk? The way they are together? Marriage means just as much to them as it means to any other couple. But of course you can't tell *them* that."

"I know," I say. "My daughter's like that, too. So . . . furious to be unique. To be original. It's a marvelous delusion. I remember when I felt that way."

"Mmm, so do I."

"And isn't it nice that it's *over*?"

"Isn't it, though?" We laugh warmly and sip our drinks.

"What do you . . . do?" I ask, after a moment.

"I'm in aerospace consulting," he says, in that nice, cordial voice of his. "I'm semiretired now. I do a little teaching, a little advisory work here and there. I was at Lockheed for twenty-five years. Then, when my wife took ill five years ago, we moved out to Tucson."

"Oh, you live in Arizona."

"Originally, it was just for the climate. But now? You can't *pull* me away."

"Is that so? It's really that nice down there?"

"I'll say. You've got your warm, dry weather. Your golfing, your desert. Your industry on a limited scale. About everything you could ask for."

"What a glowing description. The Chamber of Commerce couldn't have done it better."

"I know." He laughs. "They always say there's nothing like a convert. Of course, I like coming back up here, too." He pauses. "But tell me about yourself. Have you known uh . . . Benny, is it? Have you known Benny a long time?"

"God, yes. When he was still a busboy."

"He seems to be a great admirer of yours."

"Well, that's what you might call good P.R. Or a couple of other initials you can probably guess."

"I can guess them." He smiles. "But in your case, I don't believe them."

My God, I'm actually embarrassed by his gracious flirtation. "Well," I say, looking aside, "I have this theory that all ambitious restaurant owners are really frustrated talk-show hosts. It does something to their own egos to be always laying on the flattery. But"—I feel guilty now, having said that—"he's really a mensh. Uh, nice guy, I mean."

"Seems to be. Awfully hospitable, at least. Not often you come to rent a banquet room and get invited into a private party." He gazes around the room. "Kind of an interesting-looking group."

"Yes, well, it's the publicity crowd. Most of them come to these things for the free booze and hors d'oeuvres and then stand around talking about the tacky people who come to these things for the free booze and hors d'oeuvres." He chuckles. "But"—I shrug gamely—"it's a living."

"Sounds no more dishonest than any other," he remarks diplomatically. "Is it . . . *your* living?"

"Yes, well more or less. I've been in journalism, publicity writing."

"I *thought* you might be a writer. You have a charming way with words."

"Why, thank you."

"No, I mean it. A delightful sense of humor. I hope you won't think I'm rude if I say I noticed it immediately."

"I don't think that's rude at all."

"My wife did a little writing."

"Oh?"

"A social column for the La Cañada paper here. Then, in Tucson, she wrote commentary for Goldwater's, their fashion shows. Of course, it wasn't a real career. But she enjoyed it."

"Well, that's the important thing."

We talk a little longer. The waiter comes around with a tray of fresh drinks. I set down my empty glass, pick up a new one. He hesitates, then does the same.

"I guess I should be getting back to them now," he says. "Put in my 'fatherly grumbling' "—we smile; we have a little joke now—"before the damages get too bad."

"Well," I say jauntily, "they only get married once. Ideally, that is."

"Let's hope so," he says, with wry tenderness. "Ideally's kind of hard to find these days."

"You're telling me?"

And we laugh lightly—the shy, knowing laughter of two people who have said a little more than they'd quite planned to say.

"Lil!" Eloise Kreske waves me over. She's located some people we know. "Come join us!"

I lift up my face to gesture I'll be there in a minute.

"Well," I say, "I'd better say hello to those people. You know: free booze, free hors d'oeuvres, *awfully* tacky." He laughs. "It was very nice talking to you . . . Louis, wasn't it?"

He nods. "Lou. And you're Lillian." Smiling. "I didn't forget that."

"Ah, that's the scientific mind for you."

"No," he says. "In this case, I'd say that science has nothing to do with it."

We're silent for a few awkward seconds.

"Look," he says, "I'm sure there are more graceful ways of phrasing this, but: Are you free?"

"I am."

"May I . . . take you to dinner tonight?"

"Yes. That would be . . . I'd like that."

"Good." He smiles. "Let me just check in with my daughter for a moment."

"Take your time," I say, smiling. "I've got a whole drink to kill."

"There's probably nothing left for me to do now but sign on the dotted line anyway. That Miss Wong looked awfully efficient."

"*Fierce* is more like it. But I guess that makes things easier."

"Yes, well," he says, smiling softly, "it's nice when you find people who do that."

As he walks away, I light a cigarette, inhale deeply and laugh a little—in delight? confusion? What on earth am I doing here with this nice, warm, charming, square man? Why do I feel better right now than I've felt in—God, in years? And why is that feeling so . . . embarrassing?

"Li-il!" Eloise again.

I freeze for a moment. Should I go over there? *Or* should I rush to the ladies' room to put on a little rouge and comb my hair? Calmly, now. If I go to the ladies' room, which is God knows where, he might come back out and not find me. He might figure I've left.

I join Eloise and her friends. Pipe-puffing British movie critic. His Dagmar-esque wife with the animated irony, the dripping shawl, the clanking copper bracelets. Seth Silverman again (Jesus, he's more ubiquitous than the waiters) locking mezuzahs with some nose-jobbed, safari-suited little pisher who sells dirt to Rona. And all of them making the usual banter:

"You can always tell the ones from Paramount. They're still combing their hair left to right, just like Evans did."

"After the year Gulf and Western just had? I'm amazed any of them have any hair left to comb."

"Speaking of bad years—and bad pictures—did anybody go to that *King Kong* fiasco? I mean, those really dreadful little raviolis."

"That's what happens when the wops take over the industry."

"Well, at least it wasn't Chasen's chili again. Gawd, it's getting so you have to take your Rolaid before instead of after."

And yet it's talk I'm comfortable with, talk I'm good at. Was it foolish of me to accept a dinner invitation with an outsider? Was it . . . tacky?

Louis reappears. He lifts up his hand in recognition. I excuse myself and, weaving through the dwindling crowd to meet him, feel a tiny flash of contempt for the eagerness in his face. Yet it is a kindly, dignified eagerness. The man is a gentleman, I say to myself. Why must I write him off as sappy and desperate *simply* because he's interested in me?

"I thought I might phone a taxi. My daughter's taking the car home."

"Don't be silly. Let's take my car."

"Are you sure?"

"Of course."

"Now, as for a restaurant. Why don't we try one of your favorite places." So open, so willing to please.

"Well . . ."—ruling out Roy's, La Scala, places like that —"there's the Chart House. Oh, but no. It's all the way up in Malibu. Would you mind driving that far?"

"Not at all," he says heartily. "In fact, whenever I come up here I want *all* the Pacific Ocean I can get. You kind of miss it, living in the desert."

"Listen, you can miss it living here. The number of times I get to the beach in the winter, I might as well be in Des Moines."

"Take it for granted, eh?" He winks. "Shame on you."

Oh, God. Now I have a little Polaroid negative of his whole cornball life. I can see him and his wife poring over sightseeing guides at Holiday Inns: his face expectant, a camera slung over the shoulder of his short-sleeve seersucker shirt. I can see him in a pine-paneled rumpus room, whistling to the Mantovani on the radio as he dusts some handcraft fresh off his power saw. And I wonder: What on earth can we possibly say to each other that will last through a dinner? When will the mistake become obvious?

"Awfully nice detail work," he says, admiring the mahogany stand that holds up Benny's flaming torches. "Nice, solid craftsmanship."

"Do you . . . work in wood yourself?" I ask, fearfully watching my little negative develop.

"Oh, I just tinker around a little bit. My bookends"—he smiles—"would warm the heart of any sixth-grade shop teacher, I guess."

Okay, see? I say to myself as I laugh. He's on to himself. He *does* have some wit, a sense of self-parody. Don't be so anxious to nail him. Don't be so ready to have it fail. What am I afraid of, anyway?

In the car, I lean against the passenger-side door, my feet curled up under me like—my God, like a schoolgirl. He slides back the driver's seat, inspects the knobs, jolts off the emergency brake with one firm yank. His elbow propped out the open window, he maneuvers us out of the lot with a swiftness, a confidence that must surprise even the car. How long—how very goddam long—it's been since a man has driven me to dinner! How ridiculously clear all the little details of that act suddenly seem. I'm a woman. I'm on a date. I'm being, you might say, *courted.* For a second,

those three banal truths seem so stirringly, crazily novel that
I fear they are written all over my face.

"How about if I turn on the radio?" I suggest.

"Great."

Awkwardly (Ronald's the one who usually does this), I
shift the dial back and forth past a cacophony of rock and
roll and traffic bulletins and God knows what else. I finally
find something neutral and Muzaky and settle it there. "Do
you like this?"

"Mmm, well . . ." He smiles.

"Actually," I laugh in relief, "I don't either."

"How about KFAC? The classical station."

"Oh, yes. Good idea."

Without taking his eyes off the road, he leans over and
deftly inches the knob to the left. "Vivaldi." He smiles. "He's
always nice company."

"Do you listen to classical a lot?"

"As much as I can, these days. I've just subscribed to a
classical record club. And Tucson has a fairly decent sym-
phony. But my favorite music's the old Big Band sound.
Artie Shaw . . . Benny Goodman . . . Harry James . . ."

"Oh, yes, weren't they marvelous? My husband collected
those records. Ex-husband, I mean."

"You're divorced then?" he inquires, delicately.

"Yes," I say, suddenly wistful and covetous of Morty's
memory. "Divorced, and then he died just a few years later."
Why did I start on *that*? "It's funny—or not funny, really—
but whenever I have to fill out a form for a driver's license
or a charge account, I stare at the little squares marked
'divorced' and 'widowed' and for a second or two I'm not
sure which one I should check. Sometimes I think they
should have one that says 'package deal.' " I pause. "That's

when I'm feeling glib and cavalier about it all."

"Which . . . isn't all the time." It was not quite a question.

"No. Which isn't all the time. Usually I . . ." And I look over at him and we both smile, a little abashed at the unexpected corner I've pushed the conversation into. What is it about this man that makes me suddenly want to confide? "Well, perhaps we should save that for later. After we've gotten something in our stomachs."

"Good idea." He smiles, opens his mouth to speak, closes it. Then: "You know, I find myself wanting to get to know all about you, but I don't want to push. I hope I wasn't overbearing at the party."

"No, no, not at all."

"You sure?" He smiles knowingly. "I sensed you were a little annoyed at me a moment ago. When we left the restaurant."

"Oh, no, no," I lie—and probably badly. I am struck by his gentle perceptiveness.

"You find yourself—I find myself, that is—not knowing quite how to approach these things. My kids always say to me: You know, Dad, the trouble with you is you're a dyed-in-the-wool family man who doesn't really have a family any more. And it's true. Dating's something I'm a little rusty at. I'm afraid I'm a little rough around the edges."

"Well, what's wrong with that? God knows, most people you run into in this town are so slick, you break your ankle just talking to them." He laughs heartily. "No, *really*," I say. "It's *true*."

"No, I'm just laughing at the wonderful way you put it. I've always envied writers their facility with the language."

"I'm afraid it has nothing to do with my work. It's kind of a coping mechanism. A way of making very ordinary things seem entertaining. Or," I smile, "to be a little more dramatic about it, a way of not going crazy when you sometimes think you might."

"I think I know what you mean. I get that same kind of release from . . . fishing, of all things." He smiles briefly, to acknowledge the absurdity of the remark. Then he turns serious. "For about a year after Peg died, I couldn't sleep. I felt anxious all the time. I did all those things you're supposed to do: took up a church membership after twenty years, let our old friends adopt me on weekends, read mystery novels for escape. But none of it worked. I even considered going to a psychiatrist. Then I discovered a little lake—not much of a lake; a pond, actually—about twenty miles out of Tucson. I'd go there mornings with a flycasting rod and a bucket of bait I bought down the road. Just me and nature, as trite as it sounds. I was doing something mindless, and primitive, and as completely divorced from my line of work as you're likely to get. It cleared my head like nothing else could. I felt . . . well, more peaceful than I had since . . . in the longest time.

"My son Randy says it has something to do with what he calls 'centering energy,' " he goes on. "He reads Eastern religion, he and his wife both. They gave me all kinds of crazy explanations which of course, being an applied scientist, I laughed at. But sometimes, you know? I think he might have a point." He laughs warmly. "Those kids are something. Bright as the dickens, all of them."

"You sound very proud of them."

"I am. Almost to a fault. Another occupational hazard of being a semiretired widower. You tend to live through them a little bit more than you should. But then, let's not get me started on *that* again."

We smile warmly, acknowledging that both hands of cards

are on the table; we each have wounds we're clumsily eager to talk about. We must find small talk now.

"Well . . ." I smile jauntily, spoofing the awkwardness. "We could . . . you could tell me all about the aerospace industry."

"That gets *awfully* technical," he warns, eyes twinkling.

"Try me." I'm amazed at my coquettishness, however tongue-in-cheek. "Listen, you can even give me a quiz at the end. I think I have a red pencil in the glove compartment."

"Ah, but do you have a slide rule?"

And we laugh. And when we stop laughing, he says: "You know, you're very easy to be with."

"I *am*?" That just slipped out. We smile at the slip, and his smile lingers affectionately. And for the rest of the drive, the conversation takes its easy, meandering course.

He tells me about the Tucson productions of *Verdi* and *Carmen*. Do I follow opera? "I'm afraid," I say, "the closest I ever get to it is when my Spanish maid chews her boyfriend out on the phone. Maria Callas should have such pipes." He laughs, and then we turn to maids. He has an Indian housekeeper who is teaching him a few words of the Hopi language. "Yeah? Listen, that's an idea," I muse. "I have an Iranian student who lives with me. If she taught me a little Arabic, I might have some leverage with the Shell Oil credit department."

He laughs, and then we turn to the Middle East oil situation, then to politics. He's a lapsed Republican—the lapse for obvious reasons. "Yes," I wonder, "well, how does it feel having one of those crooks playing St. Francis of Assisi on the mesa next door?"

"Ehrlichman?" I nod. "Yes," he laughs, "isn't that something?"

"Every time you see a new picture of him, his beard gets scragglier and his serape gets longer. I suppose next month he'll be starring in a Dennis Hopper film."

And he laughs again (though I don't think he knows who Dennis Hopper is) as we turn off the highway and into the Chart House parking lot.

We walk to the restaurant. The salty air is cold and strong, so we pause and he helps me on with my jacket, his hands accidentally grazing my arms, my back. I look down at my feet, shocked at my own sudden shyness (Jesus, my act is easy to bust; who would have known it, Ronald?)—and even more shocked at how good and warm and overdue that simple closeness feels. But he *can't* be for me, I try telling myself. We have absolutely nothing in common but loneliness, and that's a pretty damn pathetic bond. My body tenses at the thought; I muster up *Morty's* arm, *Morty's* face, *Morty's* humor—and I clutch that ghost for dear life. And then, just like in that silly exercise class, I let all the panicked muscles collapse. Be smart for a change, okay? some voice inside me begs. Leave Morty out of this.

And for the next hour and a half, that is just what I do.

"Tell me about your life," he asks. And I don't know if it's the wine, or the soothing ocean out the window, or his kindly, interested face (he *does* look like E. G. Marshall), but the stories spill out from some file that's been locked for years.

I tell him about growing up on Bradford Street in Brooklyn. My father with his spats and bowler and walking stick: the only insurance man in Flatbush who looked like a Broadway pimp. My mother who God forbid should spend money on department store clothes when all she had to do was pull down the drapes and run them through her Singer.

And I tell him about the tantrum they both had when I

quit NYU in my second year for a copy-girl job at the old *Daily Mirror.* How I'd spent half my savings on a new dress from Wanamaker's for that first day at work, and how sophisticated I felt wearing it until the assistant metro editor tugged me gently by the sleeve, nodded to the price tag I'd forgotten to remove and said, "Sweethaaat, if you're moonlighting as a roundheel, you're some bargain. Go check your rates with the dolls on the corner." How glamorous that stinky City Room seemed—with its creaky chairs and rattling Underwoods and perspiry guys with pencils in back of their ears. The night FDR won his fourth term—my second week of work there—and how we hung over the huge console radio, and the guys who had bets riding on the muni elections dug into their hatbands for cash and passed around Stage Deli linzer tortes and 90-proof something that made me sick for days.

How grateful I was for my $24 a week, and how I spent most of it on taxis down to a little place downtown called The Village Grove Nut Club, where I bought watery bourbons for the drummer because I thought that was what a highborn moll was supposed to do. And how humiliated I was to find out from the club owner's own moll—Nora? Norma? I forget—that the drummer lived in Brooklyn with his parents just like I did. And how that put an end to *that.*

And I tell him about the *Telegram* days that followed. Really writing features this time—not just fillers and obits. The evenings at the Stork Club, the dawns at Lindy's where the Catskills-bound comics would practice their shtiks and have us laughing so hard we spat out our coffee all over the ham-and-eggs breakfasts we'd just bought them. How passionately (and badly) I learned to read the *Racing Form,* how proud I was to flash my Press Pass instead of some measly engagement ring. And how shamelessly I stood before bathroom mirrors, rouging my face and biting the insides of my jowls to give me Katie Hepburn's cheekbones. ("Don' be doon that," the Copa ladies' room attendant once warned me. "The men's gonna think you got gout.")

And I tell him about Ed Loeb, and the month I spent writing and rewriting "I Was Mary Martin's Stand-In for a Night . . . And I Can't Even Sing!" on spec for the *Saturday Evening Post,* and how despondent I was when both the man and the magazine spurned me. Then the long train ride to Los Angeles, with my tattered bravado on my sleeve and my cousin's address in my wallet. The second-rate unrequited love poems I wrote in my Pullman sleeper all the way from New York to St. Louis—and the third-rate used-furniture dealer I locked out of that same sleeper from St. Louis to the Coast.

And I tell him about those early months here. The fierce homesickness I fought, the blind dates I endured with dentistry students, the interviews with Margaret O'Brien and June Allyson I filed, the imitation S. J. Perelman (or Humphrey Bogart) I hoped I'd bump into at the blintzes stand at the Farmer's Market. Then that night at Ciro's, when that young show business lawyer sent me a note that said: "Do my glasses need cleaning, or are you really Ann Sheridan?"

And yet when I talk about those next years, that big humid cloud of nostalgia is gone. Morty was an accessory to the story, not its star. It is *my* life I am spinning out and dressing up and running with; *my* life this warm, attentive man across the table is relishing; *my* life that I'm suddenly relishing, too. And for the first time in a long time, that life doesn't seem to have stopped with the marriage. I go on and on about my publicity writing for Goldwyn, then for Decca Records, then finally—when my husband's career and the era itself required me to fade into the role of professional hostess and mother—my part-time work for that gumshoe firm that booked Vic Damone's backup band and papered the Sands and Flamingo with unknown female singers who wound up as contract players in Jeff Chandler movies.

And I leave out the depressing parts, and I leave out the unfunny parts, and when we finally finish our lobster and I realize how long I've been talking, I feel empty and full at the same time.

"*My God*, I've gone on," I apologize. "I must have bored you to tears."

"Quite the contrary." His smile is almost fatherly. "This is one of the most fascinating hours I've spent in a long time."

"Well, listen," I say quickly to stop myself from blushing, "that was the airbrushed version. Suffice to say"—I smile ironically—"there's a lot I left out. Which isn't quite so coy."

He looks at me thoughtfully. "I wouldn't call you coy," he says: slowly, significantly. "And I mean that as a compliment."

"Thank you," I say, moving my eyes down and away from his gaze.

He excuses himself to make a phone call. I hurriedly dig my compact and lipstick out of my purse. I open the compact, fluff up my hair, put on my lipstick, blot my mouth on the napkin, close everything with three quick little snaps.

When I look up, Louis is walking back down the aisle between the booths. We smile at each other like old, relaxed friends.

"I told Gail to leave the front door open," he says as he slides back in the booth. "And I called Beverly Hills Taxi."

"What? Don't be silly. I can drop you off and then drive myself back home."

"No, no. That's way out of your way. And it's late. I'm having the cab call for me at the Beverly Hilton lobby at a quarter of twelve."

I smile, touched by his quaintness, his properness, the lengths he has gone to to assure me he has no ungentlemanly intent. This is the kind of man you pray you run into when your car stalls on the road to Palm Springs; the kind of man you'd want as a seatmate on a two-engine plane that hits turbulence: solid, thoughtful, decent.

"More wine?" He picks up the bottle.

I wave my hand no. "I could get silly if I had any more."

He smiles. "I can't imagine *that*."

Oh, no? You don't know how desperate I can be, Louis. How clutchy, how cynical. You don't know how—

"Coffee? Dessert?" The waitress mercifully interrupts.

"Just coffee for me," I say.

"The same," he says. "And I think I'll try a piece of your pecan pie. With"—looking at me expectantly—"two forks?"

"*One* fork," I amend, "and one toothpick."

He laughs.

"No, really," I say. "I'd forgotten how big lobsters are getting these days."

He winks. "A little too big for their britches, eh?"

"The hell with *their* britches. I'm thinking about mine."

He laughs again. Okay, so I'm the joker here and he's the straight man; is that such a bad combination? Oh, I know he's a little corny, yet there's something comfortable and steady and appreciative and *good* about this man that is making him very appealing. Is this affection that I'm feeling now? Or gratitude?

We settle our elbows on the table and look out the window where the blackness is punctuated by tiny blinking lights on the horizon and violent sparks of white surf.

"I love that view," I say.

"So do I. Always reminds me of my years in the Navy."

"Oh, you were in the Navy?"

He nods, then smiles, a little wistfully. "Thirty-eight and
-nine. I've never quite gotten over the fact that I pulled out
right before the War."

"You wanted to be stuck in the War?"

"Sure." He smiles. "Didn't every red-blooded young American male?" And pronounces those last words self-teasingly.
Then he shifts in his chair. "They always say: War is bad
to anticipate, hell to endure, and great to look back on.
It's the looking back on I miss." I smile at the way he puts
it. "Peg was pregnant," he explains. "There were complications. I got an open-ended leave of duty from my ship.
Then when we lost the baby she went into the hospital for
a month and I was entitled to an honorary discharge. To go
to graduate school in a defense-related field. I could've gone
back to sea, but I wanted to stay with her. We'd only been
married a year. As it was, it was a turning point for me. I
started my Ph.D. work in physics and then did my war duty
at a Naval plant in San Francisco, and I discovered I liked
aviation much more than nautical sciences."

"San Francisco must have been exciting during the War,"
I say, remembering some Cary Grant movie. "All those romantic farewells at the Top of the Mark."

"Yes, yes." He shakes his head, smiling fondly. "We'd eat
macaroni for weeks in order to have one swell night on the
town like that. I'd put on my dress blues, and Peg'd get all
dolled up and we'd go out to Solari's. And when it came time
to order, we'd just *point* to the menu. Our Continental ac-
cents left a little something to be desired. And, you know,
when you're that age, even the waiters can intimidate you."

I smile. "Isn't that the truth."

"You know, it's funny," he says now, leaning back. "You get older, you get successful in your field, you're on top of all those little things you used to fumble with. But you miss a little of those early days. The struggle, I guess."

I nod. "The innocence. The way everything overwhelmed you, everything was larger than life. Oh, but I'm romanticizing."

"Why shouldn't you?"

"Oh . . . because we paid for it. With the terror, the confusion. It only really begins to look charming once it's over. Sometimes . . . sometimes I *really wish* I could live my life in the present the way I look back on it in the past. In kind of . . . selected frames. Seeing only those things I'm going to want to see when I'm reminiscing later. You know what I mean?"

He nods. "We tried to do that, Peg and I, toward the end. In fact, it almost worked."

"It *did*?"

"When you know you have just a certain amount of time left, you find you can do it. We discovered she had cancer," he explains. "We weren't . . . hopeless about it, but we didn't kid ourselves, either. We knew the odds. So we sat down and talked very seriously about how we wanted to spend the time we had left. We sold the house in La Cañada, got away from the country club and the freeways and all of that, and moved to Arizona. Little split-level in the desert's essentially all it is. I added on the den myself, and she started a little garden. We were able to putter around the house together and have three meals at the kitchen table again."

I nod, gravely, moved by his story.

"My colleagues all said: What? You're *retiring*? Lockheed's one hell of a competitive place. They couldn't understand why I'd leave once I'd gotten to a . . . well, a position of some authority there. But I'll tell you, when you spend your whole working day with computers and speaking jargon and reading scientific bulletins, you almost close off certain senses. And I wanted those senses back. I've never regretted it. And, of course, I have enough to keep me busy now. I do consulting. I give some seminars at the U. of Arizona. They've made me an assistant professor there." He smiles. "Which is not nearly as impressive as it sounds. When you've got a retirement community like Tucson, they slap a title on anyone who comes down there with any experience at all in any field."

"You mean, they have an assistant professor of linoleum installation?"

"Exactly."

We laugh—and the air is cleared of heaviness. The waitress comes with the pie and the coffees.

He winks. "She forgot your toothpick."

"So I noticed."

"Will you share some of this with me anyway?"

"Well . . . all right," I smile, giving in. "Maybe just one little bite."

As we walk to the car, he digs his hands in his pockets and takes a deep breath of air. In profile, in this dim moonlight, he looks almost rugged.

"The Dipper's very defined tonight," he says, gesturing upward.

"The what?"

"The Big Dipper. See?" And as I squint upward, he draws a squiggly outline with his fingers. Touched by his romanticism, I nod, pretending to comprehend.

"Come on," I kid him as he tips the lot attendant, "are

aerospace consultants supposed to talk so untechnically?"

"No." He chuckles. "But it'd sure as hell be a lot better for them if they could."

On the drive home, he tells me that what he does—or did —is really a very small, specialized part of the industry. Something about administrating computerized monitoring of the maintenance systems of second-something-or-other feasibility testing.

"My God," I say. "Your poor secretary. Did she get overtime just for squeezing all that under your signature?"

"My poor secretary"—he smiles—"was usually the Telex. Or the satellite radio."

"Oh you twentieth-century types," I sigh. "Really, there's no keeping up with you."

He laughs. "You can't fool the kids, though. When they were children, they'd tell all their friends, 'My daddy can put a man on the moon.' Then, during all the moonshots, they'd see me getting up and going to work every day with my briefcase, not getting anywhere *near* Houston or Canaveral. I stopped being a hero around there *fast*. But now I think I'm back in their good graces again since my consulting work is vaguely aligned with the ecology movement."

"I won't ask you how."

"No, better not. It's pretty dull, I'm afraid."

"Maybe just over my head. You're looking at someone who still slashes her zeroes when she subtracts. And once in a while has even been known to count on her fingers. To tell *time*."

He laughs and says, "Well, you certainly have virtues to make up for it."

"Thank you," I say, and he turns to smile. "Oh, it's the next right," I say, directing him to my house.

He hands me my keys as we walk to my door. "May I take you to dinner again next weekend?"

"You'll . . . be in Los Angeles?"

"Hadn't planned to four hours ago. But if you're free, I will be."

"Oh, no," I say quickly. "I couldn't ask you to make a trip from Tucson just for *that*."

"You're not asking me to."

"*Really?*" That slipped out, too. "I mean, I'm very flattered. But I'd—that's an awfully long distance to come just for a dinner date."

He smiles assuringly. "A very easy hour and a half on an American 707. I start the front page of the newspaper as soon as I fasten my seat belt, and I'm just about done with the sports section by the time we start circling down."

"Are you sure?"

"I'm sure."

"Listen, in that case, I feel I should *cook* you the dinner. But if you knew how I cooked, it would definitely not be worth the trip."

He smiles. "No, no. I'd much prefer to take you out."

"But you *will* come in for drinks and hors d'oeuvres. I have this specialty called cheese and crackers."

"Sounds wonderful."

We walk to my front door and . . . What is *this*? Who put this florist's box here?

"Ah." He nods good-naturedly. "I see I have a rival."

"No. I mean . . ." I'm flabbergasted. "I don't know who could possibly . . ."

There's no card on the outside, so I slide off the red ribbon and open the box. "My God, a dozen red roses!" I tear open the little white envelope. In an unfamiliar male handwriting:

> Fat's in the frypan
> and the hen she been sired
> And w/o you, foxy mama,
> Willy'd nevra been hired

I start tomorrow in the 5-9 A.M. slot, which still gives me plenty of daylight to fix your dishwasher. The attached, love, is an offer you can't refuse. Yo gon make yo boy the best-hyped   jivetalker-humpwalker-waxhustler-chartbuster in town. (Langston, Arna, Imamu: Forgive me.)

> Gratefully,
> E.

"Oh, he *shouldn't have.*" I smile and shake my head as I unclip the money order made out to me for $200. "A friend of mine," I explain, turning quickly to Louis. "He just got a disc jockey job. Jesus, I've never been a publicist for a disc jockey before. Oh, I'm *sorry.*" Suddenly realizing we've been standing by the door all this time. "Would you like to come in for a cup of coffee?"

He consults his watch. "I wish I could, but that taxi will be waiting in about fifteen minutes."

"Oh, the *taxi.* I forgot! Why didn't you mention it when we were driving past the Hilton? I could've just—"

"Well, I'm old-fashioned, I guess. I wanted to see you to your door."

"Well, then, let me at least drive you back to the hotel."

"Nonsense." He smiles. "It's just a couple of blocks. The walk will be good for me."

"You're sure?"

"I'm *sure.*"

And we laugh; that dialogue has become the theme of our evening.

I put my key in the lock.

"I'll phone you sometime middle of the week and we'll plan on dinner . . . say, Saturday?"

"Saturday would be fine. But this time, let *me* do the chauffeuring."

He shakes his head. "I'll be renting a car."

I smile. "You're impossibly gracious, you know that?"

"Don't say that." He smiles. "I might get conceited."

We laugh again. He squeezes my hand. And after a warm, only slightly awkward few seconds, we lean into each other for a very decorous brush of the lips.

I close and lock the door behind me, and after I hear his footsteps down the front steps, I pause in front of the hall mirror. Jesus, look at this, will you—and with these farkokta flowers, no less! Remember *Queen for a Day*, darling? Remember *This Is Your Life*?

And laughing, laughing, laughing lightly, I rush to the breakfast room phone and dial Ronald's number.

7

"FLY ME TO THE MOOOON AND LET ME PLAY AMONG THE stars," Ronald sings, making campy little pirouettes into my breakfast room.

"Oh, God. I never should have called you last night."

"Let me know what spring is like on Juuuupiter and Mars." He hugs me, then holds me at shoulder's length. "Oh, look at her, look at her," he kvells. "Yesterday a simple Beverly Hills hausfrau. Today, the next Mrs. Werner Von Braun. What a difference a day makes," he starts singing again. "Twenty-four little hours. With the sun and the flowers . . ."

"Okay, okay." I push him into a chair. "Listen, if I knew this would turn you into Tom Jones, I'd never have gone out with him."

"If *I* knew this would turn me into Tom Jones," he sighs, "I'd perform your wedding myself."

"*Wedding.* Listen to him." I laugh from the kitchen as I pour my coffee, his tea. "Ronald, I just met the man last night."

"I know, but we can dream, can't we?"

"*Honestly.*" I set the cups on the table.

"She's blushing!" He clasps his hands. "Oh, I could just *die* from loving it!"

"I am *not* blushing," I say, sitting down.

"Lil, don't be embarrassed. I think it's fabulous."

"Well, I don't know if it's *fabulous*, but it's . . . he's . . . *different*." I light a cigarette and gaze off. "I mean: He's eager. And he's not hiding his eagerness. And every time that would start to bother me, he'd say something or do something to make me like him again—*really* like him. He's so gracious, Ronald. So charming. But all night long I kept fighting the feeling that there *had* to be something wrong with him just for being so interested in me." I laugh nervously. "Isn't that ridiculous?"

"No, darling, it's normal. I felt the same way about Gary. Remember?"

"But why do we do that? Why does the contempt go up the minute we discover the other person's just as lonely as we are?"

"Because we are pros, Lil. We've become such pros at hiding our loneliness that after a while the *way* we hide it

becomes more important than curing what we're hiding."
He smiles softly. "Right, darling?"

"My son the psychiatrist. Look at you. Sitting here telling
me the things *I* used to shove down *your* throat."

"What can I say, darling? What goes around comes
around."

"Yeah? Well, I'm not so sure I like it." I pout. "No.
Seriously. Ronald?" My voice is suddenly small. "Are you
going to be hard on me if I find things I don't like in him?"

He nods resolutely.

"Even if they're justified?"

"Oh, come on, Lil. Don't start running away from it
already. Last night on the phone you were ecstatic. If you
could've heard yourself . . ."

"I know, but . . ."

"I mean, talk about *hot*. Honey, I thought my poor little
ear was going to melt. The kind of glasses he wore, how it
felt with him driving your car, how you didn't want to be
piggy and order dessert, how he stood in the parking lot
and . . ."

"*Stop*, Ronald. I feel silly."

"Why, darling? The man sounds like he is positively head
over heels."

"He does seem grateful to have met me. And I'm grateful
that he's so grateful. The only thing is: What happens when
we get past all that gratefulness? We have so little in common, really."

"Oh, you're a trouper. You'll invent something."

"I guess so. But is that what it comes down to? Inventing?"

"I was *kidding*, Lil. You know that. Now *come on*. Will
you stop being negative already?"

"I'm not being negative. *I'm not.* It's just that it all happened so fast."

"So what do you want? A slow boat to China? Darling, when lightning strikes—"

"But *is* it lightning? When you're young, it's lightning. When you're my age, his age, it's something else."

" 'My age.' 'His age.' Puh*leeese.*"

"Panic? Desperation? Foolishness? I don't know."

"Oh, *yawn.*" He rolls up his eyes, sighing lavishly. "Lil, don't you ever get tired of that phony Lynn Fontanne exit?"

"That what?"

"Oh, *you* know. Whenever you're afraid to face something good, you pull out the hankie at the footlights. Miss Melodrama here, mooning that it's too late. And *then* you turn right around and ask me to give you some tacky hairdo the twenty-five-year-olds are wearing to Pips. You're the *last* one who really believes you're over the hill. I mean, *gimme a break.*"

"Ronald"—I smile against my will—"you are fresh."

"You bet your ass I am, darling. I also happen to know your defenses."

"My son the psychiatrist."

"You already said that."

"Okay." I put my palm up in a truce gesture. "Okay, but . . . there *are* things that I worry about with Louis. *Real* things. Like . . . oh, I know this is going to sound presumptuous, but I almost got the feeling he wants to get married tomorrow. Not necessarily to me, but just to any . . . well, any 'suitable' woman. He was so uncritical of me. Like I could do no wrong. I mean appreciation is one thing, but blindness is another. And he kept talking about his wife in that poignant tone, as if—"

"Well, you always talk about Morty that way."

"Yes, but it's different."

"Why is it different?"

I think for a minute about how to articulate what I mean. "The irony, I guess. Those little footnotes in the sentences, that film that comes over your voice when you get nostalgic that says to the other person, 'Look, I'm not kidding myself. I know it was more complex than this, more painful than this, but let me just pretend for a minute it wasn't, okay?' He doesn't have any of that in his voice when he talks about her. He wasn't hurt like I was. It sounds like he had one of those wholesome, unquestioned marriages—straight out of the Robert Young show, for Christ's sake. Like he's naive about what can go wrong because he's always lived a life where things *didn't* go wrong. Illness, deaths, the kids growing up and leaving you—those were his crises: the normal, blameless, natural ones. But people's neuroses didn't get in the way. People's neuroses didn't *exist*. Ronald, what's going to happen when he finds out *mine do?*"

"Oh, darling, don't be afraid."

"Is that what I am?"

"I think so." He nods, gingerly. "A little bit."

I take a deep breath. "It's just that . . . Oh, I don't know. You go years desperately wanting a certain kind of flattery. Or thinking you want it. And then when it comes out of left field like this, you get terrified. You go overboard doubting it and overboard believing it at the same time. God, Ronald, there were moments last night when I felt I was holding my breath. Like any minute it would just come pouring out of me: how strange it felt to be treated like that, to feel so womanly again. I had to keep my jokes going one step ahead of me, like some advance security battalion. And every so often he'd say things like . . . oh, I forget what they were exactly," I fib, "but things to the effect that I was attractive, or witty, or *whatever*. And I'd look up and say,

"I *am?*" " I laugh. "I became sixteen years old all over again!"

Ronald smiles.

"But it didn't humiliate me, for some reason. He made it so easy for me to accept myself, somehow. Ronald, the whole time I was with him I felt attractive. I mean, *really attractive.*"

"So you finally took the gum out of your ears? I mean, God, darling, I've been telling you that since I met you."

"I know." I smile gratefully. "Except now it's different. Now I can almost believe it a little."

"Well, it's *about time.*"

"The only thing is"—I laugh softly—"it was almost more comfortable when I couldn't. You know what I did last night, after I called you? I'm almost embarrassed to tell you. I took my hand mirror up to my face and I . . . talked to myself. I posed. I recreated little parts of our conversation over dinner. Things he laughed at, things that impressed him, things that . . . *sounded good.* I said them again in the mirror and I watched my eyes and I watched my mouth and I thought: 'You *are* okay, Lil. See? You are' "—I mumble the words in embarrassment—"vivacious, attractive, *whatever.*" I look up abruptly. "I mean, isn't that ridiculous? *Isn't that just the most pathetic, ridiculous thing in the world?*"

He shakes his head reassuringly, leans over to pat my hand. "Darling, I think it's just *fabulous.*"

"You *know* it's ridiculous. Now say something funny."

He is silent, smiling like a proud uncle—embarrassing the hell out of me with his refusal.

"*Come on, Ronald.* Where are you now that I need you?"

"Uh-uh, darling. That's where you're wrong. We *don't* need me now."

"Yeah?" I smile wearily, gratefully, raising my coffee cup to my mouth. "Well, do me a favor? Stick around for when we do."

I open the door and Louis hands me a dozen yellow roses. "I thought the ones from your disc jockey friend might be drooping by now."

"Oh, aren't you sweet!" We kiss briefly. "Thank you. They're lovely."

Smiling, he steps in. "*This* is lovely," he says, surveying the living room. "Did you decorate it yourself?"

"Basically, yes. Though I had a lot of help from a friend of mine who kept me from going overboard. Left to my own devices, I would've stripped and gold-leafed everything. The fireplace logs included."

He chuckles lightly and steps down into the room. "Do you play?" he asks, nodding to the piano.

"Oh, God, not in years." I plunk a few keys. "See? It's shamefully out of key."

"Just a simple tune-up, I imagine, would do the trick." He plunks a few keys, then a few more.

"Hey," I say, "not bad."

"Well"—he smiles—"not good, either. It's been years for me, too."

"Listen, why don't I just put these in some water and get you a drink, and you can get started on Beethoven's Fifth."

"Will you settle for Chopsticks?"

"Sure." I smile over my shoulder as I walk to the kitchen with the roses. "I'm not a snob."

I set the flowers in a vase, the vase in the sink, and turn on the tap water. I lift my chin to the mirror above the sink, fluff the hair Ronald's just combed out and sprayed. I step back and adjust the shoulders of this Trigère copy the sales-lady at Allardale's talked me into. Should I have worn something simpler after all? He's just wearing a sports jacket and from my glimpse at his bare wrists as he plunked the piano keys, a short-sleeve shirt underneath. Oh, why did he have to wear a tacky short-sleeve shirt? Okay, Lil. Okay. *Enough.*

I carry out the vase of flowers in one hand; the tray with the pâté, the Brie, the imported crackers with the other. He has made himself at home in the center of my couch: leaning back, his palms flat on the cushions on each side, his ankle crossed over his knee.

"Here we go," I say, setting the tray down. "Now. Scotch? Vodka?"

"Scotch'll be fine. With just a splash of soda, if it won't be any trouble."

I walk across the room and fill two glasses with ice from the bucket on my portable bar. "How was your flight?" I ask, turning as I pour the scotch.

"Excellent." Smiling, he makes a little A-OK sign with his thumb and index finger. "Not a bump."

"I'm a terrible chicken about flying," I say, pouring the soda. "Whoever sits next to me pays the price."

"I'm sure not," he says with a wink.

"Don't be so sure." I hand him his drink and set the decanter of scotch on the coffee table. "Have you ever heard a Jew try Hail Marys during takeoff and landing?"

He laughs. I sit down. We clink glasses. "Cheers," we say, almost in unison.

"But then flying must be second nature to you," I say, leaning up against the arm of the couch, "with your work in the industry."

"As a matter of fact, it used to be just the opposite." With the quickness of apology, he shifts against the other arm of the couch, leaving a civilized space between us. "Back when I was with Lockheed, whenever I'd have occasion to fly Boeing —vacation or what-have-you—I was the company man all the way." He smiles. "Didn't let a detail escape my attention. Quality of the seat belts, faithfulness to schedule, even the landing pattern."

"You lost me on the landing pattern. *Non*-pro, remember?" We smile. "No, but seriously. I find all of that fascinating. What did you think of the Lockheed scandal, if I may ask?"

"Well, that was kind of an overblown incident. Not that it wasn't deplorable, but this kind of thing's been going on for years."

"Really?" I ask, surprised at my own coquettish, feigned naiveté.

"Well, sure. Any time you've got a big multinational corporation, you'll have your favors. Under the table or over." He smiles. "Kind of depends on whose table it happens to be."

"Well," I say, "I'm just glad I sold my stock in time."

"Can't blame you there." He smiles, then leans in and spreads some pâté on two crackers. I tuck my legs up under my skirt and wonder if he, too, is wondering what to talk about next.

"Do you still think of yourself as a company man?" I can't help but ask.

"Not really," he says, shaking his head thoughtfully. "No. I've got colleagues I still stay in touch with, and I suppose there's a certain loyalty left. But I've been enjoying being a free agent these last five years. Of course, where I live makes a difference. If I were still in Los Angeles, I might be like the retired cop who walks over to the station house in his sleep. But then"—he smiles—"if I were still here, I wouldn't have retired."

"And you like it, being retired? Oh, what am I saying? You told me you did."

"Yes, I do. When you've spent years with computers and systems management, you kind of relish a change."

I smile to myself at the awkward redundancy of last week's conversation. But then, it was my fault for asking. He bites into his cracker and I sip my drink slowly. Are we left to grope for small talk, to go in circles now that the opening banter is over? Is the fact that he flew all the way in from Tucson to be with me sitting here like a third, shuffling presence in the carefully cleared space between us?

"Wonderful pâté," he says.

"I'm glad you like it."

"Peg tried her hand at it a couple of times. Making it from scratch. Now that was a job."

"I'll bet it was. This one came in a can. My only job was not breaking my fingernail while I opened it."

"Well." Nodding to my hands. "It looks like you succeeded."

"I do have one or two minor talents in the kitchen." I smile. "Have some cheese?"

"Thanks, I think I will. You?"

"A tiny piece."

He leans over and takes the small knife to the triangle of cheese, and I notice one of those college alumni rings on his finger. His feet are flat on the rug, splayed out slightly, the trouser legs hiked up a bit to reveal short socks under his black tasseled loafers. I wince inside.

He sets the cheese wedge on the crackers, the crackers on the cocktail napkins, turns to hand me mine. His smile is so warm and kindly, I feel petty for my callous appraisal of his clothes.

We each take a bite. The crackers splinter.

"Guess I miscalculated the stress factor." He winks as he picks up the crumbs from his lap.

I smile as I brush the crumbs off my lap, and I remember myself at Jurgenson's this afternoon spending ten minutes deciding which crackers to buy. I stifle a laugh at my own earnestness.

"What's so funny?" He smiles knowingly as I pour us each another shot of scotch.

"Oh . . . nothing."

We lean back and take conspicuously long sips. All right, our smiles say, we've acknowledged the awkwardness. Now let's try to relax.

"Your daughter?" He nods to the gallery of photographs on my antique chest.

"How'd you guess?"

"I'm just the same." He smiles. "And I've got three."

"I'll have to hide half of those in a couple of weeks," I say. "She's coming in from New York for a visit, and I'm not sure she's entirely outgrown her loathing of seeing herself in past lives. She's sixteen in that one." I point to the bright-faced cheerleader on the left. "And nineteen in that." I point to the assiduously unsmiling Berkeley girl on the right. "God, the 360-degree change they can cram into three years."

"I know what you mean." He stands up and walks to the chest.

"Now she's somewhere in the middle," I babble on, feeling suddenly anxious that he's looking so hard at the pictures. "I guess all those years of finding herself paid off in temperance, if nothing else. Although if the way she uses my

Bonwit Teller charge account is any indication, there are still a few areas she's not very temperate in."

"She's very pretty." He turns. "She looks like you."

"*Really?* Thank you."

"The same laughing eyes. Even in this one the eyes are laughing." He holds up the Berkeley shot.

"Are they?" And do mine really laugh? "I'm glad to hear it. I always think of that particular time in her life as unhappy. Confused. Due to me, actually."

"How so?" His face is concerned as he sits back down on the couch.

"Oh," I say, after a long sip of scotch, "her father and I'd just divorced, and I was not in the best possible shape. I was—" No, don't say "having a nervous breakdown." "I was upset. The usual post-divorce thing. And there she was away at school, testing her wings while I was pulling on them. The more I tried to hide how much I needed her, the more obvious my neediness was. I'm afraid I was quite a burden on her."

"Are you sure?" he asks gently. "Maybe the real burden was on you. For feeling that you didn't want to be a burden in the first place."

"That's a thought." I smile, slyly, gratefully. "How'd you ever get so perceptive?"

"Am I?" His smile is faintly sad and ironic. "Thank you. Although I kind of wonder about it myself."

"Why?"

"Same reason you wonder about your daughter being happy. Guilt. Guilt that I was insensitive for too long a time." He takes another sip. "I kind of drifted through the marriage without giving much thought to how my moods affected Peg, or the kids, or what have you. Didn't even think about how they were feeling a lot of the time. That's what I meant by the occupational hazards of my line of work. You seal yourself off from all that. Peg was the family diplomat. If one of them had a problem with school, if they squabbled with each other, she tended to that. Got it all smoothed away by the time I got home and then gave me a neat synopsis along with the evening paper."

"Like an executive briefing?" I smile.

"Exactly. To tell you the truth, I never appreciated what a tough job it was on her: just placating four . . . well, four very stubborn people. In fact, I didn't think of it as a job at all. Then, when she took ill, all kinds of things were going on and I couldn't afford not to see them. Our oldest, Alison, was quitting college to get married, which Peg didn't quite cotton to. Randy was off in his second year at Colorado. And Gail was about to start UCLA just at the time we decided to move to Tucson. They all felt guilty to be abandoning their mother just at the time they felt she needed them the most. But Peg was the one who had the real burden." He looks at me significantly. "*She* felt guilty that *they* felt guilty. And suddenly *I* became the troubleshooter." He shakes his head slowly. "I think I had more heart-to-heart talks with them in those first four months than I'd had in all the twenty years before. It was kind of like picking up a mop and broom after a lifetime of never cleaning a house. And finding a lot of dust in some very unexpected places. I checked books out of the library on family relations. I talked to our minister. It was quite an education."

"It must have been."

"So"—he smiles—"if you say I'm perceptive, thank you. But it was very late in coming. And I'm still learning."

"That's so nice," I say, cocking my head to one side.

"What is?"

"Your attitude. Your eagerness to . . . well, 'grow,' as

they say." Am I being condescending? Oh, please, I hope that's not what I'm being. "I mean, the classical record club, the Hopi language, everything."

He smiles. "You remembered all that?"

"Well, yes. I admire it. The desire to change your habits, to learn new things. I'm afraid I'm just the opposite."

"With that life story you told me the other night?" He winks reassuringly. "I'll say not. You seem to have tried everything."

"That's not quite what I mean."

"What do you mean?"

"It's more . . . our attitudes. They're different. How to explain it?" I think for a second as I drink. "My friend Edith took me to a UCLA lecture once. The speaker was one of those silly human-potential movement types. You know, with the wreaths and the robe and the beard? The ones that look like Talmudic scholars auditioning for Queen of the May?"

Louis laughs.

"But he said one thing that stuck with me. He said that after the age of fifty, people either try hard to change the way the twig's been bent, or else they try very hard to fortify the bentness. I think I do the latter."

"In what way?"

"Oh, with my cynicism. My sarcasm."

"You don't seem cynical to me."

Oh, Louis, why can't you see what's in front of your eyes? Are you trying *that* hard to replicate Peg?

"Well," I finally say, "I'm not that way *all* the time, but given the choice of embracing something new or making fun of it, I'll make fun of it any day. Viciously, sometimes." I look at him challengingly. "I *like* being that way."

"I like the way you are, too," he says, smiling hospitably.

Oh, why did I feel the need to forge a distinction between us—especially with such childish defiance? "How did we get on *that*?" I ask, with a nervous little laugh.

"We were talking about your daughter. Those pictures."

"That's right. My daughter." I put a cigarette to my lips; Louis leans over and strikes a match. "I just talked to her on the phone the other day. You know how they get when there's something a little wrong? When they need to come home and be mothered a bit, but they can't bear to admit it?" He nods. "It was one of those conversations. She was the one who mentioned coming out here. She said it in that rush of words that as much as screams, '*Don't ask*, Is something wrong?' And I know not to ask. Because if I so much as let on that she needs me for some reason, she won't come."

"She's a proud one," he observes.

"Yes, she is. But there's more to it than that—that whole ritual we go through on the phone. Her insisting on paying the plane fare and my cajoling her to let me put it on my credit card. And then her insisting on paying me back and my saying, 'Of course, darling, of course.' But both of us knowing that I'll never accept her money and that she'll tend to forget that she offered. And . . . oh, I'm babbling."

"No, no," he urges gently. "Go on."

"Well, it's . . . sometimes it's like the connection between the two of us is so intense, we have to use all the phony little gestures we can find just to keep it from burning. Oh, I don't mean to be that dramatic, but, you know, a single mother, a single daughter: there are just so many echoes, so many pressures on her to feel she's inheriting my fate. Just being an only child she felt them. After the divorce, she felt them more. Then, when her father died, it was as if whatever buffer there had been was gone, and the only way she could keep from seeing my face in her mirror was to move clear across the country. Not that that's the reason she gives, but it's part of it, I know." I finish my drink and pour myself more. "There are things she's watched me go through that she's hell-bent not to repeat, neurotic patterns she's furious not to duplicate."

"But you're not neurotic," he says.

"*Everybody's* neurotic!" The words come out more irritably than I'd expected. "I'm sorry," I say quickly. "I didn't mean it that way."

"It's all right."

"It's just that . . . all I mean is: I could be reading into it, but when we talk like that, I hear her saying between the lines: 'Mother, let me come home and take from you what I need. But don't you dare acknowledge that I need it. Because if you acknowledge that I need it, then I'll have to acknowledge it, too. And then I'll never be free of you.' " I turn to him quickly. "Do you know what I mean?"

"I . . . think so," he says, uncertainly. Then he pats my hand. "You know, Lillian, you're a very intense woman."

"Nah. I'm as glib as they come."

"Okay." He smiles and turns up his hands. "You're as glib as they come."

And we laugh together at his indulgence. Oh, Louis, why do I arch my back so? Why—when your kindness prods me open like this—do I snap you away? What am I trying to protect? What am I so goddam afraid of?

"What?" He asks softly.

"Hmm?"

"You looked like you were going to say something."

"That . . . I guess I could use some dinner."

"Agreed." He smiles, fishing the rental car keys from his pocket. "Agreed."

Of course he would take me to Lawry's—with its gleaming chrome roast beef carts, its famous salad dressing, its cushions and bibs for children. I smile to myself as we slide into the booth, and I imagine him and Peg and the kid driving in from La Cañada for birthday dinners here. There is a charm —even an integrity—in the innocence of his courtship, his unshakable sense of being a family man. I glance over my menu at the young suburban couples across the room, then at Louis' eyes. The creases around their lids are magnified in the flame of the match he's just struck for my cigarette. Leaning in to inhale, I feel an unexplainable surge of affection for the man.

"I don't know if I should risk another drink," I say. "That last little bit of scotch made me embarrassingly . . . oh, don't know . . . cranky and maudlin."

"You weren't embarrassingly anything. You were just being yourself."

"Or one of them, anyway."

"Well"—he winks as he hails the waitress—"that just makes you all the more interesting."

I lean in and smile. "Louis, has anyone ever told you you'd make a marvelous country doctor?"

"What?" He laughs good-naturedly. "Never heard that one before."

"No, really, I mean that as a compliment. There's something in your manner. It's comforting, warm, wry—but a little folksy, too."

"Is that how you'd describe me?" he asks, not unpleased.

"Listen, when I'm a little high, I'll say anything."

"Liquor does take the edge off things."

And there *are* edges, my slightly bleary smile assents. Jagged parts of ourselves that could never possibly fit; others that are all too glaringly congruous. How did I manage this when I was young? How did I keep things light and playful?

"Well"—I shrug—"perhaps in an earlier life you were."

"A country doctor?" I nod. "Come to think of it," he plays along, "I do remember this little black bag. And a knack for handing out lollipops."

"See? And they said reincarnation was bunk."

We laugh. Then he looks up at the waitress.

"A very dry manhattan," he tells her. "And . . ."

"Oh, what the hell. I'll live dangerously."

"Attagirl." And to the waitress: "A scotch."

"You know," he says, when the drinks arrive, "I was thinking just now about what you were saying about all those projects of mine. It's true. I have more or less plunged into . . . well, self-improvement isn't quite the right word for it. But . . . changing my life a bit, trying to make the most of retirement."

"I think that's lovely," I say quickly. "I didn't mean to imply—"

"No." He puts his hand up to stop my demurral. "You caught something, though, when you said that after the age of fifty—or, in my case, sixty—some of us try so hard to change."

"Oh, that? Listen, never trust me with an aphorism. Especially a bad one."

"It's true, though. I have tried that, I guess. The only thing is, it doesn't entirely work. You try to build diversions into your life. You try to build comforts into your life. But once the novelty's worn off, they don't do the job they're supposed to do."

"Which is?"

"Which is to replace what you've lost." He pauses for a long sip, then looks at me. "I miss companionship," he says, with a dignified honesty. "I've been used to sharing my life all my life, and now it seems that however many hobbies I throw myself into, they don't quite do the trick. It's a little like trying to kill one kind of virus with massive doses of another kind of vaccine." He smiles. "To be—as you'd say—dramatic about it."

I smile. "As I'd say."

He takes another long sip, then lays his elbows on the table, gazes off. "I remember this one Saturday a few months ago. I'd just rigged up a hammock out in the backyard. This one patch of the yard we'd always kind of neglected. Put out some lawn furniture, but that was about it. The former owners had put in some cheap concrete and we'd never even bothered to tear it out and put in anything nicer.

"So about six months back, I took it on. Ripped out the concrete, planted some dichondra, sank in some tile work as a footpath. Made some beam trelliswork to enclose it. Even bought a birdbath. Everything had to be *perfect*," he says, self-mockingly.

He shifts back in his chair and takes another drink. "Anyway, putting up the hammock was kind of like the cap-off to the whole production. The 'christening' of my 'patio.'" His playful grandiosity makes me smile. "I nailed up the hammock. Then I went in the house and turned up the classical station so I could hear it outside. And I fixed myself a pitcher of lemonade, and brought it out with a glass and a book and a couple of magazines. And I set them all out on a little table by the hammock. And then I sat in the hammock, kind of bounced a bit, testing out the beams. And that was okay. So," he goes on—drawing out the story, between sips, with a showmanlike deliberateness—"I lay back down, and I tested it out in terms of reaching for the lemonade and pouring it into the glass. And sure enough, the table was too far away. So I got back out of the hammock and moved the table about a half foot closer. And then I got back into the hammock and lay down and rocked a little to test it out in terms of knocking over the pitcher of lemonade. And sure enough, it was a little too close for comfort."

"So you got back out . . ." I smile.

"I got back out and I adjusted the table until it was *just right*. And then I got back in the hammock. And I lay down. And I crossed my legs and looked up at the blue sky and listened to the Chopin and poured myself a glass of lemonade . . . *and I wanted to burst out laughing!* I realized what it must have looked like to someone watching: me fussing around like that for the last half hour, getting every little detail down just to be lying in that damn hammock. Boy, did I want to laugh."

I smile.

"But then I remembered," he says softly, "that's the kind of laughing someone else does *for* you. You can't do it for yourself. It's just not the same thing."

"I know what you mean," I say, thinking instantly of Ronald.

"It's the damnedest little things you end up missing," he muses over his near-empty glass. "The big ones you're prepared for. But it's those sneaky little ones that just catch you right off guard." He downs the rest of his drink. "Well," he says, slightly abashed, "enough of that."

I sip my drink quietly. The big chrome cart is wheeled to our table like an embarrassingly ostentatious gift. I remember what a kick Andi, at eight and nine and ten, used to get when the carver, as he is doing now, opened it with a flourish and sharpened his knives and smiled.

"Our special prime rib," the carver begins, with a suave, salesmanlike cheer. "With your choice of fresh creamed spinach or buttered peas. And, of course, Lawry's trademark: Yorkshire pudding."

"Doesn't that look marvelous," I say as he carves. "And smell marvelous."

"Yes," Louis says, raising his eyebrows hopefully, "doesn't it."

An hour later, we walk up to my front door.

"I'd ask you in for a nightcap," I say, "except Sima has an early class and I try to keep the house quiet."

"I better be getting back to Gail's anyway."

I nod and take out my key.

"I'll be coming in again next weekend. On business," he assures me, with a knowing smile. "Can we do this again?"

"Yes. But let me make the dinner this time."

"No. I don't want to put you to the trouble."

"It's no trouble at all. I'd enjoy it."

"This time it's my turn to ask: Are you sure?"

I smile. "I'm sure."

"Well, thank you. I'll look forward to it."

"Thank *you*. For tonight." And then, uncontrollably, I slap my hand to my forehead and shake my head and laugh. "My God, Louis, listen to us! We're so . . . *polite*. Like two of those little Japanese wind-up dolls that just keep bowing to each other."

"Yes." He smiles ironically. "Aren't we."

We stand like this for a second. Then, urgently, he clasps his arm against my back and I lean into him. And cheek against cheek, we rock back and forth: slowly, triumphantly, sheepishly—See? Now that wasn't so hard, after all, was it? —like two stubborn people making up after an argument.

We draw apart, brush lips gently. I look away, put my key in the door.

"Good night," he says.

"Drive carefully."

"I'll call you in the middle of the week." He pauses. "I'm nothing if not predictable."

"Listen," I say as I step inside, "predictability is a very underrated virtue these days. I'm all for it."

We smile, then impulsively reach out and squeeze hands in some warm and final promise. My eyes close for a second. The comfort rushes my blood like adrenalin. I open my eyes and close the door on his kind face, his courtly—almost pious—nod.

I lock the door, set down my purse on the hall table, walk around flicking off lights. Hall first, then den, then living room: precisely, somehow, the pattern I used when I'd darken the house after Andi'd come in from a date.

In the living room, I pick up the scotch tumblers, half-filled now with melted ice, and set them on the tray. I look at the leftover pâté, the French cheese, the ivory-handled cheese knife, the fancy cocktail napkins, and I smile at the hostessy earnestness, the frantically denied care that went into all of this. I shake my head, as if to force all the crazy feelings into some clear and dignified design. I am *too old*— okay, Ronald: "mature," then—to feel so unbalanced: to feel scared, delighted, skeptical all at the same time. Am I prepared for the next step with this man? Where is the grace I always expected?

I load everything on the tray and carry it into the kitchen. I pick up the phone, dial the first three digits of Ronald's number, set the receiver down. I sit for a moment in the darkness of the breakfast room, light a cigarette, stare at the sputtering black-red ash. Then I stub out the cigarette and walk into the bedroom. I pull down the shades. I zip myself out of my dress, take off my bra, my hose, my panties. Solemnly, timorously, I walk to the full-length mirror.

There. Not so very bad after all, is it? Why, then, am I always afraid of looking? Why must I just happen upon it by accident: brushing past the mirror on the way to the bathroom, the closet, the drawers, turning my eyes quickly and shamefully away?

Those five days in the hospital after my hysterectomy: Is that where the aversion started? I remember that shapeless white gown, how I pinched its back flaps closed even as I lumbered, alone, from my bed to my private-room toilet: shuffling in those paper slippers along the cold floor like a little old coolie. I ached, I dripped, I feared that I smelled. Anesthetized against the pain, the whole middle of my body felt sodden and boneless—as if I'd lost all the shape and pride under my flesh.

I dreaded that final postoperative checkup. Flat on my back, I obediently hiked the gown up to my waist under the sheet draped over my shaved, ironically pink and girlish mound. I put my feet in the stirrups, slid all the way down, and looked to myself, in that mirror they so hospitably provided, like a woman about to deliver—or a capon about to be stuffed.

The young doctor made bright small-talk as he kneaded my breasts, took my blood pressure, frowned into my pulled-open eyes. I smelled fruity gum on his breath and was suddenly, sharply embarrassed by the intimacy. Then, very decorously, he peered under the tent of swaddling and, with those cold chrome tools, poked around in my useless cavity while his stethoscope swung like an amulet. I stared at that goddam amulet for the life of me: to keep from wincing, bolting, crying out. He was young enough to be my son; to invite his calming words would be to surrender the rest of my dignity.

"You're healing beautifully," he finally announced. "Just about ready to go home now."

"Thank you," I said.

And when he left me alone to dress, I lay still for a moment: feeling sewn up, sealed up, spayed.

Of course it was absurd to go for that easy symbolism. I *knew* that. I knew that so goddam well that my psychiatrist's cloying kindness only angered me more. "You'll still be a woman, you know," Dr. Fleischer reassured me before I went in. "Of course I'll still be a woman!" I barked back. "I don't need you to tell me that." But I knew what he meant—and it was true. All those months before the surgery —the bleeding, the discharge, the poking, the pain, the having to walk into pharmacies and buy boxes of Kotex ("For my daughter," I always explained): my body humiliated me, inside and out. And desire became the sharpest humiliation of all. Did I even have the right to feel it ever again? To expect it to be felt for me?

Ronald was my savior. Together, through mirrors unlike this one—mirrors that stopped at the neck—our heads bobbed like Punch and Judy, lathering words and shampoo. Plucking, snipping, teasing, preening, lacquering: the language of a sweet and sad avoidance. Did I understand then that I'd written off sex?

Besides, toward the end with Morty, what mattered most was the touching, anyway—tired, preoccupied, almost unconscious touch. It was our Braille, our bond, our twenty years' history. No one likes to admit it, but the true passion leaves you so fast you forget what it felt like in the first place. Then come the years of faking that passion—violently pretending you're both still new. Finally, the act itself becomes mercifully incidental: the small, quick center of a larger, richer thing.

How do I think of Morty and me in bed? What do I miss the most? The two of us propped against pillows in the old bedroom, watching Merv Griffin, a plate of toasted bagels between us. His hand would come to rest in the hollow of my nightgowned lap, or quietly on my thigh. I would hunch my shoulders and slide down an inch and silently he would lift up his arm to take me under wing. All he had to do was crook his neck and wince and I know just where to rub his back: how high, how fast, how hard. Sometimes we just held hands—loosely, absently, like children at a school crossing. Or mindlessly drummed our fingers on one another's skin. I remember how he used to drum: always the three middle fingers, like the fierce gallop of some amputated horse. "You with your Hi Ho Silver," I once said. "It tickles."

"What does?"

"This."

"You know what *you* do?"

"Hmm?"

He made semicircles with his index finger on my leg. "Shearson Hammill quotations."

"How'd you guess?"

"The nine and the 0 at the end."

"Sherlock Holmes here." I nudged him. "Listen, it could be worse. I could've dialed Sylvia's number."

"True," he said, as I burrowed down under his arm and felt the familiar give of his flesh under his familiar silk pajamas. "True."

Have I mourned that precious history all this time? Is there time enough to have a new one? Do I want to? Can I let myself?

I stare back now at this awkward, naked woman in the mirror—so nervously straight-backed, so fleshy, so worn.

So absurdly and secretly virginal.

THROUGH THE TWO CLOSED DOORS THAT SEPARATE US, I HEAR
the hearty rush of water. I stand up from the breakfast table,
plug in the coffeepot, put the croissants in the oven. As I
move, I feel a faint scratching inside the neck of my caftan.
Jesus, I forgot to remove the last sales tag. I pull up the back,
pick up the kitchen scissors, turn my neck as far around as
it will go and snip the string.

Look at me, will you? Wafting around in a brand-new silk
caftan at ten on a Saturday morning, makeup on, house
straightened, fixing a Continental breakfast and listening—

for the first time in years—to the sound of a man using my shower. If I were watching myself in a TV movie, I would almost be touched.

But I am not watching myself in a movie. I am trying to load last night's dinner plates into the dishwasher without getting the wide silk sleeves of this caftan wet. Gentleman that he is, Louis had helped me clear the table.

"No, come on, you're the guest," I said, trying to keep him seated.

"Nonsense." He smiled gallantly as he stood. "This was always my specialty."

"Well"—I smiled—"far be it from me to refuse expertise."

We talked and laughed easily as we moved past each other between kitchen and breakfast room, plates and sponges in hand.

He didn't ask where things went; his gestures were practiced, unbachelorly. He seemed relieved by the domesticity of it all. (If he only knew how rarely I did this glorified hausfrau routine during my marriage, much less after.) He was much more relaxed throughout dinner than he had been in our two set-piece evenings at restaurant tables. He loosened his tie as he opened the second bottle of wine, rambled on charmingly about some old Benny Goodman album his daughter had found for him at a Venice flea market, how it reminded him of his days at the aircraft plant in San Francisco. He rose slightly and leaned across the table to help himself to seconds of the veal I'd made from Ronald's recipe. As he ladled, I watched his contented, thoroughly unselfconscious face. I could so easily imagine it at the head of a long family dinner table, a napkin tucked in at the chin.

But I was comfortable, too. After we cleared the table, I brought out the brandy, slipped off my shoes, and tucked my feet up under me on the couch.

"Shall we see who Carson has on tonight?" I asked, picking up the remote control switch.

"Sure," he said, smiling.

I flicked the set on. "Damn it, it's still got that strange tint."

"It is a bit green."

"Well, listen," I shrugged, "McMahon can use the color."

He chuckled, then asked: "Would you like me to try to fix it?"

"Please. Be my guest."

He walked over and knelt by the set, fidgeting with the knobs. It struck me that I had never seen him from the back like that: squatted on his heels, elbows thrust out, his shirt pulling out from the waistband of his pants. I had only seen him standing, sitting, walking. We were more informal now than we'd ever been.

The cuffs of my white pants slapping against the floor, I walked barefoot into the kitchen, got out the raspberries I'd bought for dessert, put them on a tray with two bowls, two spoons, a pitcher of heavy cream, a little stack of cocktail napkins.

"Oh, that's much better," I said, placing the tray on the coffee table.

"If it gets like that again," he said, pulling up his trouser legs to sit down, "just turn the color-control knob a tad to the left."

"A tad." I smiled. "Is that like an inch? Or more like a millimeter?"

"Somewhere in between," he said, smiling back.

"Have some." He was looking inquisitively at the raspberries. "Go ahead. Use your fingers." I winked. "I won't tell."

He smiled, leaned over, grabbed a handful, and popped them into his mouth like nuts.

I was tickled by his uncharacteristic jauntiness. "Hey, you're pretty good at that."

"We used to do this as kids—with blueberries. The trick was to get them just before they'd ripened, then pitch them into your mouth and make them snap in your teeth. We put bets on who could get the most snaps from the farthest shot in the fastest time without missing a one." He laughed lightly, warming up to the memory. "We'd all end up looking like we'd gargled with fountain pen ink."

"Come on." I smiled challengingly. "Let me see."

"Well . . ." He winked, as if feeling foolish. "Raspberries don't pop."

"Aw, that's just an alibi."

"Tell you what," he said, patting my knee—enjoying this middle-aged Becky-and-Tom Sawyer silliness as much as I. "Next time I see you, I'll bring a bag of unripened blueberries."

"And I'll bring a stopwatch."

He laughed, then stopped laughing and turned to me with a look of soft appreciation. "It's always so easy being with you, Lil. I let myself go more than . . . well, than I have in a long time."

"Well, thank you."

"No, I mean it."

"Thank you again." I smiled.

He didn't. His eyes were questioning, deferential. Unconsciously, I made the little shift of my shoulder that gave him my answer. Slowly, solemnly, he took my hand between the two of his. The act was grave and formal—like a proposal, or the prelude to a difficult confession.

And later, after the tenderness and the awkwardness of it all, we settled at opposite sides of the bed for sleep, and I knew it had been a mistake. I woke at four, again at five, finally at seven. Each time I was curled at the edge of the bed, as I never am normally: my back to Louis who sprawled, like Morty always had, his nose pointed toward the ceiling, nostrils widening and contracting like bellows.

But this wasn't Morty beside me. This wasn't even the Louis I knew who smiled and winked and spoke wistfully of his wife over the safe barrier of restaurant tables: my escort, my flatterer, my suitor, my date. This was suddenly a stranger in my bed: a nude, sad-faced, sleeping man with two painful-looking red dents by the top of his nose where his glasses had been. His eyes looked much smaller without the glasses; his face puffier, more ordinary. He lay slack-jawed, urgently inhaling and exhaling the dreamed fragments of sixty years of a life I had nothing to do with at all, would never be able to more than politely understand. Start an intimacy now? The futility of it all—the sharp invasion I felt by his presence —woke me, and woke me, and woke me again.

Finally, I got out of bed, dressed and made up while he slept on. I felt so silly measuring my moves in the bathroom: turning on the tap water while I used the toilet, squinting nervously against the harsh early morning sun to get my eyelashes on straight, my rouge even (Ronald, where are you now that I need you?), wondering how I'd cover the unfinished part of my face if he woke and called out good morning and I had to go back in the bedroom. But of course he wouldn't do that. As there had been a nervous modesty last night, there will be the same now. He will dress decorously behind closed doors, too, and say good morning only after he's assembled himself for company. How do the kids do it?

Lolling around in their juices, soaping each other's backs, prancing around fearlessly, making coffee in the buff? We are not kids. God, we are not.

He has shut off the shower. I bring the coffee, cups, croissants to the breakfast table. I remember the flowers he brought me last night—a mixed bouquet this time; he selected each one from his garden himself. I go into the living room to get them for a centerpiece.

As I walk back into the breakfast room, carrying the vase, he is gingerly sitting down at the table, dressed as he was last night. Rustling in this silk caftan at this ungodly hour of the morning, holding these flowers, I feel a little ridiculous.

"Some grand entrance." He smiles.

"Isn't it, though?" I laugh. "All I need is a door to fling open and I'd look like a bad take-off on Loretta Young."

"No, you look lovely." He rises to kiss my cheek.

"Did you sleep all right?" I ask, like a hostess to a guest in the next bedroom.

"Like a baby." He smiles and sits down again. "Oh." He looks up. "I didn't know what towel to use so I used the blue one. And I couldn't find a hamper so I folded it up over the shower door."

"Oh, I should have told you to use one of the big white ones."

"Well, those looked too nice to get wet."

I smile as I pour him coffee. Louis, you are such a decent man.

We sip quietly. I put the croissants on our plates. After a moment or two, he says: "I've been thinking all morning about how much I'd like to show you Tucson. Will you be my guest for a week?"

"Oh . . . I . . . My daughter's coming in next Thursday for about three weeks."

"After she leaves, then? If you can't get away for a week, three or four days perhaps?"

"Perhaps. Thank you. I mean, *yes.*" I pause. "Louis?"

His coffee cup poised in front of him, he looks up expectantly. Such a kind, warm face. I *can't* say: "Louis, this just doesn't feel comfortable yet. Let's not rush it."

So I say: "What would I bring? Clothes, I mean. Is it very warm this time of year?"

"No. Our Marches are pretty much like they are here. To be on the safe side, you might tack on ten or twelve degrees, that's all." He smiles. "Do you have any sugar, by the way?"

"Oh, *sugar.* Of course. I forgot." I stand and reach for the bowl. "When you take Sweet 'n Low, you tend to forget about the rest of the world."

I hand him the sugar bowl, he spoons two teaspoons in. I start laughing in spite of myself.

"What's so funny?" He looks up, smiling.

"That . . . here we are like this, and I don't even know how you take your coffee."

"Well," he says, thankfully blind to the irony in my tone, "there's plenty of time for us to learn all that."

The presumption stings. And yet, he is not being smug—just . . . innocent. He squeezes my hand. I smile up briefly, then lower my eyes back to my coffee. When he leaves, I will take off this farkokta silk caftan and get into something more comfortable. I wish to hell Ronald weren't in San Diego for the weekend. How easy it would be just to get in the car and go up to his house and lie around looking at his magazines while he putters with his plants and croons to his cat and bitches at me for not tucking cotton in under my hairnet at night.

"Habit is a funny thing," I muse.

"What do you mean?"

"Oh, like my forgetting to put the sugar bowl on the table."

I think he knows that's not what I mean, but he smiles politely anyway.

🍁

Gate 80.

I wedge between the man with the two-year-old bobbing on his shoulders and the young long-haired couple, their palms tucked into each other's back jeans pockets as if for safekeeping. When Andi would come home from Berkeley, I always double-parked outside PSA Baggage, my L.A. *Times* propped open against the steering wheel, as if I were simply waiting in line at a car wash. Her absence was only temporary then; we didn't need the ceremony.

Now it's different. I stand here at United Arrivals among this flock of eager "loved ones": our chins jutted anxiously at the parade of deplaning passengers.

And this is when I get nervous. What if I am expecting too much? On one of these rarer and rarer trips, she will walk off the plane and in some sharp, final way, I will know that she doesn't belong to me any more. Instead of the flash of emotion in her face there'll be a calm, cordial smile. "You didn't have to bother," she'll say. "You could've just waited at the loading zone. Or I could've taken a taxi." My heart will sink for a minute, and then I'll adjust.

"Andi!" She's craning her neck in the wrong direction. Rolled-up jeans over boots, a silk shirt with a floppy wool scarf, a trench coat over her arm. Oh, she looks wonderful! "Andi! Over here!"

She whips around and in that flash of recognition, that

smile, that awkward, excited maneuvering of her two big tote bags, I know everything's still all right.

We hug and kiss. Her earrings poke through her soft hair; she wears a new perfume; she is tall in those boots.

"You look wonderful," I gush as she bends to pick up her hand luggage.

"So do you."

"Really?" I laugh nervously.

"Really." She smiles.

"Let me see." She stands indulgently still as my eyes scan her face, feature to feature. "You're wearing eye liner."

"I always wear eye liner. *You* just always forget."

She insists she can manage both her tote bags. They bang against the sides of her legs as we walk down the long white tile tunnel to Baggage Claims. With bright, slightly studied animation, she talks of her flight (bumpy the last hour, garrulous pilot, a movie she'd already seen), the New York weather (three inches of snow last night "but I like it, Mom, *really*"), the copy-editing job she will almost definitely be promoted to. With every turn of her face toward mine, she cocks her head to flip a shank of hair out of her eyes. She gets two paces ahead of me, stops to wait, gets two paces ahead, stops to wait, again and again.

"Christ," I say, "I feel like one of those wooden ducks you pull along on a string. I must be getting old."

"No, you're not." She smiles. "I'm just used to walking fast."

She hoists her suitcase off the revolving drum, hails a skycap with an imperious flip of the arm, puts her hand graciously over mine when I try to tip him for her. I'm an adult now, all these gestures are meant to inform me. A sophisticated Manhattan lady. I smile to myself at the effort in her aplomb. She always uses such *energy* in redefining herself

—as if every two- or three-year transformation were achieved with a great sucking in and holding of breath.

But then, when she gets behind the wheel of my car, that breath is released. She fiddles with the levers as if reclaiming a favorite girlhood toy (sometimes I think she comes home just to drive the damn thing) and becomes my daughter again.

"I've got an idea," she says, adjusting the rearview mirror. "Let's stop at Joe Allen's for a drink."

"I don't have enough problems? You have to turn me into an afternoon drinker?"

"Sure, why not?" She smiles. "It's very chic these days." She shifts into Drive. "And I've got another idea."

"What?"

"Let's put the top down. *Please?*"

I want to hug her eager, suddenly childlike face. Instead, I groan. "You can always tell a New Yorker." (She loves that.) "Listen, if my hair turns into macrame knots on the freeway, *you* explain it to Ronald." And, with secret delight, I watch her relish the wan sun in her face while the convertible hood collapses behind us. Then she releases the emergency brake, turns the radio instantly and loud to the station she has listened to since she was fourteen years old, and we're off.

"I'm a little worried about you," I kid as our Bloody Marys arrive. "You've been back in town forty-five minutes and I haven't heard the words 'sterile, tacky wasteland' once."

"Oh, God," she laughs. "I *did* use to always say that, didn't I?"

"And we drove down Pico, no less."

She smiles. "The trouble with mothers is that they never

forget your growing pains. They catalogue every absurd
remark you ever made."

"True," I say, smiling. "Listen, for a small price I'll burn
the file. Deal?"

"Deal," she says, and we laugh.

Yet something is troubling her. I can tell from her preoccupied eyes, the way she is toying with that swizzle stick.
"It's Peter, isn't it?" I want to ask, of the young writer she's
seeing in New York. But I can't let her know how easily I
can read her face. (That, too, is part of the deal.) So I wait,
while she tests the water with small talk; then, finally, she
admits, a bit guiltily:

"This is a ploy, this vacation."

"How so?"

"The day I called you and said I wanted to come out?
I had just decided I should seriously consider breaking up
with Peter. I'm here because I want him to miss me, to stop
taking me for granted."

"There's nothing wrong with that."

"Oh, sure there is. It's a game."

"So it's a game. You use that word like it's one step below
grand larceny."

"I guess so." She smiles, vaguely comforted. "But I can't
help feeling that my game on top of his game will turn the
whole relationship into double bullshit."

"Could we have that in English?"

"I just can't figure out what he *wants* from me. We see
each other two, three nights a week, but he's still so tentative, so evasive. And, Mom," she says, as if asserting her
virture, "I am *not* possessive."

"Relax darling. I believe you. It's even okay if you are."

"He just has to *imagine* I'm possessive," she goes on, getting wound up, intense. "It does something for his masculine ego. I can sense that he needs me, but I can also sense that he's angry with himself for needing me. Whenever I try to get close to him, he gets very sharp and diffident, like I'm lunging in for the kill. But if I'm detached, if I'm *not* there for him, he gets petulant and insecure. It's turned into a power struggle. And he's trying to make it so he comes out the winner. *Really*, I can't stand for that, can I?"

I smile at her proud face. "In my day, we used to let them pretend they *were* the winners. That probably sounds pretty awful to you."

"Not awful," she says, trying to be polite. "But a little dishonest. Unhealthy."

"I guess we weren't so tough on ourselves then. A relationship didn't have to be honest or healthy or anything else it seems to have to be today. It especially didn't have to be a 'relationship.' "

I wait for her smile, but it doesn't appear. "Well, people just know themselves a lot better now," she says instead, with a touching absoluteness. "I'd never go into a relationship blindly again. I'd have to know the odds first, where he's coming from and where I'm coming from."

"I used to have a daughter." I sigh. "Now I have an executive training manual."

"Come on, Mom. I'm serious."

"That's obvious, darling. I just wish you wouldn't be— not *quite* so much. There's too much time for that later. Listen"—I shrug—"if love were so easy, it wouldn't be any fun."

She frowns, as if to tell me how quaint I am. "I'm not sure I *am* in love with him. I basically distrust that word. Half of the times I've used it, I've really meant 'dependence.' "

"Well, dependence *is* part of it. You can't change that."

"But that's just *it*. Peter would like to. He'd like to pretend he doesn't have a dependent bone in his body. When I first met him, he had this vague pipe dream of taking a year off and going to live in Israel. Now whenever we're with friends, he brings it up, as if he's leaving tomorrow. He's not leaving tomorrow. If I know him, he'll never get it together to go. But he uses it as a wedge between us, a way of telling other people I'm not curbing his great adventures. And a way of telling me he's not committed. It really makes me angry."

"Why let it do that? Why not just laugh at it to yourself?"

"*Laugh* at it?" Her tone suggests I've proposed a sacrilege.

"A little, sure. As long as *you* see through him, you've got half of it licked."

"But I want *him* to see through him."

"Maybe he will. I hope so. But I'll tell you something, darling. That's no guarantee, either. I remember the night your father proposed. Men still did that, back in the Paleolithic Era. Actually, he didn't propose in words. He just pulled a little box out of his pocket. And when I opened it and saw the diamond, he said, 'Nothing personal, you understand. I just thought your glove was awfully loose on that finger. And if I *do* decide to join the French Foreign Legion, we go halfsies on the pawn deal.'" I smile, remembering. Andi smiles, too.

"See?" I say. "He saw through himself enough to make fun of himself. But what did that mean in the long run? So it turned out it wasn't the French Foreign Legion. It was a younger woman instead. Should I have held my breath all those years? Should I have made myself crazy looking at his ulterior motives through some magnifying glass so I'd be sure I'd never get hurt? Or at least know in advance

when the hurt was coming? I could have, I guess. Maybe I
should have. But you know something? I'm glad I didn't.

"Andi," I say softly now, "I just don't like to see you so
grim. Be cautious, yes. But not *so* cautious that you can't
enjoy things for what they are."

She nods, comprehending but not agreeing. "Well," she
says, taking the napkin off her lap, "I think I'll go check out
the music."

I smile to myself as she stands up. They don't really
change, do they? It's a movable feast, that bravado of theirs.
She talks about her love life now with the same urgent,
righteous certainty she used to give to politics: her Ideas as
breastplates. If only they could really protect her.

I study the way she stands at the jukebox, then walks to
the ladies' room. There is a self-consciousness to her posture,
a touchingly feigned arrogance. As she walks past the table
of young actors, she looks at her feet, brushes her hair out of
her eyes with the hand that isn't clutching the strap of her
shoulder bag. She will never believe she is as truly pretty
as she is—and will never stop pretending she does believe it.
I glance at the young men's faces as she passes. They notice
her. She *is* desirable! I feel, all at once, ashamed of myself
for looking and angry at myself for doubting it.

"You invest in her too much," Dr. Fleischer used to say.
"You over-project." But how can you not? How can you
just let go?

I remember one night when she was three and a half and
woke me with a wail. I hurried into her room. "I'm scared,"
she said, as I gathered her soft, damp body against me. "I
saw monsters."

"Sssh, it's all right." I kissed her flushed face. "It was just
a bad dream."

"But what if the monsters come back?"

"They won't," I said softly. "Not with me here to scare them away."

How automatic those words were; how instantly she believed them. I watched her eyes roll shut as she stabbed her wet thumb in her mouth and sank back to sleep in my awkward arms. Her breathing was unusually hard and deep. Coming from behind, I remember thinking, such a gust could propel her tiny body down the street. I don't know how long I sat like that—an hour? an hour and a half?—penitently uncomfortable at the edge of her bed: trying to read her dream on her face, cradling her awesome trust. Finally, pious and deliberate, I set her slack head on the pillow. I tiptoed out and went back to bed, fully expecting to be awakened by her scream: "Mommy, you lied! The monsters came back!"

Why is it that now, too many years later, I am still waiting for that accusation in one form or another? Doing nudgey little things to possess and provoke her—like staring at the young men watching her, and now, as she sits back down, opening my mouth to say: "Now don't take this as a criticism, but I was just noticing that your hair's a little long in the front. As long as you're here, do you want to call Ronald? Have him give you a little trim?"

"Maybe." She shrugs. "We'll see."

"He'd love to see you, anyway."

"Great. Fine." She goes back to her Bloody Mary.

"It's not that I don't like your hair, Andi. *I do.*"

"I know you do." Her voice is over-solicitous. "I know you do."

We smile, a bit sheepishly.

"You remember them, too," I say. "Those fights we used to have when you were at Berkeley? How come we always picked hair to fight about?"

"Oh, God, I would have fought about *any*thing then."
She laughs a grand, parental laugh at her long-ago self. "I
was *awful.* So stubborn and pompous."

"Well, listen, I didn't make it any easier on you."

"Mom, no. Why do you say that?"

"Oh, the whole thing with your father. I let it eat at me
too long." I scan her face for agreement, but it wears a tact-
ful neutrality. She can't *really* have forgotten. Didn't it scar
her life, seeing me so flattened? "Andi, don't you remember
what a basket case I was?"

"You're being unfair to yourself," she says, with a warm,
even distance. "You were legitimately hurt. Those things
take time to heal."

I smile widely into her face. She nods back, taking my
smile for gratitude. It is gratitude, but more than that, it's
a sudden understanding of how all these things—the pride,
the earnestness, that innocent and self-protecting condescension—have helped her survive. Good for you, darling. *Run
with them.*

The waiter lays the check by my drink. She reaches over
and picks it up, lays down her own Master Charge on top.

"Oh, Andi, *no.*"

"Uh-uh-uh." Her hand proprietously over her credit card.

"Well, thank you, dear."

I put on my lipstick as she leans over the receipt, ball-
point poised, considering what to add. Now don't overtip
him, I want to say, like you did the skycap.

But of course I say nothing.

She flips her hair back over her eye as we stand up.

"Now what shall we do about dinner?" I ask gaily, as she
helps me on with my jacket. "Go out to the Hamlet? Eat
in?"

"Can we think about that later? I just ate on the plane."

"I know, but you should eat a little something. Because with the liquor and the jet lag—"

"I'll eat. Don't worry." She squeezes my shoulder indulgently.

"And let's give Ronald a little call. Not a whole haircut, just a little trim."

"We'll eat, we'll call Ronald, we'll do *everything*," she assures me, in sarcastic, placating singsong.

"You'll always be fresh with me," I say, after a beat, "won't you?"

"Mmm, probably."

We smile. She holds the door open for me.

"My God," I say. "Such service she gives her old lady. The check, the coat, the door. Where's the sedan chair?"

"Mmm, not yet. I figure you can still make it on foot."

"You're goddam right I can." We smile as we walk to the car. "You're goddam right."

She sits, two hours later, on her knees in front of the open hall closet: unfolding her clothes from the suitcase and handing them to me. I slip them on wire coat hangers, and, fluffing out their creases, imagine her New York life.

"Peter," she says casually, handing me a snapshot tucked in her makeup case.

"He looks a little like Gabe Kaplan."

"Not really, but I know what you mean. The Jewish Afro." She peers at the picture over my shoulder. "I'm always telling him: 'Don't you *dare* get it cut.'"

I turn around and see her still studying the picture.

"I think you *do* love him," I say.

"Oh, I don't know." She sighs, as if fatigued. "First I want to be my own person."

"But you *are*."

"Not as much as I want to be." She looks up abruptly. "What are you smiling at?"

At your wonderful, strident faith, darling. At that exquisite illusion that it's all so conquerable, that everything exists to be improved. "Nothing, really," I say. And then it's not so charming any more. "Andi?"

"Hmm?"

"If I ask you something, will you tell me the truth?"

"Sure."

"Do you get this attitude of yours from the way things were with me and your father? Do you ever look back and think: 'Look at the mistakes she made. I don't ever want to repeat those mistakes.' *Do you?*"

Anxiously, I follow her eyes through her thoughtful silence.

"No, not really," she finally says. "Not like that, anyway. I mean, they weren't just your mistakes. They were both of yours. Sometimes I wish you'd both been in therapy so you'd know why you were doing things."

"What things?" I ask quickly. "What *did* we do?"

"Oh, you were always taking emotional swings at each other without knowing why, or where. Like he'd lose his temper over some little inconsequential thing because he knew he could get to you that way, that you'd worry about it for hours. And you'd get back at him with your anxiousness. Calling that stockbroker every other minute, asking the same questions over and over again when you were really looking for a deeper validation."

"I did ask the same questions over and over again, didn't I? I remember once he said: 'Lil, you repeat, repeat, repeat. You'd make some man a great automatic rifle.'"

"Yes, but he meant that kiddingly. Affectionately."

"*Did* he?"

"Mmm hmm," she says softly. "He did."

I smile at her gratefully, then I sit down on the rug beside her and stare at my lap. "Was he happy, those last years?" I ask when I look up. "I could never ask you then. I didn't want you to be caught in the middle any more than you already were. And I knew if I asked you, you'd feel pressured to say that he wasn't. But now I really need to know that he was. Not for me so much as for him, if you can believe it."

"I can believe it," she says, with the softness of genuine understanding. "Was he happy?" She mulls it over. "I wish I could say he was as happy as he tried to pretend he was."

"What do you mean?" I ask, a little too quickly.

"Oh, he loved her. Or rather, he was infatuated with her. I mean, why not? She was young and beautiful and docile and everything. But Daddy was a creature of habit, you know? And every so often I could see little . . . breaches of his habit, little things she'd do that made him feel . . . well, like kind of lonely for the past."

"It's hard to start a new life after a certain age," I find myself saying. "In a funny way, I give him credit for doing it."

"I remember one night we were sitting around in their living room after dinner. Alana brought out this cheesecake for dessert. From Pupi's, I think it was. She walked out in those high-heel thongs of hers in that corny sarong she was always wearing with this cheesecake on this fancy tray. It was really a lousy cheesecake."

I laugh at the image—and the loyalty.

"And he looked up at her," she goes on, "and said, 'Ah, a cheesecake! I was beginning to think *you* were the only one around here.' And he went on and on about what a great cheesecake it was and how long it had been since he'd had cheesecake. But the whole time he was eating it, I could see his face getting . . . you know, like little kids' faces get when they get the wrong kind of bike for Christmas and they're too polite to complain? And I knew he was thinking about all the chocolate marble Per-Al's cheesecakes we used to bring home from Canter's every Sunday, and how we ate them right out of the box the minute we got home."

I laugh at the memory. "Each of us with a spoon, pretending we were just taking a nibble while we put the groceries away."

"And then we'd be very civilized and cut off all the ragged edges of what was left and you'd wrap it in Saran Wrap and put it in the refrigerator 'for tomorrow.' "

"Some 'tomorrow'! By the end of the day, there'd be twenty separate knives with licked-off cheesecake on them at the bottom of the sink."

"And this tiny little sliver of cake left wrapped up again and again in all that Saran Wrap—and always in the exact same spot on the exact same shelf of the refrigerator. And then Alberta would come in the next morning and think it was some ancient piece of cheese and throw it away."

"The hell she did. She ate it for breakfast. Along with the leftover pastrami."

"She did? That's never what she told me when I looked for it after school."

"Yeah? Then she was a better liar than we were," I say. And we laugh.

"Those were fun, those Sundays at Canter's," Andi muses. "Remember how I used to always beg you to let me hold the number? And I stood there with that little plastic card in my hand feeling so important and the guy behind the counter would go 'tventy-vun . . . tventy-two . . . tventy-tree . . . *Ver* is tventy-tree?' And you or Daddy would hoist me up and I'd wave the number up over the counter like it was some winning lottery ticket and place our order."

"Which you always got wrong."

"*Always.*" She laughs.

"Your father used to say, 'Can't we trade this little pip-squeak for the kid down the street? I bet the kid down the street knows the difference between a water bagel and an egg bagel.' "

We both laugh now. Sitting on our knees with the clothes and hangers and opened suitcases all around us, like two overaged sorority sisters regaling an old, shared beau.

"People don't really kibitz any more, do they?" I say. "I mean, they're funny in different ways now, but they don't really . . . kibitz like they used to."

"Peter kind of does. He goes through all these mira-mira routines with the Puerto Rican guys on his block, and he jives with the black guys at the deli. 'Hey, Le-Roy, I wanna big rocebeef samwich. I mean, a biiiig rocebeef samwich.' Sure." She smiles fondly. "He kibitzes."

"I think you do love him," I say, smiling. "Just a *little* bit?"

"Why are you so anxious for me to love him?"

"Why not? It's such a nice feeling."

"Except I want to know where he's coming from first."

"But you never really will, you know," I say softly.

"No, that's not true. It's possible for people to read each other's motives and to read their own and—"

"Andi." I want to shake her, but my voice comes out a plea instead. "Andi, don't kill it with all that analysis. Please? Go for broke while you can. You won't always have the opportunity. *Now* you have it. And even in ten or twelve or fifteen years you will. But when you get to be my age . . ."

"Mom." Now it is her voice that is pleading, solicitous. "Mom, you're not too old."

"I know," I say, embarrassed at where this has brought us.

"Of course, I'm not." I pause. "I've been seeing a man, as a matter of fact," I finally decide to admit.

"*Really?*" Her whole face comes alive with supportive excitement. "How terrific!" And I'm suddenly reminded of how much she wanted me to remarry nine years ago; how easily she thought it could be accomplished, how petulant she became when it wasn't. "Who is he? What's he like?"

"He's a very nice man, Andi. I'm not sure if he's for me, but he's a very nice man."

"Then why isn't he for you?" It's a challenge, not a question, and I'm touched by her well-meaning vehemence.

"To tell you the truth, I wish I knew. For one thing, he lives in Arizona."

"Well, you could move."

"Not so easily."

"Oh, *sure* you could."

"Take it easy, dear. First of all, he hasn't asked me to. But for another thing, you can't be quite so carefree at my age. You don't have time for too many experiments and mistakes any more. Not that that's *bad*," I say quickly, studying her concerned face. "It's just . . . different, that's all. People are in a little more of a hurry to get things settled. You have to make decisions faster, and for different reasons."

"What kinds of reasons?" she asks, with the sudden fearfulness of someone still innocent of compromise.

"Oh . . . comfort, common sense. The other person's kindness. Their simple willingness to have you." I smile reassuringly. "They're not bad reasons."

"No," she says eagerly, her voice a little too high. "They're not bad reasons."

"They're not." I shrug—jauntily—to convince us both.

"You already said that," she reminds me.

"We both did."

We smile, we look down at our laps. Then I lean over and fluff her hair. "I'm glad you're here," I say softly. *"Not* that I want you to stay, you understand . . ."

We both smile at the lie. My smile lingers; hers is tender, quick, abashed. Then, as if the affection is too threatening, she looks away and springs to her feet.

"Do you have any eggs?" she asks.

"Of course."

"Cheese?"

I nod.

"I'll make us an omelet."

"That's all you want for dinner?" I follow her into the kitchen.

"I ate on the plane." She opens the refrigerator door. "I told you."

"You have a wonderful figure, you know," I say, standing at the kitchen door.

"Thanks."

"You *can* have more than an omelet, if you want. We can go to the Hamlet, or for Chinese food. Whatever you want."

"This is fine," she says, removing the eggs.

"Whatever you say." I shrug, sit down, stand up again. "You need a little help?"

"I'm fine, dear, just fine."

"There's some Swiss in there. And some Muenster."

"I see them," she sings back, annoyed.

"And some onions."

"I see them too-oo."

I smile to myself at her fierce impertinence.

"Andi?" I walk over and awkwardly hug her moving shoulders. "Don't let him get you down—Peter."

"He's not getting me down," she says, straightening her back to shake me away. She takes a knife to the onions. "He just . . . has to learn . . . not to . . . take me for granted."

Her words are as crisp as her slices. I realize I am peering over her shoulder, so I back up against the stove. As she cuts, her chin is high, her hand is steady. With arrogant little cocks of her head, she flips that silly strand of hair away. Tears will never come to her eyes from these onions—or from anything else—if she has her way. God bless her.

"Andi?"

"Hmm?"

"Do you want an apron? That's such a nice blouse, you might—"

"Mom." She turns and puts her hands on my shoulders, speaks with the dulcet appeasement you use on an overwrought child. "Why don't you just relax . . . and set the table . . . and the omelet will be ready in a minute."

"Yes, your highness," I hum back. Smiling in spite of myself, I turn to open the silverware drawer. As she starts to grate the cheese, she is smiling, too.

9

GOD, IT'S NICE TO BE LIVING WITH SOMEONE—SOMEONE YOU'RE comfortable with, someone you know. I mean *really* know—not in the eerily polite way that Sima brushes against me during the day: eating her oily meals with rabbit-like silence and speed, whispering Arabic over the phone, padding around obsequiously, erasing herself as she goes. I mean know like I know Andi—with all that sloppy, uncivilized, taken-for-granted ease.

We have conversations from room to room, not needing each other's faces to talk. She makes a chicken salad for our

lunch and we stand in the kitchen nibbling it out of the
bowl before finally carrying our separate plates to the breakfast room and pushing aside the morning papers to eat.
Yesterday, I sat on the toilet seat lid, talking to her while
she shaved her legs. I watched her bend over, that firm taut
calf propped up on my makeup stool, slowly moving the
razor up and down—and she became nine years old all over
again, tying her toe shoes for the Mark Boyd recital. They're
always so bittersweet, these brief visits of hers.

But this time it's different. Or so I keep telling myself.
Louis calls from Tucson every other day, and between those
calls I find myself taking that great hulk of sentimentality
and trying, almost frantically, to transfer it onto him. Yet
when I talk to him on the phone I can't work up that same
feeling. His voice has changed somehow. Something is settled,
he seems to assume, now that we've shared a bed. I am coming to visit him in Tucson after Andi leaves next week,
and in the meantime he wants to prime me for his life. I
can understand that. But why do I hear a certain smugness
in his patter where the lovely vulnerability used to be?

He goes on and on about the golf games he's played, the
concerts he's attending, the rhododendron he's planting—
and I find myself responding with that anxious niceness of
someone desperately trying to pretend she's not bored. Sure,
he may have rambled on about Peg before, but at least that
talk was touching. Now her name has vanished from his
conversation—in deference to me, I suppose—but all these
other names have started spilling out instead. Jaunty, chunky
Noah's Ark names—George-and-Ann, Grace-and-Roy, Walt-
and-Fran—like some goddam salt-and-pepper set collection.
They want to have us for cocktails, for dinner, for lunch at
the club. *What* club? I always thought of Louis as the self-
sufficient desert widower, the poignantly abandoned family

man. Now, suddenly, he's someone else: the fortified community bachelor, properly and confidently choosing a mate. God, I know what married couples are like with their widower friends: pampering, possessive, watch-out-she-doesn't-try-to-take-you.

"I'm nervous about going to Tucson and meeting his friends," I tell Andi.

"Mom," she says patiently, "relax, okay? If you're anxious you'll just act phony, and that's the worst thing you can be."

"I'm nervous," I tell Sylvia.

"Nervous shmervous." She flaps her hand. "So you go on the Stillman for four days before, and you buy yourself some decent clothes for a change. And no divorce from Morty. He died on you, *capisce*? No second wife, no lousy settlement, you still belong to Hillcrest."

"I'm nervous," I tell Ronald.

"Nervous?" He laughs. "That's a scream. Honey, they're all mayo on white. You're a hot tamale."

"*You* say that. And for years I could make fun of them, too. And you know why I could make fun of them? Because I avoided them. But I only avoided them because I couldn't compete in their world. Now here I am, back on the auction block and hell of a lot older than when I got knocked off the first time."

"Oh, listen to her. Miss Tupperware all of a sudden. Darling, gimme a *break*. You can't stand those stiffs and you know it."

"You're right," I finally admit.

"And, anyway, who cares about them? You'll have Louis."

"Yes. Of course. I'll have Louis." But what if I find out he's one of them, too?

I rush to answer the door on the second ring.

"Who is it?" I call out.

"Salvation Army, love."

I open the door and Edwin lumbers in behind a huge box of that record company gimmickry he gets flooded with week after week now.

"Alas," he says, "on the higher echelons they call this paltry offering payola."

"Yeah?" The box lands with a thud on my breakfast table. "Well here we call it dreck."

But I fish through it anyway. "Andi might want these." I pull out some albums. "Or Sima." I pull out a handful of brightly logoed T-shirts. "Maybe the gardener can use this." I pull out a cellophaned clot of rubber tubing.

"Love, it's a Sony headphone attachment, not a garden hose."

"So he'll take it home anyway. They're both Japanese."

"Marvelous, Lil." He laughs. "I can always count on your hermetic sense of utility."

"You mean my Semitic sense of greed." I continue rummaging. "Oh, Edwin, whatever happened to the old days when they sent bottles of good liquor and invitations to wonderful parties?"

"Say no more." He fishes in the box and extracts a spangled satin loincloth.

"Dear, I didn't say *stag* party. Or does Frederick's advertise on the station now?"

"No. Read the label."

Glittermania! it says. *Be our guest opening night for a disco explosion your mind and body will never forget!*

"You have to wear these to get in, I suppose?"

"Nah. Just fling them at the chap at the door. Like Leslie

Howard cuffing a chum with his kid glove."

"With all these goddam sequins? I'm afraid I'd scratch up the poor shmuck's face. But thanks, anyway." I drop the loincloth back in the box and gesture for him to get it off my table. "Try the Cedar-Sinai Ladies' Auxiliary. They give a receipt."

"Oh, tote that barge, lift that bale," he hums, hefting the box back up. "And to think two years of writing *Mondo Negro* would come to this."

"That's the breaks," I say, opening the front door.

"In iambic pentameter, yet."

"Listen, you want to be back in that little room in New Jersey, drinking your Spanish rotgut?"

"Not on yo life, Mama. Ise payin' my dues, Ise solin' my shoes, and if push come to shove I be singin' the blues. In the midnight hour. With all yo love tumblin' down. And I got a woman way cross town who rolls her jelly till the sun comes roun'. Amen, and can I get a witness?"

"Dear." I pat his cheek. "Hasn't anyone ever told you that brevity is wit?"

"Ah." He winks. "But embellishment is the quintessence of soul."

I begin to close the door.

"Say, listen, Lil?"

I open it again.

"Why don't we all go. Make it a party."

"Go where? What party?"

"That discotheque. You, me, Ronald, Gwynneth, your daughter? We could shake our proverbial booties."

"You'll shake yours maybe. I'll just wish I were home watching the eleven o'clock news."

"Come on. I owe you a night on the town."

Sure, sure. Him with his golf games and rhododendron, me with my house of the sequined loincloth. The family that plays together stays together.

"Well . . . ?" Edwin asks. "Shall we?"

I pause to think it over. "Edwin?" I finally ask. "In all the time you've known me, have I ever turned down something that's free?"

Thumping music is pumped out onto the sidewalk where young parking lot attendants jump around, zooming the Mercedes' and Porsches into the showcase lot next door.

"Jesus," I say, sheltering my eyes from the glare of the crisscrossing kliegs as I get out of the car, "if I knew they were redoing an old Metro premiere I'd have brought my dark glasses."

"And I'd have brought my Jean Harlow fox," Ronald says, helping Andi out. "Oh, *God*, darlings, will you get a load of this truckload of pansies? I haven't seen half of these old dolls since the glory-hole days at the old Santa Monica pier."

"The *what*?" I ask.

"Nothing, darling, nothing," he sighs. "Just scenes from my flaming youth."

"This'll be fun," Andi says. "I hardly ever get to discotheques in New York. Peter calls it seventies Muzak and he's, you know"—a great show of disdainful apology—"one of your typical prejudiced straights."

"Darling, I don't blame him one little bit." Ronald pats her arm reassuringly. "If I weren't in the fruitbowl myself, I'd keep as far away from it as I could get." She laughs, amused and relieved. "But, tonight," he goes on now—bidding us, with a little flourish, to link our arms in his—"*tonight* this old queen is gonna kick up his heels till his garters pop. Cause in six more days, when Gary moves in, it's off with the boogie boots and on with the apron."

"Six more days?" I say. "I'm surprised you haven't started clocking it backwards—in minutes."

"A *countdown*." He laughs. "Oh, I love it! She's talking like an aerospace bride already!"

"I am not." I pout at their mirth as, linked arm in arm, the three of us wend our way to the entrance through the crowd. And *what* a crowd. Shimmying young men giggling wildly while dressed for the front lines at Guadalcanal. Young Bel Air matrons in ripped T-shirts with razor blades around their necks and paper clips stuck through their ears. Nice Jewish boys gripping each other's shoulders and whispering "gross," "percentage," "option," while the sweet young things on their arms lick their lips a lot and glance around madly for the man they met at Hef's party last week who's casting the commercial for Earth Born Shampoo. Old queens disguised as Franchot Tone, young fags disguised as Daytona mechanics, and underfed groupies with eggplant-hued lips and platinum crewcuts, little engraved butterflies winking on their collarbones by the straps of their long satin nightgowns.

"Lillian Resnick," I announce to the young girl in the gold lamé jumpsuit who's bobbing to the music atop the high chrome stool at the door. "We're guests of Edwin Henderson."

"Oh, you're with Willy Gee, outa*sight!*" She peers through her yellow sun visor into the dark noisy room. "Rafael!" she calls.

A bright-faced young waiter, nude except for that spangled loincloth, appears and beckons us to follow him. I stare at his greased and glistening chest. If I just focus two inches above his navel, I can see well enough to put on my lipstick.

"What did he do?" I whisper to Ronald. "Take a bath in Turtle Wax?"

"Baby oil," Ronald whispers back. "The better to hold the pawprints with, my dear."

"Yeah? Well, in that case, I'm glad I didn't wear my mink."

I jolt against the barrage of music and blink against the strobes as we ribbon our way through the jammed room, ducking the gyrating dancers as we go. I keep bumping into the huge mirrored pillars, the gigantic palm fronds, the eight-foot-tall wicker cages filled with squawking parrots.

Our polyurethaned Roman waterboy finally leads us down an aisle of white chaise longues, each piled with lolling, slumping bodies. In the middle of the last one sits Edwin, a denimed patriarch flanked by his new cronies. To his left is LeeAnn DeFarr, balancing her two-story turban like Carmen Miranda's pineapple tray. (Ronald whispers: "And who do we have here, darling? The Nefertiti of Watts?") On his right: the blond hippie sound engineer in a MIDAS MUFFLERS T-shirt, sucking on a stick of marijuana with the ardor of a breastfeeding infant; and, next to him, two black men—one skinny, one fat—in identical ruffled body shirts, medallions clanking like cowbells around their necks.

"Greetings, love!" Edwin stands and kisses me. "Hello, Ronald." He nods. "Ah, and you must be Andrea." He extends a courtly hand.

"Yes." She smiles and shakes it. "I really like your show. I *love* old R&B." She sits down between Edwin and the sound engineer. "There was a piece in the *Voice* a while ago analyzing Curtis Mayfield's lyrics. How, you know, if you put them next to Dylan's . . ."

Oh, my dear daughter. Leave it to her to strike up a serious conversation in the most unlikely places.

And leave it to Gwynneth to come teetering over in her spiked-heel mules, singing along with that song that's been deafening us—"Oh, misery, oh, oh, cherchez la femme . . ." while shimmying her little bosoms out of her half-unbuttoned beachcomber shirt.

"Ooooh, hi, Lil, hi, Ronnie," she interrupts her Gallic translation to coo.

Ronald cocks back her sombrero and frowns. "You know, dear, we really *must* do something about that hatband mark. Unless you're pushing for a tattoo of the Equator."

"Oh, you." She pats her hat back in place, then whispers suggestively. "Hey, listen, I've got some dyyynamite Ritties. And some Ludwigs."

"Do I have to keep telling you? I'm on the wagon." Then to me: "It keeps the left side of her brain from rotting to think up nicknames for pills."

"That's what she's talking about?" I whisper back. "Pity. I thought maybe she'd gone straight."

"I only wish. You haven't met the latest one. Some phony old Transylvanian countess. I mean, talk about burnt-out old lessies? Honey, this one's the mother of them all. Where's Miss Dietrich tonight, dear?" he leans over to Gwynneth to ask. "Mounting her collection of horsehair whips, or biting some twelve-year-old's ankle?"

"Oona? She's up there dancing. We have like this real European relationship."

"Come again, dear?" I ask.

"Oh, like she's into the whole existential flow," she explains, rapturously Buddha-faced behind her sunglasses. "You know, like she's got her drift and I've got my drift and if they happen to connect, like rilly incredible, you know? But if not, that's cool, too. Catch you later type thing."

"Gwynneth." Edwin bends over and pats her knee. "Your eloquence is getting impossibly baroque. You really must stop reading Proust."

The sound engineer passes the dregs of his joint to Gwynneth, then leads Andi up to the dance floor. Gwynneth prongs the nub between her fingernails, then takes an orgiastic slurp. LeeAnn DeFarr, who's been casing the room, nudges Edwin and whispers: "I just saw my new Karmann Ghia walk in."

"Hmm?" He's puzzled.

"Two suckers from Capitol Records. Baby, get yo act together, you hear?" She gives him a big sisterly pat on the head, stands up and smooths the layers of that batik tourniquet she calls a dress, and leans in to smile her farewell. "Good vibes now." She winks. "Party hearty."

"Someone ought to tell that doll," Ronald mutters, "that Artra Skin Tone Cream splotches in artificial light."

"Why, Ronald," Edwin marvels, "how very astute of you, old boy."

"Well, *really*." Ronald's hands are on his hips. "I didn't go to cosmetology school on Adams and Crenshaw for *nothing*, you know."

Amos and Andy close in on Edwin now, their bodies throttling like idled engines.

"Man, you gotta hear it," the skinny one says. "I'm tellin' you, number one with *two* bullets."

"Is gonna turn platinum so fast gonna scratch up yo whole needle," the fat one picks up.

"Yo whole *box*."

"Azz right."

"What it is, what it is."

They slap each other's palms and double over in laughter.

"Sonny and Bubba are songwriters," Edwin explains. The two bend over and shake my hand, Ronald's hand, Gwynneth's hand as solemnly as guests in a receiving line. "They specialize in, shall we say, mobile technological abstractionism."

"Yeah, like we wrote 'Freeway to Your Heart,' " the skinny one offers. "The Ovations went gold with that."

"And 'Soul Locomotive' for the Invincibles."

"And 'I'm Takin' Off My Hard Hat at the Construction Site of Love' for the Dynamic Majestics."

I nudge Ronald. "And they said Cole Porter was dead."

"Okay," Edwin concedes. "Let's hear the new one."

The skinny one leans back and starts explaining. "Well, like we figure like with the economy hippin' up and all, folks is out spreadin' a little more coin than they used to."

"But they dowanna be burned or nothin', neither."

"Thazright. And that whole philosophy applies to the man-woman side of the spectrum of our spiritual endeavors, too. You dig what I'm layin' down, bro? You follow my swallow?"

Edwin nods wearily.

"So," the fat one says, as they both lean in, fingers poised to snap, "we got a . . ."

"*Close*-out!" they sing together. "Close-out! In the de-part-ment store of love. Shoo-wap-doo. Close-out! boom-boom-boom. Close-out! In the de-part-ment store of love."

"You've got a credit card to my de-vo-tion . . ." the skinny one warbles.

"In the ba-ar-gain basement of my-y e-mo-tions . . .": the fat one.

"Satisfaction guar-an-teeeeed . . ."

"Cause when you hand-del-in' my merchandise you'll know I aim to please. We got a . . ."

"*Close*-out! boom-boom-boom. Close-out! In the de-part-ment store of love. Shoo-wap-doo. Close out! boom-boom-boom. Close-out! In the de-part-ment store of love."

"Fire sale on my-y af-fec-tion . . ."

"Cost reduced on my good lov-in' pro-tec-tion . . ."

"Girl, you pulled the price tag on my soul . . ."

"And the cash register in my heart is ringin' out of control. We got a . . ."

"*Close*-out! boom-boom-boom. Close-out! In the de—"

"Okay, okay." Edwin throws up his hands. "Just send me the demo."

The two proceed to slap his back heartily and wrench his right arm into a series of complicated handshakes.

"Oh, darling, you *must* have them perform at Louis' next garden party," Ronald gushes, under his breath.

"I would. Except I don't think they know any old Gogi Grant tunes."

"So? Honey, at least they can make the barbecue sauce."

Amos and Andy disperse. Edwin goes off to join LeeAnn DeFarr across the room. And a bony, onyx-ringed hand comes slithering down Gwynneth's cheek. Smiling blissfully, she licks one of its fingers, then blows a kiss upward to the tuxedoed figure it's attached to.

"Lil, this is Oona," she says.

"Allo," the woman breathes in an ominous baritone while stabbing a cigarillo through some secret point of entry in her bank of anthracite hair. Then she blows the smoke out in three neat little O's, dips her face under the sombrero and blows the fourth O up Gwynneth's left nostril.

"Zees borce me," Oona hisses throatily to Gwynneth, the two of them huddled under the sombrero like Gene Kelly and Debbie Reynolds in *Singin' in the Rain*. "I hate ven you can how you say smell ugly pipple's svet. *Come.*" She crooks her pinkie through Gwynneth's hoop earring and stands her up. Gwynneth wiggles her fingers farewell. Ronald

sighs. "Oh, chàin chain chain," he sings. "Chain *of fools*.
Darling, there but for fortune . . ."

And we lean back and laugh wearily, two punch-drunk
prom chaperones viewing the puerile madness from the
wings.

"Look—there's Andi." I point to the spot on the dance
floor, smile at how her body stays taut and precise despite
the concerted abandon in her face. "I know. Don't tell me.
I'm a mother hen."

"*You* are? Honey, I *swear* I never thought I'd see the day
when I could stare at a coopful of hot little chickens and not
want to budge off my egg."

A bare-chested young waiter sets down the tray of drinks
Edwin ordered for us. Ronald picks up a glass. "To bliss,"
he sighs.

"Let's just make that . . . contentment," I amend, raising
another.

"God, darling," he starts in euphorically, "remember exactly one year ago? After your birthday party?"

"What do you mean *exactly* one year ago. I've got thirty-
nine more days left before I'm fifty-five and I'm going to
squeeze twenty-five hours out of every damn one of them."

"Yes, but remember how bitchy and miserable we were
then? Kvetching about how we'd never get out of our loneliness?"

"Hmm, I do. And how we were too neurotic to let anyone into our lives." I turn to him—suddenly, briefly buoyed.
"We *have* changed, haven't we?"

"Have we ever, darling. Have we ever. We were so off
the wall then we even talked about getting a beach house
together."

"Oh, God, that's right. Me as Anne Morrow Lindbergh
with the farkokta seashell collection."

"And me as your lisping beachboy, combing out your snarls at ebb tide. Oh, Lil, were we ever a scream!"

The music fades now from the cacophonic thumping to something with swirly violins. " 'Love's Theme!' " He claps his hands. "How oldy-but-goody." He turns to me formally and juts out his elbow. "Ginger?"

"Fred?"

And arm in arm we stand and work our way to a minuscule patch on the dance floor. Ronald does some rhumba-like foxtrot that I'm trying my damnedest to follow.

"The *hips*," he whispers. "Honey, shake your moneymaker."

"Like this?" I'm confused.

"Lil, this is the hustle, not the hora."

"Well, it doesn't help with you kicking my toes, for Christ's sake. You're scratching up my nail polish."

"Thank Gawwwd."

"What do you mean thank Gawwwd, damn it?"

"Lil, I don't quite know how to break it to you, but hot coral went out with Virginia Mayo."

"So what color should I get, then?"

"Just leave it to me." He pats my back as we clunk awkwardly among the gracefully synchronized couples. "Tomorrow we will go to my wholesale supplier and I will find you something *so fabulous* every matron in Tucson will turn positively avocado in envy."

"Yeah?"

"L'Oreal, I think. And we'll do your fingers, too."

"Oh, Ronald . . ." I smile up at him thankfully.

"The *hips*, Lil. Work your hips! I mean what do you think you are—a pogo stick?"

And as he shakes his head impatiently and as our knees

bang at all the wrong intervals and as the violins build to a lilting crescendo, I close my eyes to the perfectly mated bodies around us—and the strobes, and the palms, and the Turtle Waxed waiters and the parrots and all the craziness that how-in-God's-name-I-don't-know has somehow become my life.

And I lay my head on Ronald's shoulder and smile.

Andi's going back to New York tonight; I'm leaving for Tucson tomorrow. We pack together, side by side: our suitcases open on my bed, a mound of tissue paper and bottle of wine between us.

"Jesus, I feel like your college roommate," I say. "Who gets to keep the broken-down bookcase?"

"You can have it. But I get the Fillmore posters. And the marijuana plant."

"Ah, and I always thought you were so virtuous up there."

"Like hell you did."

And we laugh and sip our wine. (How come the easiest moments of every visit always come at the very end?)

"They'll mildew like that." I nod to the clump of just-rinsed lingerie she's wrapping in a roll of paper toweling.

"No they won't." She tucks them into her suitcase.

"You should've let the cleaning girl do them. She would have dried and folded them, too."

"Mom, the cleaning lady doesn't have to do *everything*, you know." She turns and sees me smiling. "What's so funny?"

"You with your laundry these past three weeks. Soaking, wringing, squeezing. And in that Indian shmatte, no less. I'd walk into the kitchen and think I was on the banks of the Ganges." I pause. "You know something? I'm really going to miss you."

"Oh, but I'll be back." She smiles with unthreatened generosity, then starts to pull at the stubborn zipper of her suitcase.

"I know you will." My smile lingers on her profile as she tugs. "Here. Let me." And I force the zipper around its halting rectangular course. "See? There are one or two things your old lady's still good for."

"There are lots of things," she says.

And that, too, comes at the end: the tribute-paying, the flattery. Partly her guilt at leaving, I guess. Partly her relief to be going back to her own life. And partly, as she told me the other day, the fact that she can appreciate me better when I'm 3,000 miles away. Only kids can say something like that with a straight face. God bless them their wonderful presumption that the bedroom's always waiting, the refrigerator's stocked, the love's undiminishable.

"*Voilà.*" Finished with her packing, she sits on the edge of my bed and pours herself a little more wine.

"We're like the tortoise and the hare," I say as I putz around, addled by the profusion of clothes I've taken out of my closet. Blouses, slacks, skirts piled all over each other on my chairs. Slippery in their cleaners' plastic, they keep sliding to the floor.

"Why don't you just take them out of those bags?" she asks, as I bend to pick a jersey off the carpet.

"Oh, because then they'll get creased in the suitcase." I pace around the room, counting combinations of pants and tops on my fingers, embarrassed at her seeing me so vain and confused, wondering if she can read it on my face: *It's been thirty years since I've packed to visit a man.*

"What about this?" I hold up a mint-green sundress I bought at Saks two summers ago.

"You don't need it."

"But it gives me a nice waistline." I press it against me and look in the mirror. "Then again, it's two years old." I lay it down. "But it could be very warm down there, and for the afternoon . . ." I pick it up again. "Oh, what am I doing, mumbling to myself. I'll ask Ronald." I lay down the dress and dial his number for the third time in an hour. And for the third time in an hour it's busy. "He must have taken the phone off the hook." I hang up. "Gary's moving some of his things in today. I guess they don't want to be disturbed. I'll ask him tomorrow when he comes to do my hair."

"Mom." Her voice is calm and serious. "Why don't you just put it back in the closet? You're taking too much already."

"Am I?"

"Sure. *Look* at all this. You're only going away for four days, you know."

"You're right. It looks like I'm making the Atlantic crossing. In 1905. Oh damn, and I wanted to give a kind of jaunty impression."

"Don't worry about the impression. Just go for comfort."

"*What* comfort? I don't know Louis well enough to be comfortable. I don't know these friends of his he keeps talking about. It's different at your age. You look great in everything. You just throw in a couple of T-shirts and you're set. But I've got to think about what I look best in, and what's appropriate, and—"

"Hey." She puts her hands on my shoulder and silences me with an almost maternal smile. "The sky won't cave in if you don't look as absolutely perfect as you want to. Don't get so heavy about it, okay?"

"Get a load of this!" I laugh nervously. "*You're* telling *me* not to get heavy?"

"Yes, *I'm* telling *you*." Her adamance forces me to attention. "Listen, all my life, whenever something was bothering me I'd play it out on you and you'd . . . you'd put it in perspective. You'd say *one* little thing, make *one* little crack that was like"—she casts around intensely for a way to put it—"like this hatpin in my big balloon of self-importance, of melodrama, of . . . *whatever*. Look, I know I resist your advice. I *do*. And I probably always will. But it sticks with me on some level, in case you didn't know."

"*Does* it? *Really?*"

"You're damn right it does," she says with a little smirk, broadly imitating my voice. "I mean *look* at this chozzarai!" She nods theatrically at my open suitcase. "You're just going to a little farkokta golf town, not to the Paris collections, for Christ's sake. This purse, that purse. You wanna spend the whole time chauffeuring your goddam lipstick? And all these shoes. Who do you think he invited down, a centipede?"

I smile and shake my head at her little performance. Whoever said imitation is the loveliest form of flattery was right. "Oh, Andi. You *are* fresh, my dear."

"Of course I am. I'm your daughter, aren't I?"

And when I lean in to hug her, she doesn't, for once, pull away.

An hour later, we drive up to the United loading zone. Andi gets out, summons a skycap with that wonderfully imperious flip of her arm, and while he takes her suitcase from the back seat, she leans through the car window. Awkwardly, hurriedly, we kiss good-bye.

"You've still got that hair in your eye, dear."

"And you've still got too much in your suitcase."

I pat her cheek and smile.

The skycap staples her baggage claim tags to her tickets, tells her what time, what gate. Avoiding my eyes, she leafs through her purse for his dollar tip, turns to follow him.

"Wait!" I call. "I almost forgot!" And as I stick my hand out the car window and press a check for $200 in her hand, she pouts just long enough for us both to start laughing. Then I open my mouth and jut my chin as if to—

"Mom, I've gotta go," she calls, and blows a grand impersonal kiss as she turns and saunters toward the terminal. I watch her click purposefully in those high-heeled boots of hers, her blazer flared out over the lovely, tight little fanny that protrudes from her pressed and tapered jeans; her back straight despite those two tote bags hanging from her shoulders, her stride even, her *New Yorker* and *Four-Gated City* tucked under her arm. She doesn't pause on the linoleum mat, as I would, waiting for the automatic doors to fully open before venturing further. Instead, she keeps walking, keeps walking, entering them at the precise moment they spring back to receive her. What is the age you stop believing the waters will part for you? Whatever it is, just give her five extra years of it—*please.*

Two cars honk impatiently behind me, but I don't budge until she's finally obscured from view in the ticket line. "Morty, you'd be proud," I hear myself saying as I shift into Drive. "However else we screwed up, we did okay where it counted. We really did okay."

The eight o'clock freeway traffic is heavy, but I feel peculiarly peaceful during the long, bumpy ride back. Home, I call my service. A message from Louis: "The ticket will be at American at 1:00. Looking forward." A message from Ronald: "Coming at 10. Wash it first." I try to call him, but his line is still busy. Ah, love. Ah, sublime domesticity.

I pour myself a brandy in some vague rite of celebration for whom—Ronald and Gary? Andi and me? Louis and me?— I don't know. I doze off in my chair, open my eyes, stumble into the bedroom, roll back the sheets, set the alarm clock and lay myself down.

❦

I fling the door open on Ronald's ring, ready for his rapture. "Well, if it isn't the merry . . . Ronald!" I'm shocked by his downcast eyes. *"What's the matter?"*

"Talk about egg on your face? Darling, say hello to a mushroom omelet."

"Gary?" My heart sinks.

"There's been a postponement."

I close my eyes for a second. "So that's why your phone was busy all night."

"We were talking a long time."

"Five goddam hours?"

"Nureyev must have knocked it off the hook afterward."

"And what were you doing that you didn't notice? Jesus, your pupils are the size of pinheads."

"So I took a couple of Ludes. Lil, I had to calm down."

"Oh, Ronald, *what happened?*"

"What happened," he sighs, sinking into the breakfast room chair, "is he spent a couple of days with his parents, and he started getting nervous covering himself. See, he thought he'd tell them he wasn't getting a phone for a while, until he could figure out a way of breaking it to them."

"They still don't know?"

He shakes his head. "But it's not his fault, *really*. He's told me about them. Straight as flagpoles, darling. And he's their only child. And the father had a heart attack five years ago."

"Well, Gary didn't give it to him. It's a father's job to accept his son. It's not Gary's—"

"I know, I know, but it's *not easy* for him. We've discussed it. Oh, Lil," he pleads, *"he's not bad."*

"I *know* that," I plead back. "He's *lovely.*"

"He always said, 'I never made the choice you made. I never closed that door behind me. You're braver than me, Ron.' " He laughs a sad, affectionate laugh. " 'Brave?' Can you believe it? I thought, *this* shivering nelly? But that's just it, Lil. He had a way of seeing me that made me feel maybe I'm not such an old ass after all."

"Of course you're not! And stop talking about him like he's dead. The thing with the parents will work itself out."

He shakes his head. "It's not just that. After he saw them, he had some introductory something-or-other with that new agency here—the one he was all set to work for? And they said something about the close 'social climate' of all the staff members and their 'spouses.' Don't you love it, darling? They really talk like that!" His little laugh fades. "But it made him more nervous. So he called the psychiatrist he used to see and made an appointment for 'crisis counseling.' He's telling me all this on the phone last night and I say, 'Gary, I don't want to know from social climates and crisis counseling and spouses. Fuck all that jargon! Do you love me or not?' "

"And . . ."

"He said, 'I don't know.' " For a heart-stopping second, he leaves it there. "And then he said, 'I mean, yes, I do, but I'm confused and I have to have a week just to think.' "

"See?" I rush right in with my bundle of frantic hope. "So it's *not* over, darling. He's just sorting out his feelings, that's all. Oh, that's *so* normal, Ronald. You know: the last-minute jitters . . . the storm before the calm . . . the last mile is the hardest . . . the—"

"Really, Lil, we must get you a job doing needlepoint samplers for Knotts Berry Farm."

"Okay, okay, but they're clichés because they're *true*. Listen, did I ever tell you about the night before Morty and I got married? Honestly, he was so edgy, I thought—"

"Thanks, dear"—he cuts me off with a grim little smile—"but no. He wants out. I can feel it, Lil. I can feel it all the way down in my queer little bones. If I weren't such a damn fool, I'd have let myself see it a week ago. But no, this old gelding just couldn't take his blinders off."

"Ronald, *don't*."

"We'd be talking on the phone and I'd ask him, 'Should we rent a U-haul or can you get everything in your car?' 'Did you file the change of address card with the post office?' 'Should I pick up a desk chair for you?' And the way he answered . . ." He shakes his head. "Honey, those feet were so cold, you could taste the ice through the telephone wire. That voice was so full of guilt he didn't know if he was coming or going. But I let myself pretend it was just his naiveté, just his awkwardness. I couldn't face the truth, Lil. I *didn't want* to face it!"

"So you let yourself assume the best for a change. Is that so shameful? Is that such a crime? I remember when you never allowed yourself *any* hope, when you wrote yourself off as so worthless that every affair was a joke on yourself before it even started. I mean, *look* at you now! You've finally gotten yourself to a point where you *expect* things to work, where you know what you deserve and—"

"Darling, please. Spare me the consolation prize. My poor nerves can't take it right now."

"But I *mean* it. I'm not just saying it to humor you."

"I know you're not." He pats my hand gratefully.

"And it's *not over.*"

He nods wanly. "It's not over," he recites. Then he sighs grandly. "Oh, why wasn't I born with Aretha's voice, darling? I could sing the blues for days." He glances at his watch. "Well, enough of this." He picks up his satchel and stands. "Shall we?"

"Relax a minute." I beckon him to sit down again. "Let me make you some coffee."

"Nah. My stomach's a wreck as it is."

"Some soft scrambled eggs, then."

"Lil, *come on.* We don't have all day. You've got a one-thirty plane."

"Oh, the hell with the plane."

"*What* did you say?"

"I said the hell with the plane. I can always catch a later one."

"Sure, and flush one of the most important days of your life down the toilet so you can suffer along with me? Well, no thank you, darling. I'm not buying any of it. That's just a pissy excuse and *you know it.* You want to keep yourself down, Lil? You want to keep yourself lonely? Well, go ahead, darling, but don't you use me as an alibi. I'll ask you something *you* asked *me* once. You said, 'Ronald, are we in love with our own misery?' Well, pet, if these last six months have taught me anything, they've taught me that I can live very well without that particular love affair. And you can, too. Now we are standing right up." He pulls me up. "And we are sitting our little tush on the bathroom stool." He pushes me down the hall. "And we are going to comb through this wet little birdsnest here . . . and trim you . . . and set you . . . and cook up your rollers." He sits me down in front of the mirror. "And you are going to forget every word of this conversation . . . and get your hot little bod on that plane . . . and shimmy off that ramp at Tucson like Ann Miller greeting the troops in Korea. With fireworks, darling, with—" He frowns as he fingers my hair. "Oh, God, Lil. Don't I always tell you: *creme rinse?*"

"You always tell me creme rinse."

"And don't I always say towel drying just tangles it up?"

"You always say towel drying just tangles it up."

"And will you for God's sake use that number-seven comb I stole for you out of the goodness of my heart?"

"Such a martyr." I smile as he flaps out the plastic cape and tucks it around my neck. "Suuuuch a martyr."

An hour later, I stand still, as ordered, while he circles me slowly, pulling and tucking at my clothes, dabbing my makeup and hair.

"I feel like a store window dummy on changing day."

"Well, at least now it's Magnin's, darling. That dowdy old thing you wanted to wear was pure House of Nine."

"My dear, I'll have you know I bought it at a very expensive boutique."

"I can't leave you alone for a minute, can I? Oh, damn. Close your eyes a second." I obey, and with a licked pinkie he leans in to rub away a smudge. "I swear, one of these days we are going to *have* to find you a greaseless moisturizer. Now open."

I open. He does a little more dabbing. *"Finito!"* He stands back and nods at his work, then steers me to the closet and opens the mirrored door. "Now is that fabulous or is that fabulous?"

"Oh, *Ronald*." I turn from side to side, admiring what

I see. "You're a love." I turn and blow him a little kiss as he bends to pick up my suitcases.

"God, darling, what do you have in here, barbells?"

"I know, I know. I'm taking too much. Here, let me—"

"And wrinkle up that hot little outfit? Not on your life."

So I walk ahead of him and open the front door. He lumbers down the steps with the suitcases, slides them into the back seat of my car. I'll have them ticketed into baggage before I park in the American daily-rates lot.

I go back inside for my purse and sunglasses, turn off the lights, write Louis' number for Sima and leave it by the breakfast room phone. I feel a strange sense of finality as the front door clicks locked behind me.

"You're sure you're okay?" I ask, gripping his hand as he opens the driver's side door for me.

"Of course, darling."

"You've got Louis' number. If you feel like just talking . . ."

"Lil, I am going to be fine. *Just fine.* Now don't forget what I said about the electric rollers. Two on each side for ten minutes and you'll positively sparkle."

"I wish I could believe it."

"Come on, Lil, you'll knock 'em dead."

"That's not what I'm referring to."

"Will you *stop* worrying about me? I mean, darling, I've got so much to do these next few days, I don't even have *time* to be upset. I've got to send Raulito his Easter present, I've got to cut back my plants, I've got to dye back this absolutely dreadful henna job that Jackie Stein got on Monday, I've got—" He sees me smiling at his bravado.

"Okay," I say. "I'm convinced."

"Now you just go on out there and"—wiggling his fingers—"*rip* it *up*, sweetheart. *Shine* it *on*. Give it all you've got."

He leans through the window to kiss me, and before I can say anything else, he walks back to his car. We start up our motors together. I idle mine for a minute, as if waiting for something. But he makes a sharp U and is off in the opposite direction. So I pull the emergency brake and start slowly down the street—toward Olympic, and the freeway, and the airport.

10

HE IS, OF COURSE, THE PICTURE OF THE CHARMING HOST—
right there at the gate with a kiss on the cheek and a full
itinerary of carefully chosen plans.

"I thought we'd take a quick tour of downtown," he says,
as we walk down the tiled airport floor, "then get a little
lunch at the Tambo de Cobre at the Marriott. It's a beautiful new place. Then we'll get you home and unpacked.
Unless you'd rather do that first."

"Oh, no, no." I'm not used to him being quite this deci-
sive. "I'd love to see downtown."

"We'll be having dinner with Walt and Fran tonight.
And tomorrow I thought we could either see the brand-new
art museum—they've got a fine collection of pre-Columbian—
or go off to Tombstone."

"Tombstone?"

"Wyatt Earp's old town." He smiles. "Can't take a trip down to Tucson without seeing the genuine article. I think you'll get a kick out of it."

"Oh, I'm sure I will," I manage. Is it his fault that he's never had to endure all those tedious press parties at the Warners and Twentieth lots where they slopped out "chuck-wagon" buffets of gristly roast beef and inedible chili which, to make matters worse, you had to digest while staring at posters of Lorne Greene's face?

"I'm glad you're here," he says, holding the car door open.

"I am, too," I say, with an automatic smile.

Strapped into our shoulder belts (it's one of those cars that won't start otherwise; a big four-door with green interior), we drive up and down the streets. I squint against the sun, strain against the strap, and nod at all the examples of historic architecture he's pointing out. Later, at the restaurant, we each set down our menus, lean back in our chairs and smile a little too heartily into the void of four days that stretches before us. The silence lasts a beat too long, and just as I'm about to ask if he's heard from his daughter since her honeymoon, he asks: "How was your daughter's visit?"

Perhaps if I'd gotten a little more of my wine down, I could make a joke of our awkwardness. But right now I can't seem to find the ease, and it's too risky after not seeing each other in four weeks. So I plunge instead into a cheerful summary of my time with Andi, ending with all those fond, parental musings that give us a chance to act warm and conspiring. "You know how it is. They go to all that trouble to convince you they've become so sophisticated, but you can see through them like an X-ray."

He nods and smiles. "Isn't that the truth."

"And they have this wonderful, cocky resistance to you

until the very end, when all of a sudden they lay the roses at your feet!"

He nods and chuckles again.

And so it goes, around and around that familiar track: my voice a little too bright, his agreement a little too ready, our collusion a little too frantic, too warm. I want, suddenly, to bolt off that course and be myself with this man: to laugh and tell him about my ridiculous nervousness in packing for him, my worries about his married friends. I want him to know about the *other* people in my life—we're doing Andi to death, poor girl; there's nothing left to say about her, short of pulling out home movies—but how can I tell him about Ronald and Gary and Gwynneth and Edwin without apology, without translation?

Well, perhaps later.

"How's the chicken?" he asks.

"Delicious. The veal?"

"Excellent." He makes that little A-OK sign with his fingers. I smile at him and mean it.

All right, all right. When we reach his house we'll be able to relax.

"Just my little home on the range." He sets my luggage down inside the front door. "But I kind of like it."

"Oh, no *wonder*," I say, walking around carefully among the early American couches, the coffee tables full of quaint . . . bric-a-brac, I think you call it. "It's lovely." My voice is intimidated into a polite serenity, for here is the museum of his marriage: a family's haven, so burnished and muted and snug I expect to find Norman Rockwell's signature on the wallpaper.

"Come," he says quickly, "let's go where it's light." And he leads me through to the next room: an airy, plant-filled sun porch. "This is the room I just added on last year."

"Well, you did it very nicely," I say, touched by the room's effort at sprightliness—the fake-Italian tile, the pre-framed posters chosen for their huge bursts of red and yellow—and even more touched by the alien sleekness of the furniture: the wood stereo cabinet, the glass-top tables, the canvas director's chairs. For an instant, I picture this sentimental man flustered in some modern furniture showroom: blinking under the track lights amidst the young couples and sports-car-driving bachelors, picking the first thing the fast-talking salesman suggests.

The image makes him seem vulnerable all over again; it sends a bolt of affection through me. "This is so different" —I turn to him—"from the living room."

"Yes." He smiles proudly. "The kids saw to that. Great little interior decorators, my daughters."

"They chose the furniture?"

"Most of it. I contributed my veto power. And"—he smiles —"my John Hancock, of course."

"Of course." I force a little laugh. "Oh, look, *there* it is." I nod out the glass, over-eager with remembrance. "Your famous hammock."

"Yes, yes." We both smile. "Famous indeed."

He clasps his arm around my shoulder briefly, as if to celebrate the striking of a chord. Then he releases it and asks: "How about a drink?"

"Another? Oh, what the hell. I'm on vacation."

"Attagirl." He winks. "Might also not hurt to work up an appetite for dinner. Fran's an excellent cook." I follow him down a short hall. "She took one of those Cordon Bleu courses a while back."

"Did she?" This time the laugh is involuntary. "You mean where they monitor the oregano charts like electrocardiograms? Oh, I think that's so . . . nice." I gulp back my little blasphemy as I enter the large, cheerful kitchen. "To have a specialty like that." Peg left her reverence for cooking in the form of shelvesful of pewter and crockery and God knows what, kettles and cake plates and cookie jars: all obviously unused now but displayed here like totems in a shrine.

He pours the vodka first into a marked shot glass, then into two tumblers of ice. He neatly quarters a lime. I try to make myself comfortable leaning against stretches of counter and woodwork. I light a cigarette and cast around for an ashtray.

"Oh, here." He reaches up to a high shelf and hands me a little dish. "I'm sorry." Then he hands me my drink; we raise our glasses. "Cheers." And I realize that his smile—that same smile that always looked so wistful and yearning to me in my house—looks very different here: composed, almost self-satisfied.

"Let me show you my garden," he says now. And we walk quietly out: he with his shears, me with the cigarette in one hand, the ashtray in the other. Every few steps we pause while he explains the strain of each bud threaded to its slender pole and does a little snipping. I nod in hopefully convincing interest, as pious as a visitor on a surgeon's hospital rounds.

"These zinnias are hardy little fellows," he notes, "but the cabbage roses are something else. Got to watch them in this climate."

"My God," I say, dismissing anything saltier, "you could write a horticulture dictionary."

"Afraid not. I'm still a rank amateur."

"Another one of your self-improvement schemes?" I try to make it light.

"Well, no, not exactly. More or less an inheritance, you might say."

And I suddenly remember all that talk about *Peg's* garden.

Jesus, I feel like I'm walking on eggshells—in cleats.

He must read the discomfort on my face. "So much for the grand tour. Let's get you your drink."

"They're wonderful," I say, smiling up from the patio chaise and making a wide arc with my arm when he returns, glass in hand. "The mountains."

"Aren't they?" He takes a deep breath and turns a ceremonial half circle, the settler surveying his domain. "They become part of your life after a while. Like air and water. Something you can't do without."

"I'll bet." I smile, as genuinely touched by his romanticism as I was that first night when he looked up at the stars in the Chart House parking lot. But more than that, relieved, somehow, by his weddedness to this land.

Evening comes and we arrive at the split-level ranch home of Walt and Fran. I can tell she's trouble: one of those country club climbers who do their damnedest to look like Nancy Reagan; whose smug, precise little smiles never let you doubt for a minute that somewhere in back of her eyes she's computing your social quotient. Their home is one of those desperately proper mixes of antique and contemporary. (Showing me around, she uses the word "eclectic" three times in ten minutes.) The market value of two big paintings of fox hunts is announced by a squadron of specially attached lights, and little ashtrays that say The St. Francis, San Francisco, and Palmer House, Chicago, are positioned on the coffee table with such casual exactitude you can almost see the chalk marks underneath.

He, Walt, is a big, square-built man utterly unblemished by wit. His conversational forte seems to be numbers, as a matter of fact. He sits there in his plaid pants and cardigan sweater, laconically reeling off golf scores, scotch proofs, commodities futures and the precise measurements of their brand-new Jacuzzi—a Dow Jones machine dressed up as Perry Como.

She's the embellisher of the pair. "And not only *that* . . ." "And wouldn't you know . . ." "Dear, tell them about the man who came to *repair* it . . . ": her chirping annotations terminated with a succinct little pursing of her mouth, as if she's blotting her lipstick on Kleenex. She seems particularly fond of turquoise jewelry, clumps of which she displays, like war medals, against her white caftan and aggressively tanned skin.

"What a lovely necklace," I finally say.

"Why, thank you." She smiles down on it with such ornate innuendo you'd think she'd personally grunted each stone out of her womb. "Our women's group is working with indigenous artisans," she explains, leaning back on the couch expansively. "We've just opened a little charity boutique called Sunshine House. Jewelry, Kachina dolls, the *most* amusing little potholders and whisk brooms. I *must* take you down there. That's a definite."

Oh, God, must it be? But I smile my interest.

"This little candy dish, for example"—she points proudly with her chin—"was done by a young mestizo girl who had a rather unfortunate drinking problem before we started her in the crafts program."

"How nice." I nod admiringly. She smiles fondly. "And these?" I point daringly to some glazed ceramic eggs. "These are also . . . indigenous?"

"Why, no." Her neck muscles tighten to hold up the melting smile. "Those are Fabergé."

After dinner, while the men talk shop (he's in aerospace too, it turns out), I follow her into her kitchen and she floods the gully of her distrust of me with a torrent of information about local stables' cantering tracks, local department stores' designer departments, and local cacti's ability to withstand the humidity of being positioned on the window ledge above the new Jacuzzi. This last little discovery is presented dramatically, between cryptic pauses while she puts away the napkin rings. Turns out she's an amateur florist, too. Where the hell am I, anyway—Tucson or Kyoto?

"Do you garden?" she looks up and asks.

"No," I answer. "Unless you count a couple of philodendron I picked up at Safeway."

"Oh. They are such nice, *easy* plants. Amusing, really."

"Aren't they, though? All you have to do is spit on them once in a while and they grow." For a second she regards this as a literal statement; then her tight mouth eases into a vague little smile. "Metaphorically speaking," I hasten to add.

And I am back in her graces enough for her to confide that it's supermarket whipped cream she's serving on the chocolate mousse tonight. "You know how it is." She smiles coyly. "Once in a while you cheat."

"That's what I always say," I hum as I help her load the coffee cups on the silver tray. "Cheating is *awfully* amusing."

"They're very nice," I say to Louis as we get into his car. I feel a little guilty for the cheapness of that lie, as if it implicates him in the condescension, which is something I don't want to do.

He pauses for a moment; then, judging me to be sincere, says: "I'm glad you think so. Walt and I go back . . . Lord, years."

Lord years. Is that something like light years? No, no. Playfulness is too chancy now. You don't compound deceit with affection. So I simply ask: "Was he at Lockheed, too?"

"Hughes. We had a kind of . . . uneasy friendship in Los Angeles." My hope picks up. Perhaps he and Peg shared my take on them? "And then they moved out here—first he was allied with Honeywell in Phoenix; then he made the switch to consulting—and they kind of discovered the area for us. We became closer. You know how it is."

I nod and smile, moved by his desire to explain, to qualify, to want me to understand. Friendships with couples are always imperfect; you take what's there. Anyway, I can't judge Louis by his friends. He's not yoked to them, for God's sake.

Yet why—I wonder, as he clicks on the classical station —why can't I get away from the thought that he's still so yoked to his wife?

The rest of the drive home is filled with shuffling small talk: a smokescreen for our preoccupied thoughts with the question of sleeping arrangements. He had a guest room made up for me—an expected civility in a three-bedroom house, especially when you've got a nosy housekeeper. (And what housekeeper isn't?) It lets us both off the hook, of course. It also rules out nothing. And as we sit staring ahead in the car, the delicate quandary is as unremarked on as the U. of Arizona parking sticker on the windshield—and several times as visible.

Kids have it so much easier. They *discuss* the damn thing. They come right out with it, spitting lust and rejection at one another as if they were merely words. But we're from another time. So we hide graciously behind a conversation about Bach, about whom I know nothing more than that my daughter once played some exercise of his at a second-grade piano recital; and about whom he knows not much more than what the classical record club tells him. Oh, the sweet, labored valiance of it all.

He flicks on the living room lights as we enter the house, and the sanctity of his transported La Cañada life shrinks what intimacy we have. Probably a hotel would have been better, now that I think of it. Against its temporariness, its sterility, its absence of history, we could at least be large to each other, be equal. But here he is the host—worse, the widower. And I am the guest: the polite, potential devirginer of his past.

If that is what I can be.

If that is what I want.

I sit on the plump, cushioned couch. He sets two half-filled brandy snifters on coasters in front of us.

"This is delicious," I say. "What is it?"

"Blackberry brandy."

"Ah, like those . . . little berries you popped into your mouth as a kid."

"Yes, yes, that's right." He chuckles. And I suddenly remember it was *blue*berries he talked about. But blue, black, what difference. We are grasping now, anyway.

More small talk. Flowing in the way it flowed on our three previous dates: a little rushed, a little false, a little sorrowful. But only now do I see it as that.

"God, I'm tired," I finally say. Then I laugh. "Shows you what a great traveler I am, I can get jet lag on a ninety-minute flight."

"Perfectly natural," he says—warmly, evenly—"if you haven't flown in a while."

I wink, just as he would. "Is that your . . . prognosis?"

"You bet." He picks up the ball in all ten anxious fingers. "When someone tells me I remind them of a country doctor, I don't"—he casts around for a jaunty way to put it—"I don't fool around."

And I smile. And he smiles. Are we both smiling at the same thing: at two perfectly nice, middle-aged people trying to rescue their timidity—their ambivalence—with merry snatches of past repartee? Trying to cover the discomfort in finding they have so little to really say to each other? Trying to cover the fact itself?

His smile turns into a look of tender, tentative gravity. I would fly against this house, this past and take you—that look says. It would be the first time here, the first time since.

I close my eyes briefly, in appreciation of his silent offer. But it's more than I can take from him. And more than I can honestly give.

He kneels by the air conditioner in the guest room a few minutes later, adjusting the knobs. "There we go." He stands. "That should be just right."

"Oh, *thank* you," I say, awkward with guilt. "I'm sorry to be conking out on you like this, but I'm just . . . *exhausted*." I take a little sip of air, ready to broach the truth that stands like a presence between us, but his warm smile and quick clasp of my hand assure me that we might spare ourselves, especially at this hour. "I may just putter around a bit in the living room before turning in," he says. "But you'll be able to sleep. I'm a fairly quiet putterer."

As I awake the next morning to the sounds of him moving around in the kitchen, I know we will have to discuss it. But when? And how? *He* certainly won't bring it up; he's invited me here for four days. And I? How can I play spoiler to his hospitality? And how do I even *say* it without sounding presumptuous, ungrateful, childishly frank? "Louis, I think we're trying for something that doesn't exist"? "Louis, let's be honest with each other"? "Louis, let's sit down and talk"?

"Louis?" My voice is as high as a schoolgirl's. He is breaking eggs in a bowl as I enter the kitchen.

"Good morning." He turns, suffused with a cheer that shatters my little speech. "Did you sleep all right?"

"Like a baby."

"To coin a phrase."

"Exactly. Listen, what are vacations for if not to bring out the profundity in you?"

"I agree." We share a little laugh. "I quite agree."

I sit down at the table and pick up a bulky newspaper. The *Arizona Daily Star*.

"It's not a bad paper," Louis says. "Some rather good columnists. I saved you the crossword, in case you're a buff."

"It's all yours," I say. "I usually quit after a three-letter word meaning housepet."

He chuckles and turns back to his eggs, and I let the morning's exchange of easy warmth mushroom inside me. Sunday. The smell of fresh coffee, a big fat paper you can loll about all day with, a man standing here *making me* eggs—a man I can banter with, after all. You're giving this up, Lil? You're throwing it away? Sunday with a man, goddammit! How many years has it been?

So we don't have exactly the same sensibility, the same background. Is that the worst thing in the world? Maybe it's a relief. You're spared the bother with the intensity, that awful grappling to make the man your twin. So you screen out more. Is that so awful? You screen out, you tune out, you laugh once in a while when you normally wouldn't, you accept the imperfect volley as part of the game.

"I thought we might go to Tombstone today."

"Great." I smile, wide with new resolve. "Sounds wonderful."

"Then we've got another dinner engagement, if you don't mind."

"Oh, no, I don't mind. Not at all."

He sets the two plates of eggs on the table. "Just a little kitchen-sink omelet I work up once in a while. I hope you like ham and green onions."

"Oh, I do."

"It won't win any prizes." He ladles it out. "Except maybe an A for effort."

"Well, maybe that's the most important one," I say, thinking about our own efforts here.

I check his face to see if he understands. But, no, he is wearing that composed, satisfied look as he lifts the forkful to his mouth. The part of his plate denuded of eggs shows a rooster's crown; the little spiked sun in the distance is covered with a dollop of jam.

We spend the early afternoon inspecting "The Town Too Tough to Die": wending in and out of the Wyatt Earp Museum, the Bird Cage Theater, the Crystal Palace Saloon. We stop at a souvenirs stand and I rifle through the postcard rack. I pick up a colored glossy of a macho young cowboy in spiked boots, squinting under a ten-gallon hat. "Ten cents a dance, but the lasso is extra," I write on the back. "(Don't say I never do you any favors, darling.)"

"Dropping a line to your daughter?" he asks pleasantly.

"No. It's to my best friend." I pause. Perhaps this is as good a time as any to bring it up, to let him know a little something about my life. "He's also my hairdresser."

"You mean they're replacing diamonds?" He smiles.

"Pardon?"

"As a gal's best friend."

"Oh." I force a little laugh. "Yes. Well, you might say that."

"Shall we get on to Grace and Roy's now?" he asks, after a moment. "Knowing them, they're breaking out the cocktails already."

"Yes. Let's." I tuck the postcard into my purse. "I wouldn't mind a drink at all."

"They're a little more . . . well, outgoing, you might say,

than Walt and Fran." We are walking from the car to their sprawling adobe-esque villa. "They're locals. He's a big land developer. Self-made man, more or less. What they don't have in sophistication, they make up with heart."

Well, that they certainly have. Roy opens the door—Western string tie over a short-sleeve shirt, a barbecue apron that says EL JEFE tied around his waist—and pumps my hand vigorously as we're introduced. "So glad you finally brought her by, Lou." Big arm around Louis' shoulder. Then, back to me: "How do you like it down here. God's little acre, i'nit? Ever seen such beautiful country? Grace'll be out in a minute, then we'll fix you kids up with a drink and shoo you on outside. There is one *heck* of a beautiful sunset coming up right about now."

"Hellooooo." A large, effusive woman comes rustling across the terra cotta floor in white ruffled blouse and long plaid hostess skirt, smiling all the way and managing somehow to resemble a slightly inebriated quail on its way to a square dance. "Lillian, it is *so* nice to meet you!" She hugs me to her feathered breast.

Then, while the men go out back, she flittingly bids me follow her through a long entryway—its wall groaning with arched mounted trout, huge framed maps and crossed Spanish swords—and into a huge kitchen (I've spent more goddam time in kitchens in the last 30 hours than I usually do in a week) where a stoop-shouldered young Mexican girl stands basting steak with barbecue sauce.

"I understand you're a writer!" Grace pops open the liquor cabinet on this zesty note.

"Well, that's stretching it a bit. I'm a publicist, actually. I—"

"What'll it be?" she demands with magnanimous cheer.

"Oh." I gaze at the bottles. "Scotch will be fine."

"I'm sorry." She's pouring. "You were saying . . ."

"Oh. Nothing, really. Just that I'm a publicist. It's not the same thing as a—"

"Say when!"

"Oh, that's *plenty*, thanks." She's already given me a double shot.

"You know," she says now, pouring herself a hefty one, "I do a little writing myself."

"Do you?" I manage to inquire.

She nods gravely. "Poems. Peg did, too, as I'm sure Lou's told you."

To make matters easier, I nod my head yes.

"Of course hers were better than mine. She did some writing for Goldwater's so she had more of a professional hook into things. I'm just a homemaker, essentially."

"There's nothing wrong with that."

"Oh, yes, there is," she says, after a long swallow. "The kids grow up and leave you. We have three. Lou's probably told you. Almost the same age as his. We got friendly through our middle daughters." Well, that's a consolation. "One, two, three, they leave. Like . . . like dominoes falling." For a second, I'm afraid she's going to jot that one down, but her long, contemplative look suffices. "Not that I'm not happy for them. I couldn't be happier! But it leaves you with all kinds of time on your hands. Carmen, *un poco mas salsa.*" The Mexican girl nods. "It leaves you with all kinds of time on your hands and you kind of wish you'd applied yourself earlier, taken the big leap, as it were." She turns to me suddenly. "Have you ever read Edna St. Vincent Millay?"

"Not in years, no."

"Peg always said, 'Try doing something. Give it a whirl.' She was a real go-get-'em girl. Always had a project. I'm more introspective, more concerned with inner things." Yes, like the inside of that glass. "Could I ask you . . . Would you mind taking a look at them?"

"Pardon?"

"My poems."

"Oh. Yes. Of course."

She rustles out of the room, comes back quickly with a flowered loose-leaf binder from which the indices SOUPS, DESSERTS, MAIN COURSES have been removed. "You . . . are . . . a . . . dear," she says, shuffling busily through the pages. "Of course they have to be typed first. I'm getting myself a little Smith-Corona electric. Do you know *The Writer* magazine?" She doesn't look up for an answer. "I find it awfully valuable. They have a long, long list of markets. Here." She clamps open the rings. "You're *sure* you don't mind?"

"I don't mind."

I reach for the piece of paper she hands me, but she doesn't let it go. "This one isn't exactly polished," she explains. I nod. "And the places where there are question marks in pencil, just disregard them." I nod. She releases the paper. *Thoughts*, I begin to read the flourishing longhand. "I do want to trim them down a bit, but I understand that you really should let the first draft stand for a while first." I nod again. I start again. *Thoughts*. "And, please, you can be perfectly honest." I smile long and reassuringly into her desperate, guileless face.

Thoughts

> Thoughts
> on a winter's (wintry?) morning
> ~~of the new day dawning~~
> Betwixt (?) the past and the present
> The yesterdays
> and tomorrows

of
  my
    life

Thoughts
of the day unrolling
and the bluebirds strolling (?)
on the window ledge
So free from care and strife

Thoughts
of my life in chapters
Pages ever turning
turning
  slowly
    turning
Held (Bound?) by true love's glue

Thoughts
taking off on wings, dear
soaring through the clouds, dear
Flying straight
  to
    you

"Well," I manage, "you seem to have a definite sense of
rhythm."

"You really think so? I'm *so* relieved. You don't think the
rhymes get in the way? I read somewhere you shouldn't have
rhymes and blank verse in the same poem."

"Well, I think that's"—her desperate eagerness allows me
no less—"at the discretion of the artist."

"Oh, I'm so glad you said that. Actually, I'm very insecure about these." She leafs through the book again, un-
clamps a page, pauses, clamps it closed again. "Well, I won't
bother you with them now. You've been *so* nice, *really*.

Let's go outside and join the fellows. Now," she says, escorting me outside, "*tell* me about *you*. You have a daughter, I understand. You know, I have *always* admired women who could manage motherhood and work at the same time. Barbara Walters, for example. Now *there* is a supergal. Do you know her, by any chance?"

And so it goes for the next hour. She babbles on incessantly, her plaintive gaiety rising with each drink. Meanwhile, El Jefe spends great amounts of energy stoking the barbecue flames and asking if I've ever seen mountains quite so purple, steaks quite so juicy, guacamole quite so rich. When I close my eyes I could swear I am listening to every Cal Worthington Dodge commercial ever made.

And I am closing my eyes a lot—a few seconds at a time, for relief. And I am bracing myself with drink after drink. Louis knows something's wrong. His face wears a look of quiet, dignified regret. It's not you! I want to say to him. It's not your fault. It's not even their faults, these ridiculous people. It's nobody's fault.

"Carmen!" Grace calls. "*Vamos a comer. Hagamos la mesa!*" Then she follows the Mexican girl back into the house, the quail after the Chihuahua. Roy stands across the patio, turning the steaks on the grill with the pride of a football coach prepping his stars before the last quarter.

Louis and I are alone under the string of hanging lanterns. "Are you all right?" he asks.

"Yes, yes." That schoolgirl octave again.

"They can be a little overpowering," he begins.

"Don't apologize. Really, it's fine." *It's not solicitude I need now, but laughter.* Oh, he is charming, he is genteel, he is considerate, he has made me feel like a woman again in a way that may never leave me. He is all of those things— *really!*—all of those things. And, damn it, he is so very very impossible for me to be myself with.

"The two of them helped me through a difficult time," he explains.

"I *believe* it. I can appreciate that."

"They mean well."

"Oh, I know, I know."

"You're sure you're all right?"

"I'm sure."

"You are sure?"

"I'm positive. Really. Please don't worry."

We stop for a moment, our mouths half open, each preparing the next reassurance, the next little Japanese doll nod. We notice the effort together. It is probably the first truly mutual moment we've had since I've been here.

"You're smiling," he says. "What's so funny." But it isn't a question at all.

So I answer with all the tenderness that irony deserves. "Oh, Louis, we are so polite."

And the looks we exchange are as healing as they are mournful, telegraphing every sentence that went carefully unsaid the last day and a half.

"I'm so sorry, Lil," he finally says, softly.

"So am I. Really. So am I."

I ring Ronald's doorbell at twenty of twelve the next morning: my bags in the back of my car; my eight attempts at phoning him from both airports foiled by that busy signal again.

"Who is it?" he calls out in a cranky voice.

"The mailman. The Avon Lady. Russ Tamblyn, for crying out loud. Will you open the goddam door?"

The chains clank, the lock tumbles noisily and he stands blinking puffy-eyed in the doorway, his plaid Bill Blass pajamas hanging wrinkled from shoulders to feet.

I don't think I've ever been so happy to see him.

"What the fuck? God*dam*mit, Lil, you're supposed to be—"

"Supposed to be what?" I ask calmly. "Supposed to be turning myself into someone I'm not? Supposed to stay there two more days just to keep up a sweet, polite charade? No, darling. He's got too much integrity for that. And so do I."

He closes his eyes and shakes his head bitterly. "Look at the two of us, will you?"

"*Yes*, look at the two of us! We did every damn thing we could do. We *tried*. Don't you see?"

" 'Don't I see.' You know what I see? I see a tired old faggot who just lost the best thing he ever had. And I see a fabulous woman who *stupidly* threw away her chance for—"

"Look, dear, I did not come all the way over here to listen to this self-pitying crap. Now are you going to ask me in for a cup of coffee, for Christ's sake, or do I just stand here on your doorstep another twenty minutes making like a goddam Jehovah's Witness?"

"Oh, would that you could be. I swear, if anybody needs salvation right now . . ."

"Well, I can't help you with that, but will this do?" I reach into my purse. "I was going to mail it to you. I forgot."

He stares indifferently at the front of the postcard. Then he turns it over and reads what I wrote. The trace of a smile fights its way onto his bleary face. "Oh, how *fabulous* of you, darling," he finally says. "You *know* how much I always wanted to be Annie Oakley. And to *think*," he sighs, "I thought I'd never get a chance to wear my calico bonnet again."

"Now you're talking. *Now* you're talking, darling."

And I smile as I rumple his hair and follow him into the house.

11

SOME BIRTHDAYS YOU CAN IGNORE, EVADE, EVEN INVERT IN YOUR mind. But not the one yesterday. I mean, what can you do with 55? You turn the goddam numbers around, it's no different. You turn them upside down, you still can't get out of it. It reminds me of when I was in the hospital after my hysterectomy and the orderly wheeled in my dinner tray. Starved, I picked up the tin plate warmer with the thumb hole in the middle ("like Chasen's already," Sylvia said) and there was this scrawny-looking fish with its eye still in. I was damned if I was going to eat something staring at me like that, so I took my fork and turned it over. But there was an eye on the other side, too. So what did I do? I ate it.

And what do I do now? The same thing.

But for some crazy reason it's not so hard to accept.

Sylvia's taking me to dinner at L'Ermitage tonight. "The Buffy Chandler crowd might be there," she says. "Wear your tunic from Saks."

Edwin sent me a dozen lilies of the valley ("My poet's sense of literalism, love, though Burbank you're decidedly not") and dedicated a record to me on his radio show yesterday— "Just Friends," the song Morty and I danced to that perfect night at the Mocambo all those years ago.

Edith enrolled me in some UCLA extension course called Emotional Centering in Urban America. "The lecturer's so marvelous," she gushed. "He teaches you how to own your own tenderness." "As opposed to renting it?" I asked.

Andi sent me a photograph of herself to put on my piano. Framed, no less. Peter shot it. And her hair—my dear, wonderful girl—her hair is still in her face.

Gwynneth gave me a long silk scarf in a Theodore box: one of those endlessly unrolling Isadora Duncan models in a dreadful print which I was about to exchange before Ronald told me she shoplifted it. "So what do I do with it now?" I asked him. "Gift-wrap a diving board?" "Honey," he answered, "sell it to Kareem Abdul Jabar as a necktie. The Muslims are *all* wearing suits these days."

I even got a card from Louis. "I'll always treasure you as a friend, Lil," he wrote, beneath the artsy Norcross sentiment, "and I'd love to call to say hello the next time I'm in town." I sat smiling over that card for a long time, thinking that I wouldn't be at all surprised if he does call—in six months, or eight months, or ten. And that I'd be less surprised if he weren't engaged by then to a very nice local woman. And that I will have no regret or sorrow or falseness in my voice when I tell him how happy I am for him.

As for Ronald's gift—the one we're getting for ourselves—we are going to look for that now. I pick up my keys, my sunglasses, the scraps of paper with the directions from the rental agents. "Two bedrooms?" they'd invariably asked. "There'll be children, then?"

"No. No children. Just my brother and I. Oh, but there will be a cat."

I pull up to Ronald's gym, put the top down, lean my head back into the warmth. The large double doors open and I turn and squint at the lean male bodies moving in and out: a blurred parade of T-shirts and wheat jeans, neckbeads gleaming in the late April sun.

The leather seats grow hot. I shove the cans of Fresca and the foil-wrapped grapefruit into the glove compartment. I lean back and savor the length of the minutes, the sound of passing cars, the unseen eyes of their drivers.

The sound of his shoulder bag against the car door opens my eyes.

"Lil," he whines, "those streaks are going orange. I told you to bring a scarf."

"Scarves make me look like a Tarzana housewife."

"That's because you don't know how to *play* with them. Come on, bend over."

He unties his blue paisley neckerchief and whips it around my head. Purse-lipped, he sets to work: his arms crossing and recrossing in front of my face, their blond hairs tickling my nose. Tiny tracks tug at the corners of his eyes; excess flesh bulbs his nose, flaps from the bones of his jaw. That little gold stud in his left earlobe—the one he'd stopped wearing all those months with Gary—shines like a tiny beacon of hope.

"There!" He bends the rearview mirror my way.

I frown. "I look like Yasir Arafat without the mustache."

"You look very chic is how you look."

"May I remind you, my dear, that I am a Chosen Person?"

"You are a Chosen Person, but I am a colorist. Now quit bitching, darling, and drive."

I turn on the motor and we head west.

"What are we looking at first?" he asks, as I make the right, then the left, onto Wilshire.

"The duplex in Trancas."

"Trancas, how fabulous! There is this *adorable* like hunk of muscles in the lifeguard tower there."

"Great. We won't have to spend money on a mover."

"Arms like tufted upholstery, I *swear.*"

"Or on a couch, for that matter."

"Oh, to be crushed by that doll . . ."

"Listen, don't get your hopes up. The one in Malibu looks like it's more in our price range."

"In that case, darling, I'll just have to learn how to jog."

"I'm hungry," I say, after a few minutes.

"You weren't lifting hundred-pound weights. I am *famished.*"

"I brought grapefruit and diet soda."

"Oh, God."

"Oh God is right. You want to stop at McDonald's?"

"Oh, but Lil, I'm so flabby. I cannot show my face in Studio One again until I get rid of those silly rolls on my middy."

"You want the grapefruit?"

"No," he sighs. "Let's go to McDonald's."

"But *just* this once."

"Oh, absolutely, darling. We'll be *so good* this summer. No sweets, no snacks. We'll make ourselves positively *sylph-like*."

"We'll paste a picture of Sophie Tucker on the refrigerator as an incentive."

"Sophie Tucker, my ass. We'll paste one of Daryl Hall."

"Daryl Hall?" The name sounds faintly familiar. "I think that was the name of my old Shearson Hammill broker. The one who duped Morty and me on Cuban-American Oil."

"Oh, darling," he laughs, "you *are* a gem."

He leans back in his bucket seat and lifts his face to the sun. I keep my eye on the rush of cars pouring in from the San Diego off ramps and Veterans Boulevard. The noise finally passes; the traffic thins; the bluff at Ocean Avenue looms ahead, its palm trees growing clearer and bigger with every block. The air turns cool and salty and clean. Renewing? Invigorating? Replenishing? Oh, what the hell, let's say all of that.

Ronald turns on the radio. "Oh, I *wish* I were born with Aretha's voice," he sighs. "I wish I had a body like Sylvester Stallone. I wish I was up in that lifeguard tower in Trancas right this very—"

"I wish I had a cigarette," I say.

He lights one of his own, passes it to me, and in the perfect sunshine, the perfect silence, the perfect peace of muzzled complaint, we drive on to the beach.